· TOUCHSTONE ·

A Death-Bed Confession that Withered a Mother's Heart. 20 years had passed since Edith Caterson's twins were born; the debonair Tony and the stolid Sandy, fine men but so unlike one another. And now, twenty years later, because she loved both boys she could bear to learn that one of her babies had died at birth and another substituted. But then came the horror! Then arose the so poignant, ever-haunting question, a question that life could not answer and only death assuage! The greatest tragedy that can befall a mother.

The enigma that surrounds Edith Caterson's two boys and her mother love that faces this riddle so courageously will keep you absorbed to the very end.

A book for all women — mothers especially.

· TOUCHSTONE ·

BY

BEN AMES WILLIAMS

AUTHOR OF "SPLENDOR," "ALL THE BROTHERS WERE VALIANT,"
"IMMORTAL LONGINGS," ETC.

NEW YORK

E. P. DUTTON & CO., INC.

8537

First Printing   . . Jan., 1930
Second Printing . . Jan., 1930
Third Printing . . Jan., 1930
Fourth Printing . . Jan., 1930
Fifth Printing . . Jan., 1930

I

THE big limousine, taking its sober way through the press of more modern cars, wore a ludicrous sort of dignity. It was one of those relics of ancient days still sometimes to be seen; it towered like a caravan; its black flanks, like the cheeks of a vain old dowager, were meshed by tiny cracks beneath the enamel surface which they wore; its trimmings were polished till they shone; and the brass lamps high on either side gleamed in the sun. The ponderous vehicle was at once long out of date and always of the moment, a monument of conservative respectability. Built in those days when automobiles were still to a great degree a product of hand work, it was even now sound in wind and limb, fit for any duty that might be demanded. It was, if you like, an anachronism; yet there was in its bearing no suggestion of a sense of inferiority. It moved imperturbably among the swarm of more modern cars, holding to a steady line, forcing others to make room. It assumed a haughty individuality, like a queen advancing with a high and heedless disregard through the thronging courtiers who fell humbly back on either side.

This car was no degenerate descendant of a splendid line. It was itself an ancestor, and as such to be revered. Mrs. Caterson had for it an amused yet reverent affection; and though she might now and then, for the sake of greater convenience, use another car, she was never so much at ease as when she sat in the high body of this limousine, as though she were perched upon a pillion, with the familiar nape of Richards' neck five feet in front of her eyes.

Caterson himself did not always agree with her feeling for the limousine. He said as much now. "We might better have used the sedan, Edith," he remarked. "This old lady is awkward to handle, when the traffic's bad."

Mrs. Caterson shook her head, smiling faintly. "It's old habit with me, Joe," she reminded him. "When I want to be particularly splendid, this is my way of doing it. We're in plenty of time. The game doesn't start till two."

He nodded. "Oh, yes," he agreed. "Time enough." They were blocked by a cross street, waited till the whistle bade them on. He looked at her, saw how radiant she was; and his eyes warmed. "Lady, Lady!" he chided tenderly; and when her glance met his: "Cheeks like that, at your age! And your eyes!"

"Well, I am excited," she admitted happily. "Feel my heart, Joe." She drew his hand against her bosom. "Why shouldn't I be? With two sons on the team?"

"You weren't as bad as this last year," he argued.

"It was just Tony, then," she reminded him. "And we didn't know until the game how wonderful he was. Now there's Tony and Sandy too, and me their mother, Joe! Imagine! Me!"

"Who else?" he protested gently. "For that matter, me their father, too!"

She shook her head at him. "That's not so wonderful," she retorted. "Being a father isn't a full-time job. But I've been their mother every minute of their lives for twenty years."

Her eyes suddenly were shining, and he gripped her hand. She was, he thought, incredibly youthful of countenance, incredibly lovely. Her cheek was as smooth as it had been when first he met her, and her eyes as clear. Only in her eyes there dwelt sometimes the shadows of the passing years, as cloud shadows drift across a sunny field. These eyes of hers were curiously quick to happy tears, but he had never seen her weep for grief, or from sheer nerves, as women do; she wept only when she smiled. . . .

The traffic grew more and more dense about them; they moved by fits and starts, a car's length at a time. Richards at the wheel drove straight ahead, making no attempt to weave in and out of line; but sometimes he was slow in accelerating, and at one such moment a horn sounded behind them, and an open roadster swirled past and cut in front of them with an impudent flirt of its wheels. Mrs. Caterson cried in quick recognition:

"There's Nina! And Mr. Buckel!" She smiled at some thought of her own. "Tony sent her his tickets," she remarked.

Cross traffic had halted them again; and the girl

in the car ahead turned to wave her hand. There was something elfin in her countenance; she had an olive skin, dark arching brows, dancing eyes and a warm, laughing mouth. She made now some pantomime, unintelligible to them, and laughed, her shoulders shaking with her own merriment. Her father beside her turned and lifted his hand, and then the block broke and the cars moved on. Almost at once, Nina found a chance to slip past a slower vehicle and dart ahead, leaving them behind.

"She drives like an angel," Mrs. Caterson remarked; and her husband smiled his assent.

"She's a fine girl," he agreed. "I haven't seen one as nice for a long time." He looked down at his wife again. "Not for—let me see—twenty-four years," he assured her smilingly; and her hand curled happily through the crook of his arm.

There is for the dullest sensibility something about a big football game which quickens the heartbeat painfully. The season of the year may have something to do with this, for your properly conducted game falls on an Indian summer day. There is frost on the ground at dawn; not enough to make the gridiron muddy, but enough to crisp the grass, and to remind you that sterner weather is just around the corner. This is autumn's keenest charm; this warning that for all the present's loveliness, a worse season is to come. The consciousness of impending danger produces an exhilaration, an almost intemperate delight; and the senses seize gluttonously on

these pleasures of gay sun and crisp airs, so soon to
be withdrawn.

Such a day, with crackling frost on the morning
grasses, and a bright sun at noon, and a football
game as the shadows lengthen, is full of a happy
flurry and haste. The interval between breakfast and
the lunch that must be eaten early is incredibly brief;
luncheon is swallowed whole, lest by some mischance
you be late for the initial kick-off. You decide to allow half an hour for the journey to the Stadium;
you allow, for safety's sake, an hour. You crawl with
the converging traffic till it clots and stands still; you
leave your car in marsh or fen or in someone's back
yard or on the nearest dump; you walk the last half
mile, shout this and that to familiar faces in the
crowd, hear the distant and then the nearer rumble
of the cheers, make haste lest even now you may arrive
too late, and come to your seat at last a full half
hour before the appointed time.

Richards drove Mr. and Mrs. Caterson to the
gate nearest their seats on the east side of the
Stadium; and Mr. Caterson appointed with the man
a rendezvous where they might meet after the game.
Richards touched his cap, and the limousine moved
soberly away. They turned toward the ticket takers,
and Caterson fumbled in his pockets, and Mrs.
Caterson laughed at him, wagged her head, cried:

"Joe, you always turn pale at this stage. You
always think you've forgotten the tickets! Poor
lamb!"

He dug deeper into that stubborn pocket. "By Gorry, Edith, I have forgotten them this time," he insisted.

She shook her head. "You looked at them twice on the way over," she protested. "You're feeling in your overcoat pocket, dear!"

So he found them, and grinned ruefully; and they surrendered themselves to the tide that flowed slowly toward the gates. All about them there were pressing young bodies, quick laughter, the shuffle of feet on the gravel, the gasp of a girl lifted off her feet by the crush about her. Outcries! "Hi, Bill! H'are you? How the folks? Tha's fine. See you inside!" A twelve-year-old boy holding his ticket tightly in both hands, looking up out of the deep gulf between the coonskin coat on the man in front of him, and the stout dowager behind. "Get your winning colors!" An aeroplane spinning overhead; the line of taut throats below upturned faces as everyone watched its passage. A crumb of gravel in your shoe and no chance to take it out. "Hold your own tickets, everybody! Hold your own tickets!" The bright new two-by-four railings that guided this mass of people into single files. Individuals like cherry pips squeezed out of the mob and spinning through these aisles. The shuttling throng inside the gates, a ticket in each person's hand, eyes scanning the numbers above the Stadium portals. A young woman elaborately gowned, alone, elaborately pretending to be unconscious of the eyes upon her, waiting for someone. A middle-aged couple, furred to the ears; and on the right arm of the man a slender girl in her teens; and at the woman's side a boy three years younger, with his mouth open. "Program! The only way to tell the players. Names and numbers of all the players." A boy and a girl eating hot dogs. A small man with three steamer rugs, stumbling along behind three large, well-upholstered women. A man with two boys stopping to speak to some acquaintance. The boys wandered on, and he raced after them in a sudden panic lest they stray away. As Mr. and Mrs. Caterson moved toward their own portal, a program vendor bawled in their ears: "The only way to tell the players!"

"The idea!" Mrs. Caterson protested, and her eyes were swimming happily. "As if I wouldn't know our boys unless they were numbered!"

But Caterson bought a program, and on second thought, he bought two. A moment later they came to their proper portal.

In the half-gloom under the Stadium, they ascended the steep stairs and emerged abruptly into the blaze of the sun. They had a momentary sense of insecurity; the concrete tiers descended so abruptly from where they stood to the field below. An usher shouted: "Up! Up! Keep moving!" They climbed, and there was a sea of faces spread before them, from which now and then a familiar countenance, like a breaking wave, uplifted. "Hi, Joe!" "You Joe Caterson!" "This Tony Caterson any kin of yours, Joe?" Friendly raillery, and Edith's cheeks bright as the sun, and Caterson grinning good-

humoredly. Then they found their seats, and relaxed in quick obscurity, themselves in turn now calling to those who were still climbing the steep aisles.

Edith's eyes fastened on the field where two score
figures dotted the turf, and footballs boomed and
spiraled, and men went through a dumb show of
swift, darting runs, dodging imaginary tacklers. Her
hand tightened on her husband's arm; and he looked
at her and saw the tears streaming down her cheeks,
and her lip between her teeth.

"There's Tony, Joe," she cried. "There!"

"Sandy, too!" he discovered.

She whispered: "They won't get hurt, will they?"
Then shook her head, answering her own question.
"Of course not!" Pressed close to him. "Will they,
Joe?"

He chuckled. "I'll back either one of them," he
said proudly. "They're a tough pair."

The two became fixed in a rigid attention. About
them the stands filled; the roar of cheers resounded;
bands appeared and blared loud melodies; the aeroplane still circled overhead; friends called greetings.
But neither Mr. nor Mrs. Caterson were conscious
of anything about them, until at last the boys on the
turf down there trotted toward the portals, vanished
from their view.

Then three or four men in white knickerbockers,
one of them with a new football under his arm, appeared by the goal posts and stood talking together,
carefully unconscious of the crowd.

Mrs. Caterson said helplessly: "I can't bear this

last five minutes, Joe. I always think it will kill me. My heart's pounding so!"

"Read the program," he suggested, and handed one to her, himself began to riffle through the pages of the other. And abruptly he exclaimed: "Here are their pictures, Lady! Here's Tony!"

"And here's Sandy!" she echoed; and she read aloud, almost crooning the words: "'Alexander Caterson, right guard, twenty-one years old, five feet, ten inches, a hundred and eighty-nine pounds.'" To her husband proudly: "Sandy's gained weight, Joe."

"'Anthony Caterson,'" he retorted, from the program. "'Right half back. Twenty years old. Six feet, one inch. A hundred and seventy-eight pounds.'"

She looked across his arm to see the record, and her eyes, after a moment, faintly clouded. "They still pretend they're different ages," she pointed out. "I don't suppose anyone in college even knows they're twins."

Her husband hesitated. "That reminds me," he remarked. "Brady of the *Transcript* came in to see me yesterday, to ask whether they were or not. He promised not to use the story, but it's bound to leak out somehow."

"I don't see why they—make a secret of it," she said wistfully. "It's as though they were ashamed!"

"Well, they don't look alike," he suggested. "And if people did know, someone would always be saying: 'Twins! Why you're not a bit alike, are you?'" He hesitated. "The books say that twins who don't resemble one another never do care to talk about it," he reminded her. "They're twice as common as the ones who do; but usually people never even know they're twins at all."

She nodded. "But I do wish our boys were more congenial, Joe," she confessed. "It makes me unhappy, sometimes." Then she came swiftly to her feet, hands unflung; for the whole Stadium was suddenly a mass of cheering maniacs. Down there at the junction between the concrete and the wooden stands, a little knot of jerseyed figures had sprinted out upon the field; and the very skies were roaring.

Mrs. Caterson took herself in hand. She was the first to sit down. "I must, Joe," she confessed. "I have to be perfectly calm, or I'll just burst before the kick-off." He was still on his feet, and she tugged at his arm. "Did we win the toss?"

Someone behind them called: "Everybody down!" Everyone grudgingly did sit down, and each one settled himself as carefully as though he meant to stay sedately quiet throughout the afternoon. Mrs. Caterson looked along the rows of faces; she became brightly conversational.

"I can't look at the field, Joe. You tell me what's happening! There's Nina, and her father, just two rows behind us. Oh, and Joe, there's Ruth Elcess. She looks badly! I'm afraid she's ill. Do we kick off? Lend me your handkerchief. I've got to blow my nose or I'll scream. Why doesn't he blow the whistle? What are they waiting for? Oh-h-h-h-h!"

The boom of toe on pigskin; the pound of feet;

scattered cries; a great roar as the runner was borne to earth.

And Mrs. Caterson settled herself with a relieved sigh. "There, it's begun!" she exclaimed. "Now I'm all right, my dear."

So turned her full attention to the game.

II

AN hour later, upon pandemonium fell sudden sanity again; the half ended, the teams trotted toward the exit that led to the locker building, and the massed thousands along the concrete tiers rose and remembered that their throats were raw, their sides were aching, their muscles cramped and sore. Men tried to speak to their neighbors and could only croak hoarsely. Everyone moved this way or that, and many drifted down toward the exits. But Mr. and Mrs. Caterson stood happily silent together; and then Nina Buckel came swooping down from her seat two or three rows above to hug them both, and to dance up and down between them, and to cry:

"Wasn't he wonderful, Mrs. Caterson? Wasn't he glorious?"

The girl's eyes were shining; she laughed infectiously, and she tugged at them furiously, and she exclaimed:

"You don't act a bit excited! Why don't you jump up and down and yell? I should think you'd be so proud!"

Mrs. Caterson said happily: "He was fine, wasn't he, Nina?"

"And he'd have scored another touchdown if he hadn't slipped that time," the girl insisted, as though someone had denied this. "When he gets started,

they just can't stop him, can they? They just can't
hold him at all! And he runs so easily. He doesn't
seem to go fast. You can't see how he does it, but
he's past them before you know."

Mr. Caterson said judicially: "I saw Grange play
once, in Columbus. Tony today reminded me of
Grange. Like a ghost, drifting down the field."

"He's better than he was last year," Nina announced. "He just gets better all the time, doesn't
he?" She clung tight to the older woman's arm.
"Aren't you proud of him?" she insisted. "Aren't
you just all swelled up about him?"

Mrs. Caterson smiled gently. "After all, Nina,"
she reminded the girl, "I've always been proud of
Tony. I've always thought him wonderful. I suppose
I would anyway, of course. That's the way mothers
are, you know."

Nina's eyes were suddenly thoughtful. "Sandy was
good, too," she said uncertainly. "He played a wonderful game."

"Did he?" Mrs. Caterson asked eagerly. "I
couldn't always be sure which was Sandy. So often
there was just a heap of men, with him underneath
them all."

"But Tony was by himself, alone against them
all!" Nina cried. "Oh, I couldn't breathe, watching
him. When he'd wait to catch those punts, and two
or three men racing down on him, and the sun shining on his helmet! And when he got away from
them, I screamed. . . . Didn't you hear me
scream?"

Mr. Caterson chuckled. "I think everyone screamed except his mother, Nina," he said whimsically. "She took it out in pounding me. I'm black and blue all up and down one side."

Below them on the gridiron the bands moved to and fro; they formed alphabetical patterns; they marched and countermarched; the drum major fired a pistol, he twirled his baton, he dropped it and a great laugh rose. Nina's father came down to join them. A small, keen man with a crisp mustache and alert gray eyes, he said briskly:

"Well, Joe, you're an All-American father again, eh?"

Caterson's broad, steady mouth widened in a pleased smile. He was a heavy set, solidly built, grayhaired man with twinkling eyes that belied the stolidity of his countenance. "He did well, didn't he?" he agreed.

"And Sandy was fine, too," Nina insisted, watching Mrs. Caterson.

"I never saw a better tackle than that one Tony made," Buckel commented. "Three interferers between him and his man." He chuckled. "Did you see how he passed the interferers, Joe?"

"Dove between them," Caterson replied; but Buckel shook his head.

"Shrewder than that," he retorted. "He feinted them out of position. I saw his eyes. He looked behind them, and hesitated, as though the runner had changed his course; and they checked just long enough to give him a clear shot at his man. You know, it takes genius to be able to think, at a moment like that."

"I didn't see that," Caterson confessed. "Yes, a cool head." His eyes were glowing. "Drop in this evening, Will," he suggested. "The boys will be there for an hour or two, and some of the youngsters are coming. Nina, bring your father and mother along."

Nina laughed happily. "Don't worry, I was going to," she assured them. They watched the bands again, and the girl joined in one of the songs. Those who had gone out during this intermission were returning; and Nina and her father sought their seats once more. Incredibly soon, the teams reappeared. Over yonder, the sun was dropping swiftly now; the top of the Stadium drew a black shadow sharply across the field, almost to the foot of the stands where the Catersons were sitting. The jerseyed figures distributed themselves; and Mrs. Caterson looked happily at the scoreboard. Thirteen to nothing. That was, barring dark mischance, a margin safe enough. She could bear now to watch the kick-off; the converging rush of racing boys; the quick-massing confusion, and the whistle. The game went on.

As the third period proceeded with no advantage either way, Mrs. Caterson fell a-dreaming, and her eyes followed Tony happily, dwelt upon him lovingly. He was the most conspicuous figure on his team. Defensively, he played the safety position; and she liked the way he stood, alert and yet at ease, confident and sure, wary and audacious. She was full of a deep pride in this son of hers; she had had so many reasons for a just pride in him. Even as a baby he had been preeminently lovable and charming, full of a great friendliness, actuated always by a desire to serve and to please, at once wilful and obedient. As he grew older, these traits became more strongly marked; he learned a tender consideration for older folk which endeared him to them; he had even toward his friends of his own age a sort of deference which made them love him; and when his school life began, he showed a quick aptitude, and an originality of mind which distinguished him at once. In preparatory school and afterward in college, he was a brilliant and conspicuous figure; one of those young men for whom the spotlight was designed and intended. Mrs. Caterson, watching him now, remembered so many things about him, and always happily. Tony had never given her concern. . . .

She watched him fondly, while she dwelt among these memories. He was a flashing figure, whether on offense or defense; and it was easy for her to follow his movements. She caught her breath when, interfering for another man, he flung himself recklessly at the knees of a charging end; she could not breathe again till he came swiftly to his feet, helped the prostrate end arise. She clenched her fists when he carried the ball, winced when the tacklers bore him down, exulted when he rose undaunted. Once he started on a wide end run and raced across the gridiron directly toward her, two opposing men barring his way down the field as they sped beside him; and

Tony checked himself like a cat and swerved behind
them, as swift as light, while they floundered clum-
sily. The great roar that acclaimed his ten-yard gain
was like sweet wine to her.

The period ended, and she had a moment's peace
during this brief breathing space. When play began
again, something like despair fought for the beaten
team. Mrs. Caterson was no student of football.
The intricacies of the game were not for her. She
could only watch her son; but she sensed this new
intensity in the play, and when Tony knocked down
a long forward pass, for the first time since the game
began she screamed as these others here about her
screamed. Then he was back waiting for a high, end
over end punt; and a vast sudden hush lay upon these
thousands. The ends reached him, crouched ready
to bear him to earth—and at the last possible second
darted between them, took the ball on the run, and
wove for thirty yards through the desperate de-
fenders.

There had been no further scoring in this second
half, but now the stands around Mrs. Caterson were
crying out for another touchdown. Tony took the
ball; but he lost a yard at end. The other halfback
slid through tackle for two or three hard-won paces.
A drive at centre gained a yard. Then a punt angled
across the field, rolled safely outside at the ten yard
line. Tony fell back on defense once more.

Mrs. Caterson began to forget the game. It was
obviously already won; she was content with her
dreams. The beaten team completed a forward pass

that brought the ball to mid-field; but Tony downed the runner there, and the line held safely. Tony was back now at his own ten yard line, and another punt was coming. It was low and wide, it struck the ground and bounded end over end toward the goal line; and Tony ran warily toward it. One of the opposing ends was just behind him. These two and the ball converged; and Tony looked toward the end, and swung to block him off. Then something happened, not quite clear to Mrs. Caterson. The ball took an erratic bounce, and Tony whirled back as though to seize it, but it eluded him, bobbing along the ground. He hesitated for a fraction of a second, then threw himself again at the other man. But the end dodged him, fell on the ball as it rolled across the line.

And a terrific volcano of sound erupted from the opposite stands, while all along the east side of the Stadium a sorrowful whisper ran.

Mrs. Caterson gripped her husband's arm. "What was it, Joe?" she asked swiftly.

He hesitated, momentarily; he touched her hand. "Just a tough break, Lady," he told her.

"But why didn't Tony catch it?"

Caterson was watching the knot of players down there on the field where ran some swift argument. "Tony says it didn't hit him," he decided gravely. "But the referee has called it a touchdown!"

And he added a moment later, with a quick relief: "But they missed the goal!"

She watched him, puzzled by his demeanor, while

the teams lined up for the kick-off; and she looked back at the field in time to see Tony give way to a substitute; and she wept with delight at the great cheer that greeted her son when he trotted off the field. Sandy was still in there; she could, in the open formation before the kick-off, distinguish his shorter stockier figure. But as the play went on, and dusk drew swiftly down, it was hard to follow him, and a few minutes later, almost casually, the game ended. The teams drew into two huddling knots for the perfunctory cheers that went unheard in the vast roar of swift-loosed jubilation. Then from the east stand thousands poured down upon the field, where in the clotting darkness a twisting confusion did appear. The band was barely to be heard above the uproar, only the brave beat of the drum was clearly audible; hats were flying across the ghostly white bar of the goalposts where blue clad figures of policemen clustered vigilantly. And by and by, Nina came down to slip her arm through that of Mrs. Caterson, and they began to descend toward the exits from the stand.

Their seats were halfway up the concrete slope above the head of the stairs; and since there were others all about them, they moved slowly. Mr. Caterson and Nina's father were just behind them; and Nina, supporting the older woman down the steep steps, talked happily of the game. But before they were caught in the press of folk about the head of the stairs, someone touched Mrs. Caterson's other arm; and she looked up and said quickly:

"Oh, Ruth! How are you, my dear. It's months since we've seen you."

She turned aside to speak with this other woman, and Nina and her father waited where they were. Mr. Caterson had followed Mrs. Caterson. Mr. Buckel asked:

"Who's that, Nina?"

"I think it's Miss Elcess," Nina told him, in a somewhat lowered tone. "You know, the nurse who took care of Mrs. Caterson when Tony and Sandy were born. She's devoted to the boys, and Mrs. Caterson likes her. They've had her since, when Tony broke his leg that time, and when Mr. Caterson had pneumonia, three years ago."

Buckel nodded. "Oh, yes. I didn't recognize her. She used to be heavier, didn't she?"

Caterson, returning, heard this word. "I don't think she's well," he agreed. "She looks badly. She wanted to speak to Mrs. Caterson about something." He smiled faintly. "She's always felt a sort of proprietary interest in the boys, you know. Sends them birthday cards, and Christmas presents, and so on; and Edith sees to it that they always remember her. She's a loyal soul!"

The crowd about the exit was thinning now; they moved a few steps that way. Mrs. Caterson, after a moment, came to join them again; and Nina asked her gravely:

"Miss Elcess is sick, isn't she?"

Mrs. Caterson nodded. "I'm afraid so," she agreed. "She's been feeling badly for some time, and she's going into the hospital tonight. They're going to operate on her Monday morning. She was—mysterious about it. I'm afraid she's seriously ill." Her eyes were shadowed. "She wanted to know whether we were to be at home next week," she confessed. "I don't know why. . . ."

"You've always been so nice to her," Nina reminded her. They were descending the stairs into the darkness under the Stadium.

"And she hasn't any kith or kin," Mrs. Caterson agreed. "I promised I'd come and see her in the hospital. That seemed to comfort her."

Caterson and Nina's father were just ahead of them; they moved with the thinning crowd, and emerged into the twilight, and Caterson said over his shoulder:

"There's Miss Delevan, Edith. With Dan Lind."

Mrs. Caterson linked her arm in his, and they walked four abreast, Mr. Buckel at one end of the line, Caterson at the other. "Dan? Where is he?" Nina cried, looking in the direction Caterson indicated. "I haven't seen him since last summer. Where? I don't see them."

Mrs. Caterson laughed. "You mustn't expect to, Nina," she warned the girl. "Mr. Caterson has eyes like an owl. He's forever seeing people in a crowd. I tell him he's always looking for some pretty girl."

Nina leaned forward to call teasingly: "Is that so, Mr. Caterson? Shame on you!" But she had a swift regret that she had spoken, for Mr. Caterson did not smile in response to her jest. She saw that he was made uncomfortable; and Mrs. Caterson pressed Nina's arm and whispered:

"Sh! He doesn't like to be teased about it."

They presently separated; for Nina's car was parked in one direction, while Richards would be waiting in another. "Come about half past eight, Nina," Mrs. Caterson directed. "The boys won't come home to dinner, but they'll be there by that time. They can stay till a quarter of ten. I suppose you youngsters will be just ready to start your party by then."

"We've tremendous plans," Nina agreed. "You and Mr. Caterson ought to come with us! Dance and dance and dance. . . ." Her eyes were shining.

"We're much too old, my dear," the older woman reminded her. "And bring your father and mother."

"I'll promise to be late," Nina assured her smilingly. "You told me to ask everyone, but I've only asked six or eight people. But we won't get there till nine, anyway, so you'll have the boys to yourselves for a while. I know, you see."

"Nonsense, child," Mrs. Caterson protested, smiling. "Come when you choose, dear."

Nina lifted her hand in a swift gesture of farewell, and they drew apart. In the street outside, the big limousine loomed like an arc, conspicuous from far away. When they came to it, Richards touched his cap, swung wide the door.

Mrs. Caterson smiled at him. "Well, we beat them, Richards."

"Tony beat them," Richards amended proudly. "Yes, madam. I was in the wooden stands. He was the whole team."

Her eyes filled happily as she stepped into the car.

III

WHILE Richards maneuvered the limousine patiently among the crawling lines of cars that were leaving the neighborhood of the Stadium, these two sat for a while in silence, summing their impressions of the hours just done. Once Caterson remarked:

"There's Miss Dyson, in that car we just passed." And his wife smiled and touched his hand.

"Trust you to see her, Joe," she said teasingly; added a moment later: "Nina's a sweet girl, isn't she?"

"Fine," he agreed.

"I think Tony's very fond of her," she murmured, half to herself. "And they're sweet together."

Caterson chuckled. "Mothers have a long imagination," he protested. "Tony's got to finish college and begin to earn a living, you know."

"I'm not worrying about Tony," she assured him; and when he did not at once reply, she added quickly: "Nor about Sandy either, of course, Joe. Sandy's all right."

"I've thought sometimes that Sandy liked Nina about as well as Tony does," he remarked; and she laughed in quick amusement.

"Sandy? He's never looked at a girl. When he

starts to slick his hair, and keep his trousers pressed, I'll begin to worry. Not before."

He grinned in the darkness. "You didn't make me crease my trousers—not till after we were married," he argued; and she pressed his hand.

"Of course, Sandy's exactly like you," she assented. "Never gives a thought to his appearance, or to what people may think about him; just goes mooning along about his own concerns. Just as shaggy and shabby as you used to be." There was a smile in her tone. "You're not much better now. Oh, Sandy's your son, all right."

He was silent for a moment, said at last: "You know, Edith, Miss Elcess is the only individual I know who likes Sandy better than she does Tony. Did you ever notice? Tony's a Prince Charming to everyone else; but she prefers Sandy every time. It was so, even when they were babies; it's always been so."

She nodded. "I've thought so, sometimes," she agreed. And she added thoughtfully: "I'm afraid she is ill, Joe. Dangerously so. She didn't say as much; but you could see something in her eyes, like a prevision of horror. It made me—shudder a little."

"There's always been—sadness in her eyes," he reminded her. "Always something a little furtive about her."

Mrs. Caterson said gravely: "Jealousy, Joe! That's the hard lot of nursing folk; especially the ones who help bring babies into the world, and tend them. They love so many babies, and lose them all. And they're bound to be jealous of the—real mothers. That's why I've always been kind to her, and a little tolerant. And I'm worried for her now."

They fell silent again, their thoughts, as is so often the case with folk long and truly married, running parallel, so that they communed without the necessity of words. The nurse. These boys of theirs. Their pride in Tony. Their long concern over Sandy's casual ways . . .

It happened that it was Mrs. Caterson who put at last a garment of speech upon these reflections.

"Joe, Joe," she murmured, almost sadly. "How different they are!"

He nodded. "Tony's like you," he told her thoughtfully. "Gay, and tender, and friendly, and audacious and kind. Always like you. And I see myself in Sandy, constantly."

"The best of you," she agreed. "You love to plod away at things that interest you, and so does he. You won't work at things that don't appeal to you. You won't learn to play bridge, and you never did really know how to dance, and you're too lazy even to balance your own check book." Her tone was full of fond amusement. "And Sandy's just the same. Latin and French and Literature and such things just bore him. But you notice his marks in the sciences. You would always work like a horse at any building problem, planning a dam, or a power house, or something."

She laughed softly. "And of course he's the image

of you! You both have those broad, willing, battered
countenances, as though you'd taken a lot of hard
knocks and might take more."

"And Tony has your features; the lean lines of
blood and breeding," he agreed. "And the eyelashes
of a girl!"

"They're no more alike than—strangers," Mrs.
Caterson said, half to herself. The traffic was thinning; they would soon be home. "I don't suppose
anyone would suspect them of being twins, if they
didn't know." She hesitated. "I wish they were more
like real twins, sometimes," she confessed. "I worry,
sometimes, about the way they—jar on one another.
I wish they got along better, Joe."

"Pshaw!" he urged, reassuringly. "All brothers
fight. You have to expect that."

"But they're not even in the same fraternity," she
insisted. "And they haven't roomed together, except
Freshman year. Sometimes I think they actually hate
each other."

"Sandy irritates Tony," Mr. Caterson confessed.
"Tony gets sore at him, sometimes. But I never
noticed any—reaction on Sandy's part. He doesn't
seem to mind anything Tony says, or does either."

"Oh, Sandy!" she agreed with an unhappy laugh.
"Sandy doesn't mind anything! Sometimes I think
he hasn't any—pride, any spirit at all, Joe. I wish
he did have. I wish he did fight back, more than he
does."

He shook his head. "Don't worry," he advised

her. "Sandy may not fight back. But he doesn't give way, either. You watch him for a while. He's apt to have things his way in the end."

"He stuck to it till he made the team," she remembered. "Tony says he was hopeless, when he started in last year. I don't think Tony thought he ever would be good enough." And she added happily: "Wasn't Tony splendid today? He's sure to be captain next year, isn't he?"

"I should think so," he assented.

She asked indifferently: "What happened when they made that touchdown, Joe? When the ball rolled over the line, that way?"

Caterson hesitated momentarily. "I suppose the ball must have bounced against Tony," he said at last. "That would give them the right to recover it."

She frowned faintly, as though puzzled; said at last: "But of course it didn't matter. We won anyway."

"Yes," he agreed. "Yes, of course we won, anyway."

The big limousine wheeled into their own drive; it trundled between the high shrubs, now almost leafless, and stopped before the door, and they alighted. Caterson spoke to the chauffeur.

"You know about going for the boys, Richards?" he asked, and the man nodded assentingly.

"Yes, sir, at the hotel."

Mrs. Caterson, about to enter the house, turned to call: "And take the limousine, Richards. If you take one of the other cars, Tony will want to drive, and I'd rather he didn't. He drives so fast. You take the limousine. He always refuses to drive that."

Richards chuckled, touched his cap again. "Yes, ma'am." And Mr. and Mrs. Caterson went into the house, while he wheeled away.

IV

MRS. CATERSON stayed a long time at her
dressing table, her hands busy with her soft
fair hair, still only faintly touched with gray. Long
after it was to her husband's eyes in smooth and
perfect order she pushed and patted it, inserted pins
and removed them, turned her head this way and
that. Himself ready to go downstairs, he sat at
ease, his cigarette alight, and watched her with a
widening smile. She was so intent, so earnest, so
absorbed. Till at last he laughed aloud, and rose and
crossed to kiss her.

"I declare, Edith, if I didn't know who it was
you're primping for, I'd be jealous," he protested.
"You might be dressing for your wedding, Lady."

She looked up at him radiantly, eyes shining,
cheeks bright. "I'm dressing for my two young men,"
she reminded him. "Why shouldn't I take pains?"
She frowned at him in mock reproof. "A pretty
daughter would have made a dandy out of you, my
dear."

His eyes twisted sharply; it was as though they
clenched into twin knots like tightened fists, with a
quick spasm of pain. And she cried out tenderly:
"My dear, my dear!" For this was an ancient wound
which she had thus reopened. Before the twins, a

daughter born to them had died; that grief was alive and aching still in Caterson.

His countenance cleared and he dropped one hand on her shoulder. "It's all right, Sweet," he told her. "You are daughter and sister and sweetheart and wife to me. Make yourself lovely for the three of us. We'll have the boys to ourselves for a while before the others come."

"I thought they'd like seeing their friends," she said apologetically, answering the unspoken regret in his tone. "But there may not be anyone but Nina and Mr. and Mrs. Buckel. And they won't come till late."

"Why of course, they'll want to see youngsters their own age," he agreed. And as she rose, ready at last to go down, he gravely gave her his arm. These two had learned to preserve a certain ceremony in their lives; a certain courtliness.

They were alone at dinner, for the boys could not come till somewhat later; they finished, and in the living room, Caterson opened the *Transcript* to read the chronicle of the game, while Mrs. Caterson moved here and there, shifting a vase of flowers, putting in order a pile of magazines, setting a light to the fire on the wide hearth, listening now and then by the window toward the drive. He read a paragraph now and then aloud. Tony Caterson this, and Tony Caterson that.

"And Brady says Sandy played a whale of a game," he added suddenly, pleased surprise in his tones. "Lady, Brady says Sandy played a fine game."

"I couldn't always see what he was doing," she confessed. "Did he?"

"You remember they gained against us for a while?" he reminded her. "And then we stopped them. Brady says Sandy broke up that delayed dive at tackle that made all their gains. Here, I'll read what he says. . . . "

She protested with mock severity: "You don't have to prove to me that my boys played finely, my dear." Laughed happily. "Besides, I wouldn't understand if you did read it. You're just trying to confuse me. Joe dear, where do these roses look best; on the piano, or on the table here?"

He laid aside his paper and joined her, moving with her about the room, chuckling at her happy excitement. "I don't believe even Nina's as thrilled as you, Lady."

"Of course she isn't," she assured him. "After all, she can't have but one of them, and I've got them both." She stood for an instant in the crook of his arm. "I'll always have them both, Joe, won't I? These great lads of ours."

He kissed her softly; and she broke away from him. "They're coming!" she cried. "There they are, Joe. I hear the car on the drive."

And she fled before him to the hall and flung the great door wide, in the moment that the limousine lurched to a jarring stop before the threshold while gravel spurted under its hard-braked wheels. She stood silhouetted against the light, and what seemed like an incredible number of youthful figures erupted

from the car, and she could not see for her tears.
But someone swept her up in his arms, and his arms
were strong; she was whirled about, borne swiftly
back into the hall, kissed till she was breathless. Her
eyes cleared, and her arms tightened about Tony's
neck, and he kissed her again and set her on her
feet. Turned with a gay, sweeping bow to his companions.

"Friends," he cried. "This lovely child is my
mother, if you please. To have and to hold! Behold,
and admire!"

And swung to grip his father by the hand. Mrs.
Caterson's eyes followed him. He was so tall and
fine. . . .

There were others here; so many of them. And
she had wanted her boys alone. She felt a swift
pang. Then she found Sandy beside her; and he said
awkwardly:

"Hello, mother!" She hugged him, and kissed him
hard, held him off so that she might scan his broad
and homely countenance, kissed him happily again.
He colored uncomfortably; and then Tony brushed
him cheerfully out of the way.

"One side, fellow," he commanded amiably. "Let
these others make their curtsy to the queen. Mother,
this is Barbs Delevan, and that's Audrey Deal, and
yonder's Dan Lind. You know Barbs and Dan, of
course. Audrey here is the Dark Lady of the Son-
nets. Look at her, if you doubt me. Did you ever see
a darker, lovelier lady?"

Mrs. Caterson smiled gently as she greeted the

girl. Audrey was indeed very beautiful; yet there dwelt something brooding, almost sullen in the red curve of her lips against her olive skin. Barbara Delevan she had met before. A stocky, black-haired girl with a sophisticated and impudent humor in her eyes, she always made Mrs. Caterson faintly uncomfortable. Dan Lind she liked. He was older than her sons, but he knew the trick of youth, would wear always its bright garments. He had a grave deference toward older folk which she approved. She saw him now, greeting her husband. Sandy had drifted away into the living room. Tony was taking Miss Delevan's cloak.

"Picked these folks up on the way out, mother," he explained. "Dan said they were coming later, but I fetched them along."

"Hence these gray hairs!" Audrey Deal commented, in a slow, expressionless tone. "I don't mind hitting seventy when I'm down near the road. But I don't like to do it in a ladder truck!"

Tony laughed cheerfully. "There, mother, she doesn't like your pet hearse!" he protested. "They laughed when they saw it, so I took the wheel. I showed them the old bus is no laughing matter. You should have seen it flirt its heels."

"I can sympathize with you, Miss Deal," Mrs. Caterson told the girl. "Tony isn't allowed to drive, if I'm in the car."

"They'll scrape him off a telephone pole, some day," Audrey evenly predicted; and Mrs. Caterson felt a quick clutch of fear at her heart, laughed it aside, led the way toward the living room. Tony had disappeared; she missed him instantly, and went to seek him out. He was in the pantry, mixing a cocktail; and when she offered some gentle protest, he laughed her word aside.

"Sweet Child!" he cried. "You're not supposed to know about such things!"

"But you're in training, Tony!"

"Of course," he assented. "But there's an open season from now till ten o'clock. So we'll have to be quick, you see. Here, taste this for me. Is it right? Or what? And how?"

She could never resist Tony, save in matters of some sure concern. She made a wry face now at the sip he forced upon her; and he cried delightedly:

"Good! I can see it's exactly right! The expression of your nose, Child; them tears in your lovely eyes. Now the ice! How about some glasses, mother? Want me to get them?"

She began to arrange glasses on a silver tray. A maid appeared to volunteer some service, but Tony pushed her cheerfully aside. "Self service tonight," he explained; and when the girl was gone: "She's something new, isn't she, mother? And very nice, I'm sure. A sweet chin to chuck, behind the pantry door. Now what else do we need?"

"You didn't get hurt, Tony?"

"Not a scratch! Not a black and blue spot on my creamy skin anywhere."

"I was so proud of you," she said, almost diffidently; and he hesitated, grinned, was for a moment silent. She thought, with the quick intuition of mothers, that there was a shadow in his eyes; but if a cloud did lie there, he banished it instantly, cried:

"All right, Child. Lead the way!" And he followed on her heels, beating time with the shaker to the music of tinkling ice, singing as they crossed the hall, in a ludicrous parody:

> " 'Here comes the gin!
> 'Clear, white and thin.
> 'Oh, how it testifies
> 'When it is in.' "

Barbs Delevan met them at the door. "Please, please, pretty please!" she begged; and Tony served her.

"Now then, reading from left to right," he invited. Barbs took the tray of glasses from Mrs. Caterson; and the older woman turned uncertainly away. Her husband and Sandy were together at the end of the hearth. Dan Lind and Audrey had been dancing; the phonograph scratched for a moment and fell silent now. Mrs. Caterson crossed toward the fireplace; linked her arm through Sandy's, watching the group yonder by the door. Barbs had taken a second cocktail, Audrey was draining her glass. Tony, she saw, had not yet helped himself.

"You're all right, Sandy?" Mrs. Caterson asked. "You didn't get hurt?"

He shook his head slowly. "No."

"Your eye is swollen, isn't it? I'll bathe it for you. . . ."

"Just got a little bump! Be all right in the morning," he assured her.

Dan Lind called across the room: "Sandy, you're on deck!"

Sandy nodded. "We're allowed a cocktail, tonight," he explained, to his father, then moved toward the others. Mr. and Mrs. Caterson were left alone. She saw the sweep of headlights across the window, and went through the hall to open the door to Nina and Mr. and Mrs. Buckel; and Tony, a cocktail in his hand, came to encircle Nina with his free arm and kiss her cheerfully. But he kissed little Mrs. Buckel as cheerfully as he did Nina. Sandy greeted them more soberly. It was Nina who kissed Sandy; and Mrs. Caterson saw his slow, uneasy color. Other cocktails were poured. Mrs. Caterson inconspicuously avoided this ceremony. She saw approvingly that Tony, having drunk the one, poured himself no more; Sandy's glass, too, was set aside. She found herself by her husband's side, and whispered happily:

"You know, Joe, I like these boys of ours!"

And he chuckled at her tone.

Bob Curry appeared, with Nell Dyson and Linda Crater. This new flood of youth swelled the babble of gay voices. Tony kissed each newcomer, if she were feminine; but none of them save Nina kissed Sandy. Mrs. Caterson, watching this one of her sons, saw his apprehension give way to relief at each escape, and she made Mr. Caterson see and smile with her.

"What a sobersides he is!" she whispered. "Exactly like you, Joe. Remember?" Her eyes were dancing teasingly.

"But he'll get over it, as I did," he assured her, and laughed at her quick, responsive color. These two were not too old to call youth back again.

There was a swift, kaleidoscopic blur of conversation. Someone spoke of the speed at which Tony had driven the limousine; there were remarks upon the unreasonableness of all speed laws, and of the prohibition law, and of the training rules which curtailed the cocktails Tony and Sandy might drink. The younger folk agreed in condemning these restraining influences. The four older people drew aside, content to watch and listen smilingly. Someone mentioned the fact that the current cocktail was a good one, and had enthusiastic assent. There was, it appeared, an equally swift and extreme enthusiasm about other things. The most popular new orchestra, the latest dance record, the most recent model of a certain car. A New York night club emerged as the central topic. All these young people except Tony and Sandy knew its attractions.

"My dear," said Audrey Deal, in that slow drawl of hers. "There's something going on every minute! You don't have time to think! It's wonderful!"

Then someone else said something, and this appeared to startle and delight them. Mrs. Caterson understood, after a moment, that Barbs Delevan was going on the stage. The other girls were ejaculatory and incredulous; but Tony was instantly approving.

"Of course!" he cried. "Barbs, you'll be a knockout! I'll send you oceans of roses. I'll brag that I knew you when."

"But why do you, Barbs?" Nell Dyson asked in a cool tone. She was a self possessed young woman, sensible and level-headed. "You don't have to, and it is a grind!"

"My duty to the race," Barbs replied, with the impudent audacity which always characterized her. "Economic independence, and all that. Havelock Ellis says that when woman is economically independent she'll be free to choose her mate, unhampered by any except eugenic considerations. Hence the race will benefit. I'm nothing if not racial-minded, my dear."

She had become suddenly the centre of this circle. They were all listening to what she said; they laughed jeeringly now, in a vast good humor, and Bob Curry cried, in a sardonic tone:

"Mother of men!"

Barbs nodded amiably. "Dozens of 'em," she agreed.

Tony chuckled. "No, Barbs," he protested. "You've mistaken your calling. You're going out of your class." He expounded with the utmost gravity. "There are just three kinds of women," he argued. "There used to be only two, before we moderns came along. Eve and Lilith. The mother and the seductress." His eye, for an instant, touched Nina's, held her glance. "We've added a new category," he declared then. "The playgirl of the western world.

Good fellow well met! Three women, now. The mother, the seductress and the playmate."

Barbs looked at him shrewdly. "Where do you catalogue me?" she challenged.

Tony drawled: "I can't see you as the brave little mother! And you're rotten at games!" And their shouts of laughter were his applause.

They argued the point this way and that way; and Caterson stirred uneasily, and exchanged a rueful glance with Buckel. Men are slow to adopt new fashions of speech. These two were uncomfortable now.

The debate approached agreement. Barbs, they decided, was seductive.

"She's proved it often enough," said Audrey Deal, in that level tone at once sullen and insulting which she affected. "You know it, yourself, Barbs. You've got a rotten complexion, and a pug nose, and your eyes almost squint, and your figure's just plain bum. But when you appear at a dance, it's a mob scene."

"Technique, darling!" Barbs retorted. "Skill will tell, you know. It isn't the cards you hold; it's the way you play them."

Nina had said little, laughed often. She had a way of laughing which Mrs. Caterson thought curiously charming, her shoulders dancing up and down with her swift mirth. She was thus laughing now, standing a little aside, her arm linked through Sandy's; and she whispered something to him so that even Sandy grinned; and she called:

"What's the secret, Barbs? Give this little girl a helping hand, won't you?"

"Technique!" Barbs repeated. "If you dance with a man, tell him you're stifling, and he'll take you out of doors. Hold tight to his arm and he'll kiss you. Let him, and sigh as though you can't help yourself —and then break away. He'll dance with you again, playing for repeaters. And then other men will dance with you to see why he did. That's all there is to it, dear pupils. Now repeat the lesson after me. . . ."

Tony laughed, moved across the room. "Speaking of dancing," he cried, and started the phonograph and turned with open arms toward Barbs. "By way of illustration," he invited, and kicked the rug aside. Nina swung to Sandy. Dan and Audrey, Bob Curry and Nell. Mrs. Caterson, watching them, whispered to her husband:

"Joe, look at Tony! Did you ever see anything so beautiful?"

He nodded. "But Sandy dances the way I used to " he pointed out. "Sheer grit and perseverance."

There was a great clock in the hall; it chimed by and by the three-quarters. Tony exclaimed: "Do my ears deceive me? Can it be?" He swung Barbara toward the hall so that his eyes might confirm his ears; and these two passed for a moment out of sight. Audrey Deal called gravely:

"Now Barbs, sigh as though you can't help yourself!"

And everyone laughed, and Tony and Barbs reappeared, entirely composed. Then Tony held up a warning hand.

"Silence please! Attention! Last dance. Duty calls the striving athletes. Ladies, don't crowd. Take your turns, please."

And he caught them each in order, whirled them into the hall and back again in a dizzy sweep, releasing one and seizing on the next. Nina, Audrey, Nell. Then Mrs. Buckel. So at last his mother . . .

He kissed her roundly, there by the tall clock. "Good night, Sweet Child!" he whispered. "I told Richards. We'll drop some of these folks in town. See you at Thanksgiving!"

She hugged him hard, somehow tremulous. "Tony, Tony, don't ever forget we're proud of you!"

And then the others were about them, in the loud disorder of departure. Sandy, almost grudgingly, bade his mother goodby. He turned his cheek to her kiss; and she cried in tender anger:

"Don't be silly, Sandy. Here, son! On the mouth! There, my dear."

And added, whisperingly: "Look out for Tony, son. Don't let him be too bold!"

So, abruptly, they were gone; all these young faces, gay voices, laughing eyes. Nina went with them; but Mr. and Mrs. Buckel stayed a while. The big living room was astonishingly empty. Mrs. Caterson replaced the disordered rugs; and she took the tray of glasses and the shaker to the pantry again. When she came back, Buckel was saying:

"But the devil of it is, you can't help liking them!"

"Who?" she asked. "Young people?"

Her husband smiled and nodded. "We were just
—appraising them," he confessed. "No reticences,
impatience of all restraint, the most extreme enthusiasm over the most unimportant momentary fads, a
pedestal for any entertainment, a dungeon for any
sober thought." He chuckled. "And yet what a fine
lot they are!"

Buckel shook his head. "Those are national
traits," he suggested. "A young man and a young
nation are not so greatly different."

Mrs. Caterson urged smilingly: "We can decide
about it just as well sitting down."

But Mr. Buckel said they too must go. Mrs.
Buckel suggested that Mrs. Caterson must be tired.
. . . A few minutes after the youngsters had departed, Mr. and Mrs. Caterson were left alone.
They turned toward one another, and her eyes were
wistful and yet happy too. He pushed the logs together on the fire.

"Read a while, Lady," he suggested.

But she shook her head. "I'm tired," she confessed. "The let down, I suppose, after so much excitement. Let's go upstairs."

When they were by and by abed, they still talked
for a space, referring to this episode and that one in
the hours just gone. Her voice fell lower and lower,
sleepily; she said at last good night, and her hand
clasped his across the gap between their beds, and
held it for a while till her fingers relaxed and fell
away, so that he knew she was asleep. He lifted her

hand and laid it at her side and covered it over, and she murmured a faint word and slept again.

The telephone was on a stand in her dressing room, and the door was closed between; but the bell woke her, and she sat up in bed, startled out of slumber, terrified by this abrupt alarm. He spoke quick reassurance as he went to answer it; and she listened, puzzled and bewildered, to his monosyllabic ejaculations. She heard him make some doubtful remonstrance, heard him give at last a rueful assent. When he put the receiver back on the hook she called swiftly:

"Joe, what is it? What's the matter? What is it, Joe?"

He came to the bedroom door, said in frowning bewilderment: "I don't know, Lady. That was the matron at Temple Hospital. Miss Elcess is there. They've decided to operate at seven in the morning, instead of Monday, and she wants to see me before the operation."

Mrs. Caterson cried: "But Joe, how absurd! She saw you this afternoon."

He hesitated, shook his head. "Well, I promised I'd come," he told her.

She looked at him searchingly, but he said no more; and she somehow dreaded what answer he might give if she now did question him. So Mrs. Caterson made no further protest while her husband prepared to go.

V

CATERSON'S dressing room adjoined their bedchamber on one side, while Mrs. Caterson's was on the other. He came back from answering the telephone in her room, and stood uncertainly for a moment before he went to find his clothes. He was habitually careless and casual in matters sartorial; and tonight he was perplexed and mystified by this peremptory and disturbing summons that his confusion was even worse than usual. Mrs. Caterson had in the end to get up and help him find this garment and that; she discovered his missing garters attached to the socks he had worn this evening and in the laundry hamper; she chose his tie; she reminded him to put on a forgotten belt; she laughed at his ineptitudes.

But she did not ask him any more questions, nor did Caterson offer any explanation. Only when he was ready to go she said gaily, reassuringly, walking with him to the head of the stairs:

"There, my dear. I won't come down, but don't forget your coat."

"Yes," he assented, kissed her. "I'll try not to wake you, Lady. Go to sleep."

"Of course," she assured him. "I'm just walking in my sleep now." And she added casually: "Give

47

Ruth my love. I'll be in to see her as soon as she's ready for visitors."

He nodded and went down the stairs. She stood watching him; she leaned over the rail to see him find his coat in the closet; she called a last cheerful word, and waved her hand as he went out through the dining room toward the garage. When he presently backed the car into the drive and swung toward the street, she was at the window of her dressing room to see him go.

And she stayed there for a space after he had disappeared. She had drawn a kimono over her night gown when she got out of bed, and slipped her feet into flat sandals. When a woman puts off high heels and the strict rigor of her daily dress, she becomes curiously small and soft and appealing. Mrs. Caterson was not a particularly small woman; but she seemed so now. Her figure, motionless there by the window, was that of a child; and when she turned presently to extinguish all but one of the lights, and crossed again toward the bedroom, her sandals scuffed on the rug with a sound like faint, muffled sobs.

The night was cool, and the windows in the bedchamber were open, so she closed the doors before she got into bed. There was a bedlight above her pillow; and its bright illumination accentuated the faint pallor which had crossed her cheek at this night alarm. Her eyes were dry, but there was in them the ache of a formless fear; and she lay for a while with one arm under her head, looking straight before her at the blank wall, at the faintly moving curtains by the open window.

Then with a movement of resolution, she snapped out the light and turned on her side to sleep. At first the room was utterly dark; but the night outside was clear as the day had been fine, and by and by the starlight outlined the rectangles of the windows. Mrs. Caterson lay with her eyes closed, expecting sleep and courting it; but she was no longer sleepy, and after a while she opened her eyes again and lay watching a great star that shone through the thinning foliage of the trees. She stayed thus a long time, still as stone, no movement of her muscles reflecting the whirling confusion which possessed her mind.

But at length she freed one arm from the bed coverings and turned on the light; she propped herself somewhat higher on the pillows and chose a book from the table by her side and opened it to read. This was an old device of hers. It was often the case that if she were waked from her first sleep, she would lie awake for hours; and she had learned that to attempt to go immediately back to sleep again was to toss and twist distressfully. But if she took up a book and became absorbed in the printed page, her lids would presently begin to droop again.

So now she would have read herself to sleep; and for a page or two her eyes followed the lines, and her thoughts sought to do so. But first her thoughts and then her eyes turned elsewhere. The book fell unheeded on the coverlet. Her limp fingers still grasped it, but inattentively. Her eyes, glazed and unseeing, once more fastened on the blankness of the wall.

And her thoughts, like a horse that is at once tethered and under the sting of the lash, plunged and leaped and raced, circling maddeningly.

VI

CATERSON was a man, rough and ponderous and strong, in whom there dwelt a slow, persistent flame. He found delight in using his hands; in the slow, meticulous construction of little things and big ones too. He was by heart and blood a builder. Downstairs in what passed for his study there was a six-foot model of an ocean liner, built of paper, built to scale, built to measurement in every smallest detail, from the proportions of her hull to the conformation of the belaying pins in racks along the rail. Other things which he had fashioned were in other places, half way across the world. A dam and power house harnessing a tumbling stream to the uses of men a thousand miles away. A bridge; a dock; an office building; a cathedral; an aviation field. He was the builder, Tedlock the financier. Caterson and Tedlock was the firm name; a name to move mountains. They not only could move mountains; they had done so, or driven a shaft through the mountain's granite heart. . . .

Caterson was a builder, at home in any occupation that required manual dexterity. Something of the artist in him, too, perhaps. These traits appeared in his handling of a car; in the smooth, sure manipulations by which he turned now out of his garage into the street. Richards never drove Caterson to his office; Richards was at Mrs. Caterson's beck and call. Caterson preferred to drive himself; he had a small car which no one else ever used. It was this machine to which tonight he turned. As he swung into the street and pressed the throttle and felt the quick response of the engine he thought suddenly of Tony. Tony had this same love of driving, this passion for speed. Sandy drove when he must, but never from choice. In this as in so many other things, the brothers— twins though they were—were different.

Caterson, taking his way automatically toward the city, thought of these boys of his—as he was apt to do. There was, it had seemed to him tonight, an undercurrent of hostility between them; he had sensed something of the sort before. They had never been utterly congenial; had never evinced toward one another that almost passionate devotion which most brothers do at times display. So far as he knew, they had never had any open, serious quarrel. . . . Fisti- cuffs, yes; but these bouts were like summer showers, soon over, with no great harm behind. Yet there had been tonight, Caterson thought, something more tangible.

He slowed and stopped for a traffic light, and re- membered his errand, for a moment almost forgot- ten; and he wondered, with a quick clutch of fore- boding, what might be the answer to this riddle. There was a girl in the car beside his own; and he found himself scanning her features searchingly. He wiped his forehead, dragged his eyes away. This subconscious trick of his always disturbed him. When the light changed, he did not at once perceive it; the cars beside him leaped ahead and he followed them belatedly.

He continued for a few blocks more toward the city, then swung aside to the south, taking a street which served as an artery for cross-traffic. Temple Hospital lay in one of the suburbs in that direction, sprawling across the summit of a low hill which overlooked salt marshes, and the harbor, and even glimpsed the sea. Caterson knew the way as he knew his own front yard; for he and Mrs. Caterson had lived thereabouts in their first years together, before the firm of Caterson and Tedlock began to assume its present vast proportions, before the twins were born, before Caterson built the home where now they lived. The twins were born, in fact, in Temple Hospital. Miss Elcess had been trained there; she had come back there in her extremity.

She was, he decided, seriously ill; that much had been plain to him in the glimpse he had of her at the game. Her cheek wore an ugly, jaundiced hue; and there were shadows of agony in her eyes, and of a dreadful fear. And the woman who tonight had called him on the phone had spoken of her in that hushed tone which is the professional expression of the gravest fears. This was the hospital matron, he remembered; and when he drove into the parking space in front of the hospital and left his car and approached the entrance, he reminded himself to speak first to her.

It was by this time late at night, and the entrance corridors he found almost deserted. He turned toward the recess where the charts were hung, discovered a nurse on duty there, gave his name and said he had been summoned.

"The matron telephoned me," he explained.

"The superintendent?" she suggested. "Miss Foley?"

"Miss Foley, yes," he agreed.

"I'll try and find her," the girl told him; and she slipped silently away along the corridors. Caterson followed her uncertainly, falling quickly behind; he stopped at last, and waited, hat in hand. Other nurses passed him by, moving upon their own affairs. Then a somewhat older woman approached him, and he saw she meant to speak to him, and when she did so, uttering his name, he asked:

"You are Miss Foley? You phoned me?"

She nodded. "Yes," she said gravely. "Will you step in here a minute, please?" He followed, his heart pounding with a sort of guilt like that a small boy feels when he is summoned to chastisement. She led him into what seemed to be a small reception room, turned to face him there.

"Miss Elcess insisted that you be called," she explained. "I'm afraid it is an imposition."

He smiled reassuringly. "She is one of our oldest friends. We're very fond of her." And he added: "I hope she's not seriously ill."

"She is very seriously ill," Miss Foley assured him. She hesitated, and her tone was at once pitying and stern. "She has waited till it is too late to help her, I'm afraid." Shook her head. "I shouldn't say that. But Miss Elcess herself now realizes her condition. Doctor Bright had no need to tell her."

"You mean," he asked forthrightly, "that she may die under this operation?"

"That isn't likely," she told him. "But she may die very soon after, Mr. Caterson. She knows that. And after Doctor Bright had gone, tonight, she insisted on sending for you." She hesitated. "I tried to dissuade her. But I think she wants to ask you to— care for someone dear to her. She was insistent, and she is very ill."

He felt a quick surge of relief. The fears, intangible and unadmitted, which had nevertheless oppressed him, fell away. He smiled reassuringly.

"You need not apologize for calling me, Miss Foley," he assured her. "I was glad to come."

She nodded. "I'll take you to her," she said.

And Caterson, with a quicker stride, like a man relieved of a load, followed her to the elevator. They rose to the third floor, traversed the hall; and Miss Foley knocked lightly, then pushed open the unlatched door. Caterson was at her shoulder as she entered the room.

He saw Miss Elcess, in the high hospital bed, her head a little raised; and her aspect shocked him. At the Stadium she had looked badly; but there she had been in her ordinary garb, not greatly different to the casual eye from the throngs about her. Here, prone, helpless, surrendering, she seemed already shattered and shrunken. He checked, instinctively, in a quick dismay.

But her eyes shone at sight of him there, and she sought to smile; and Miss Foley said cheerfully:

"Here he is, Ruth. He was glad to come."

Caterson approached the bedside. "I'm mighty sorry you're like this, Miss Elcess," he said awkwardly. "Mighty sorry. Mrs. Caterson told me to give you her love, tell you she was coming in to see you soon . . ."

The head upon the pillow moved in a tender impatience, and Miss Elcess looked at the superintendent. "Go away, Miss Foley," she said huskily. "Shut the door."

Miss Foley nodded briskly. "Certainly. I wouldn't stay too long, Mr. Caterson!"

"Don't come in till he goes," Miss Elcess insisted; and Miss Foley reassured her. Caterson watched the superintendent's departure with a faint regret, once more ill at ease.

When the other woman was gone, Miss Elcess spoke to him. "Take off your coat, please, Mr. Caterson," she said, in that husky, broken voice. "Bring the chair near. Sit by the bed. I can't talk very loud." He hesitated. His hands were moist, his brow suddenly cold with a dreadful fear.

But after a moment he did as she desired.

VII

CATERSON sat down beside the bed where the sick woman lay; and he waited uncomfortably for her to speak. Her eyes had closed, and after a moment, startlingly, tears seemed to spurt from beneath her lowered lids; they darted down her cheek, across her high cheek bones in relief above the hollows illness and pain had graved there. And Caterson said slowly:

"I expect you're too tired to—talk to me. I can come in the morning, some other time . . ."

Her hand sought his shoulder; her fingers twisted in the rough cloth of his coat and fixed there. She shook her head, and she seemed to smile.

"No," she said. "No. I'm all right. I'm not—really crying. It's just such a relief."

He hesitated. "You know," he told her, in a tone of jocular friendliness, "I don't know what this is all about, Miss Elcess. I only know you needed me, wanted me . . ." She did not at once reply; and he added: "Miss Foley thought you wanted me to take care of some one whom you love. But of course," he added hurriedly, "you're going to be all right yourself, in a week or two."

She shook her head, calmer now. "Oh, no," she assured him. "No, Mr. Caterson. I'm going to die."

Her tone was steady and unafraid. She touched her body, prone beneath the blankets. "There's a lump in there, and if they leave it there it will—eat me up. But when they take it out, I'm going to die."

He was silenced, stricken by her steadfast courage. He felt her fingers twist tighter in the fabric of his sleeve; and then suddenly her eyes opened, and she moved a little, so that she was more erect, and she released her hold on him.

"I have to tell you a long story, Mr. Caterson," she said slowly.

He nodded, and something in her eyes made him summon courage too. "I want to hear it, then," he assured her.

"It's about the boys," she added, choking huskily. "About your boys."

And he thought he had known this; yet at the word a black curtain fell before his eyes, and he stared at this dark screen silently, as the audience in a theatre, when the lights are dimmed, grows quiet and stares at the curtain there about to rise. He waited, seeing nothing; and Miss Elcess after a moment began to speak, now more readily and freely. Yet was there something murmurous in her tone, as though she spoke in sleep, or from the abysses of a dark and dreadful dream.

"I was with Mrs. Caterson before the twins were born, you know," she sad gently, as much to herself as to him. "For she wasn't very well, and we were concerned for her. So I was with her for weeks before, at your home. She wanted to stay at home, but Doctor Sprague would not have it so, because he was afraid of some emergency. He wanted to have every means at hand, so he said she must come here."

She paused momentarily, and Caterson tried to speak some word; but his lips emitted no sound.

"So I was always near her, at your home. I loved her, Mr. Caterson. Everyone must love her, and I did; and I watched over her in every way. And when the time came, too soon, you and I together brought her here. You remember?" She smiled slowly, and she was for a moment infinitely older and wiser than he, as women in these matters are. "You remember how nervous you were, Mr. Caterson? You were much more trouble than she was. Oh, I had a time with you. . . ."

He did remember, so vividly. It had been worse on this occasion than when the first baby came; the girl baby who stayed so short a time. He remembered; and his thoughts went wandering in those old, tormented hours, till Miss Elcess spoke once more.

"Too soon," she repeated. "So even Doctor Sprague was much concerned. He came away from his dinner table to be with her; and he stayed with her. And you couldn't be with her, because she was distressed for you, so you walked up and down outside and smoked cigars till there were ashes and butts all along on the snow. It was March, you remember, and fresh snow on the ground.

"And you walked up and down. I could see you from the window. Till after a while there was no more time to watch you, and we all went up in the

elevator. And after we came down again, Doctor
Sprague stayed with Mrs. Caterson, while I ran to
tell you. And we were all so relieved, because she was
all right, and the babies were all right; and they were
twins, and there is always something funny about
twins." She smiled slowly, turning her head to look
at him. "It's supposed to be a joke on the father,"
she explained. "So we laughed about that, because
it was nice to laugh about something. And you came
up, but you couldn't stay but a minute, because she
was very weak and tired."

She hesitated, and her voice suddenly shook, as
though she were broken on the rack.

"You didn't go in to see your babies," she reminded him. "I couldn't take you, but I told you
where to go; but you forgot. You kissed Mrs. Caterson's hand, and she went to sleep, and you went
stumbling away, and went home. You remember?"

He was watching her with a fearful apprehension,
his cheek drawn into deep furrows; but he nodded
hurriedly. "Go on," he bade. "Go on."

"And Doctor Sprague went home, too. Poor Doctor Sprague! You remember he died eleven days
afterward? Yes. He might know, now, if he were
alive . . ." She hesitated, continued slowly: "He
went home, and he told me not to leave her, because
she was very weak. But the floor nurse came in while
I went to make sure the babies were all right. They
were in the room with the other babies. You saw
them, afterward. Little iron cribs like baskets, in
rows along both sides of the room, and a place for

cards on the foot of each crib, with 'Baby Smith' or 'Baby Jones' written on the cards. And I wrote 'Baby Caterson' on two cards for my babies. Your babies, Mr. Caterson, I mean. They were asleep. Such fine little boys." She seemed suddenly to choke again. "I remember how glad I was that they were so well, because so many twins die, you know. Almost half of all twins born do die, Mr. Caterson. In spite of everything!"

He thought, in a bewildered fashion, that there was a plea for forgiveness in her tones; but while he still puzzled over this, she went on.

"They were in the hospital nighties, that night, because we hadn't been ready for them quite so soon. But I saw that they were asleep, and well. There was another nurse there, putting another very new baby into a crib beside theirs. That baby's mother was going to die, she told me; and there wasn't any father. Some woman had been kind to this girl, had sent her here; that was all. Her baby was very small, too, as yours were.

"And I went back to Mrs. Caterson and let the floor nurse go. It was almost two o'clock by that time, and Mrs. Caterson slept so quietly; and I sat beside her so that I would be there if she needed me. The hospital was very still, that night, I remember; only once in a while I would hear a nurse go softly past the door."

She hesitated for a moment as though summoning her memories; and Caterson leaned forward tautly, laying his hand upon her arm with an instinctive gesture. But at her slow glance he withdrew it, uttered some low word.

"Mrs. Caterson woke up," Miss Elcess said then, and her voice was stricken. "She had dreamed that her baby was dead, and she woke up crying, and trying to sit up, and I had to move quickly, and hold her; for she was desperate with grief. She cried out that her baby was dead, and I told her she had two babies, and they were both fine, and tried to quiet her. She was so terribly sure, and so frantic!"

He said with a heavy nod, trying to keep his tones steady: "She told me, next day, about that dream."

"She wanted to go to her babies," Miss Elcess explained. "I had to hold her. She was so weak that it was not hard to hold her. But she was torturing herself, and I was afraid she'd make herself ill; and she was sure her baby was dead. So at last I told her that if she promised to lie quietly, I would bring the babies in to her. There was nothing else to do. And she promised, and I flew along the hall to the baby ward, to their little iron cribs.

"There was no one there, just then; just one dim light burning. I picked up one of the twins, and then the other; and the second one squirmed, and made small, spitty noises. And I started toward the door, and then I realized that the first one did not squirm or move. And I knew, even before I looked. One of them was dead, Mr. Caterson. Mrs. Caterson was right! One of them was dead."

He made a sound like a cough; like the strangling

cough of a man into whose chest a dart is plunged. And he managed speech, a word meaningless enough, no more than an echo.

"Dead?"

She nodded dumbly. "I heard Mrs. Caterson calling," she went on, in a dull monotone. "Her room was only two or three doors away, and even through the closed doors of the baby room, I heard her call. There was only a desperate minute, Mr. Caterson. I turned back to the line of cribs, and picked up the nearest baby, and put the little quiet one down in its place, and ran back to Mrs. Caterson. She was fighting to sit up, and I thrust the babies into her arms, and her face shone, and she lay down with one of them on either arm. I had no chance to think of anything except to quiet her, you see. She lay there with her face like the sun; and she would have them side by side on her right arm so that she might look at both of them at once. They twisted and made small, sputtering noises, and then they went to sleep again. And she watched them for a while, till her own eyes drooped; and by and by she, too, was asleep, with them on her arm."

She herself lay for a moment as though sleeping, her eyes closed; and Caterson there beside her, perceiving at last the clear lineaments of fact through the mists of his formless fears, became steadier. He grew calm.

"You took another baby instead of—ours," he repeated.

"Yes." The sick woman hesitated, then she said again: "Yes." And she added: "I had only a minute. I had to do something."

"You did the best thing," he told her steadily. "But—what followed after, Miss Elcess? What was the end of it?" His tone, in spite of him, rose to a keener pitch. "Please—go on," he urged.

"Mrs. Caterson went to sleep with the babies on her arm," the woman repeated. "And after a while I tried to take them, but she roused, and her arm curled to enfold them, to hold them. And when I tried again, she still would not let them go, even in her sleep. Then she woke, and lay half awake till dawn, watching her babies through half closed lids; and I saw that she was growing stronger. But I dreaded the morning, and I did not know what I was to do."

"But what did you do?" he cried, goaded now. "What did you do?"

The color drained from her pale lips. "I didn't do anything," she confessed.

"What happened?" he insisted. "What happened in the morning?" His eyes flickered, gleamed with sudden desperate hope. "Was the other one all right after all, just asleep?"

She shook her head, and after a moment she said in a slow, resolute tone:

"This is what happened. At daylight, Mrs. Caterson went sound asleep, and I could take the babies away. I hurried back to the baby room with them. I expected questions, reproaches, perhaps hospital discipline. But I met no one; only in the baby room there was a nurse bringing a bottle for a morning feeding, for a baby that was not nursing; and I saw that the crib where I had left the—other one was empty.

"There was not even a card on the end of the crib now. I put my babies back in their places, and I asked the nurse where the other baby was—without telling her anything.

"She told me it had died in the night. I remember she said it was a good thing, because the baby's mother was dead now, too, and there wasn't any father. She said it had died, and of course they had taken it out of the baby room. And at first I was terrified, and I didn't dare tell the truth; and then I knew that the truth would—kill Mrs. Caterson, perhaps. And so I kept still.

"I meant to tell Doctor Sprague. But Mrs. Caterson was ill, you know; she was very ill, for days, and they thought she wouldn't live. So I had no time to think of other things, and in the end I never told him at all."

She hesitated; she said pitifully:

"It's been a good deal to carry, Mr. Caterson. I never meant to tell you. But—it's easier, now that I have told."

"But didn't anyone see the difference?" he protested. "Didn't anyone notice it?"

She shook her head. "There isn't much difference in very new babies, except their weight, and whether they're boys or girls, unless they have black hair," she reminded him. "And your babies each weighed almost exactly the same as—the strange one. And there was no one to notice, but me. It was not a thing anyone would suspect, or look for, you see."

He nodded, soberly accepting the situation, facing the question that now must be asked. And he thought suddenly of these boys of his—these two boys who had for twenty years been his sons. Tony, tall, and keen, and lovable and fine; Sandy, the plodder, stolid yet substantial too. They had always been so desperately proud of Tony; but neither had Sandy ever given them cause for shame. Proud? Yes, infinitely proud of each one, he had been.

And now, in this moment just ahead, he must lose one of them. One was his true son, one was a stranger. It need not, he told himself, make any difference. The boys were after all both his boys, if twenty years of love and care could make them so. He tried not to ask the question; tried to argue that it need never be asked. He would not even tell Mrs. Caterson. There was no need for her to know; no need that she should ever know. He need only learn to dissemble, to support this burdensome truth alone.

But through the dark confusion of his thoughts there ran suddenly a bright illumination; it was like a lightning flash on a lowering summer day. It was a ray of light that seemed to focus pitilessly upon his head; and Caterson in this moment bowed to that sudden understanding. There was in this catastrophe a fitness which he suddenly perceived; which he accepted as his due. He would not seek to escape or to evade.

He lifted his head to put the steady question.

"Which one is—our boy, Miss Elcess?" he asked quietly. "Tony, or Sandy? Which one is our own?"

She swung to meet his glance; and in her eyes he had, even before she spoke, his answer. Yet she spoke evenly enough, bravely enough.

"I don't know, Mr. Caterson," she told him, in tones like the stroke of doom. "I was so desperate to get back to Mrs. Caterson that I—didn't pay close attention; and afterward, I couldn't remember. I don't know!"

And at her word the man relaxed in his chair. His face became expressionless; but there was that in his breast like the keen and darting bite of a white hot blade.

VIII

IT was past midnight before Caterson left the hospital. That which Miss Elcess told him had left him for a while in a sort of hypnosis in which his thoughts raced and churned with an extraordinary energy. A series of pictures presented themselves in his mind, each in its turn for a moment clear and distinct, each in its turn merging into the next one. It was as though he were looking at a moving picture film that ran very slowly, with a pause on each exposure.

Thus there passed through his mind the whole lives of these boys, these babies who had grown to young men, these individuals whom he had always accepted as his own flesh and blood. They had been extraordinarily near to him. He had felt, between them and him, close, living, almost physical bonds. He had known not only what they did, but what they thought and felt and hoped. All the long progress of their lives had tended toward this close sympathy and loyalty and love between him and his sons.

And now, abruptly and with no least warning, there had opened between him and them a gulf; a gulf which seemed in this first moment too deep to plumb, too wide to leap. The boys were suddenly strangers, looking back at him across the widening abyss. They were both strangers. Upon each one of them the taint must lie, for Miss Elcess did not know which was the true son and which the false one.

And if she did not know, then the answer was not to be found in the living world.

Caterson, at that last word of hers, at that incredible and overpowering negative, had slumped back in his chair, his body relaxed and motionless while his thoughts came sweeping down the channel of the years. And the sick woman, having spoken, waited silently for his reproaches, or for his further questioning. When he did not speak, she turned her head to look at him, to discover if she could what was passing in his mind. But his eyes were blank and empty; he was not even conscious in this moment of her presence there.

While he thus sat, and while she watched him, someone knocked softly on the door and before they could reply, came in. It was the nurse assigned to attend Miss Elcess. She approached the bedside and put a thermometer between the sick woman's lips, and she laid her finger tips against the other's pulse. She stood thus for a moment, then made some readjustments here and there about the room, removed the thermometer and, still without having spoken a word, went out again.

But her coming and her going had brought Caterson back to the present world, and when she was gone, he asked another question:

"Miss Elcess, why haven't you told us long ago?"

The woman nodded, as though she had been expecting this inquiry. "It wasn't anything I ever really decided," she told him. "I don't suppose most people ever have occasion to make any great decisions. I expect our lives are made out of little decisions, little defeats, and little victories. It always seemed that this was decided for me, just as the thing itself was taken out of my hands by the situation at the time, Mr. Caterson. I only did in each particular moment what I had to do."

"I can understand your not telling anyone then," he admitted. "I can understand your desperation and your fears, Miss Elcess. But why haven't you told us since?"

She smiled faintly, her eyes closed, her head moving on the pilow.

"The other baby had no one to love him," she reminded him. "And you and Mrs. Caterson had lost a baby. You needed a baby, and he needed a father and mother, and it seemed to me as though the whole thing had been planned to make you all three happier.

"I thought at first I would tell you some time, and then for years I thought I would never tell you; but when I grew ill, I knew I would have to tell you, somehow, before I died."

She hesitated, added ruefully: "I hope you won't be unhappy about it, after a while."

He nodded, willing to reassure and comfort her, yet still driven by amazement into questioning.

"Who was the other baby?" he asked. "Who was his mother, his father?"

She shook her head. "I didn't dare ask any questions," she pointed out. "I felt, I suppose, the way a criminal must feel, that everyone is watching him suspiciously. I was afraid any question from me would make other people curious, start some investigation.

"Only, I know there weren't any relatives. The mother who died hadn't any people living. I heard the nurses say that. They were all saying it was a mercy the baby died too."

She hesitated, smiled faintly. "You can find out," she reminded him. "You can go back to the hospital records and find out, if you want to."

But Caterson shook his head. That sleeping dog, he knew, must be allowed to slumber undisturbed.

When he left her, he had a word or two with Miss Foley in the corridors. She thanked Mr. Caterson again for coming. He made some polite and acquiescent reply, and turned toward the elevator, and so emerged at last into the street.

The night was crisp and cool, cool enough for frost. The skies were cloudless, and the stars shone there, not as they sometimes do, like a confused and milky mass, but individually, each with a radiance of its own. Caterson crossed to his car, but for a moment he did not press the starter. He sat trying to assort the confused impressions of the last hour, trying to bring order out of the chaos of his thoughts, trying to whip himself back to some certainty of mind.

He perceived and with an increasing certainty, the

crux of the problem which now confronted him. The question was, very simply, whether it were better to tell Mrs. Caterson or no; and he found himself remembering the reason Miss Elcess had given for her own long silence, and sought in similar fashion to justify himself in silence now. Through the nurse's silence had come twenty years of increasing happiness for them all. Since she had spoken, he himself could never be completely happy again; and if he were to tell Edith that one of these boys she loved was not in fact her own son, she must for the rest of her life be as perplexed and sad as he.

Even in this moment, Caterson could foresee what the years were like to bring. There would always be, like a spectre between him and his sons, the question which was the true, and which the false one; and he perceived in this situation all the possibilities of tragic grief which it must at times present. He sought by such arguments to persuade himself that he might now be silent, might keep this grim secret buttoned fast away in his own bosom, to gnaw there like the fox which tortured the Spartan boy.

And he tried to tell himself that this was his fit and proper course, that to shelter and protect Edith was his best and bravest procedure. The thought brought him some comfort; for he dreaded telling her, dreaded it with a fear beyond words. But a moment later, with a sudden clearer vision and a sterner mind, his thoughts set and locked in a new mold. He pressed the starter, waited a moment for the engine to run smoothly, and turned his car toward home.

He had made up his mind to tell Mrs. Caterson. To be silent would be to spare her, but also it would be to spare himself; and Caterson recognized in his desire to keep silence now an inner weakness, a taint of moral cowardice against which he had for all the years of his manhood sought to stiffen his soul. Here were the lineaments of an ancient enemy who must once more be beaten down.

He set out for home, and the car leaped at the pressure of his foot upon the throttle. At the first turn, he slewed dangerously, so thereafter he drove more slowly; but the relaxing of his own speed re-minded him of Tony, who always drove at a break-neck pace. He thought he and Tony were alike in this, and this thought of the resemblance between Tony and himself reminded him that perhaps Tony was not, after all, his own son.

So he came back to that tormenting conundrum. Which was the true son, and which the false? And during this homeward drive, he searched among his memories for evidence on this side and on that. He could discover only a confusingly even balance be-tween the two boys. Tony in eyes and features resembled Mrs. Caterson; Sandy had Caterson's own broad and rugged countenance. Tony had Mrs. Cat-erson's charm, her appealingly friendliness, her gaiety; but the boy had, too, something of Caterson's persistent zeal in any undertaking. Yet, of the two, Sandy was unquestionably more like Mr. Caterson. He, too, was a builder by instinct, a worker with his hands; and he had much of the shy reticence which had always possessed the older man.

Caterson found himself only more and more confused by his attempt to test and assay the boys; but in his scrutiny of their lineaments and of their characters, he came to a new and more disturbing element. He remembered the old antagonism between them. This enmity was distinct and easily to be recognized; it smouldered always, manifesting itself in small prideful ways, and there were moments when, especially on Tony's part, it flamed more vividly. If the boys knew the truth, Caterson decided, this feeling would be accented; and he thought wearily that they must never know.

Yet Mrs. Caterson must know!

He came by and by into the street that led up over the hill to his own home, and while he was still two or three blocks from the house, he saw that there was a light in the bedroom window. This meant that Mrs. Caterson was still awake; if she had slept, she had roused again, and perhaps now was reading while she waited his return. He had not till this moment realized the imminence of the necessity of confronting her, and in a sudden dismay he pulled in beside the curb and stilled his engine.

He sat there for a while in a damp sweat of apprehension, dreading the moment when he must meet her eyes. He longed for any escape from this necessity, any honest evasion or reprieve. But, as was the man's habit, full recognition of his own fears served to vanquish them. He fought them down, he stiffened his courage, he started the engine once more and continued on his way.

He had left a light burning in the hall, and when he came to the top of the stairs he pressed the button which extinguished it; so passed into his own dressing room. Their bedroom was just beyond, the door closed between. Usually, when he came home late at night and Mrs. Caterson was awake, she heard him in his dressing room and called to him. But tonight, though he listened, she did not call; and in spite of his resolution, he felt a swift relief at this, at the thought that though her light was burning, she might be asleep, might perhaps fail to rouse when he went in to his own bed beside hers. Thus that which he dreaded might with honor be postponed till morning.

He undressed very quietly, and he put his clothes away upon hangers, or in the laundry hamper, with a meticulous care entirely foreign to his ordinarily careless habit. He sought small pretexts, each one time-devouring. Thus it was some time after he reached home before, having switched out the light in his dressing room, he quietly lifted the latch of the intervening door and passed into the bedroom beyond.

But when he did so, he saw at once that her eyes were open, that she was watching him, that she smiled faintly at his cautiously silent entrance. He stopped uncertainly, astonished and dismayed, and he said huskily:

"Oh, you're awake, Edith?"

"Yes, Joe," she replied. "Yes, I haven't been asleep."

He nodded automatically, without being conscious of the gesture. The windows were open and the room was full of crisp, fresh air. And she said softly:

"Get into bed, Joe. You'll catch cold."

But still he did not move. He stood there as though paralyzed, and small beads of perspiration formed upon his brow. He stared at her unseeingly, and she watched him, and after a moment she smiled, in a fashion astonishingly full of understanding and of comfort.

When she spoke again, his ears were incredulous. He could not believe he heard aright. For she said, in a tone full of infinite wisdom and reassurance:

"To bed with you, Joe my dear! It's all right! Don't be so distressed. You see, I already know!"

IX

IN the major crises of domestic life, women are apt to evidence a greater degree of strength and of composure than do men. This may be because in such matters there dwells in woman an ancient wisdom. Affairs of birth and life and death have from the beginning been her more direct concern. She is more used to meet these three somewhat terrifying phenomena face to face and steadily.

But whether this be the cause or no, the fact remains. If the cook leaves, or hot water mars the dining room table, or ink is spilled upon the choicest rug, a man can view the matter with composure, while his wife may approach hysterics. But if there is a child to be borne, it is the woman who approaches the matter most calmly; and if Death knocks, she will fight him to the end with a calm and steady courage, and meet defeat at last with a resolution beyond man's utmost powers.

Caterson might have remembered this; might have expected that his wife would be in the face of the news he bore steadier than he. But this had not occurred to him; and least of all had it occurred to him that she might anticipate what he had to tell her, that she might be in some intangible fashion forewarned, and so forearmed. Thus her word now left him drained and weak and bemused by something he could not understand. She said gravely: "It's all right, my dear. I know." And he stared at her, and he shook his head, and he sat down wearily on the bed.

"You can't!" he protested. "Edith, you—— What do you mean? What is it that you know?"

Her eyes closed for a moment, and he thought she would weep; but she opened them again, and smiled.

"Get into bed, dear Lad," she insisted. And as he moved slowly to obey her: "No, dear. In my bed, here. We must talk together for a while."

And when he came to her, she folded him in her arms, tucked his head upon her shoulder as though he were still a child, stroked his forehead tenderly. "There," she whispered. "There, poor boy. Be still."

His cheek pressed hers. "But Edith," he whispered. "You can't—know? What she told me!"

"It's about the boys, isn't it?" she challenged gently.

"Yes. Yes, it is."

She turned out the light above their heads, so that they lay in darkness; and the darkness somehow sheltered and protected them. She said slowly:

"I remember the night I bore them, Joe. So clearly. And afterward I slept, and in my sleep I knew—one of them had died." She hesitated, and when he did not stir, she reminded him: "You know, I told you my dream in the morning, Joe."

"Yes, but it was—just a dream," he urged.

"You thought so," she assented. "And perhaps I thought so. I was willing to think so, my dear. For —the boys were there beside me in the morning. And Miss Elcess tending us all."

"Yes," he agreed.

She waited a moment. "Tell me," she said at last. "Tell me what happened tonight. She sent for you. Is she very ill?"

"She expects to die," he assented. "They've decided to operate on her in the morning. She seems to know it's hopeless, and Miss Foley, the superintendent, as much as admitted this to me. A cancer, I think . . . So she sent for me."

"I've known for many years," Mrs. Caterson repeated. "You remember how she has always liked to come to see us, to see the boys. I've seen her watching them; seen the burden in her eyes. There really is an understanding between women, Joe."

And she added softly: "I didn't know on the surface of my mind, perhaps. I learned to forget that old dream. But it was always there, waiting to be remembered. Waiting to explain so many things."

And a moment later she said in tender chiding: "You must have seen in her attitude all this time that something was wrong, my dear; must have seen that something tormented her."

"I didn't notice, particularly," he confessed; and she smiled in the darkness there beside him at the blindness of this man, and of all men.

"She told me tonight what happened," he said at last. "The whole thing!"

"Yes?"

"There was—another baby born in the hospital that night," he explained. "The mother—I don't know whether she was married, and the father dead, or exactly what the story was. Miss Elcess never dared ask questions about it afterward. But there was a boy baby, and it happened he was a very small baby, as ours were. Some woman had befriended the mother, sent her there for proper care. The baby's crib was beside those where our boys were laid."

"I see," she assented; and for all her steady courage, there was an ache in her grave tones.

So in a hurried rush of words he made clear the whole. She did not speak during this recital; there was no need of her prompting. Once begun upon the tale, his tongue ran swiftly. He had thought there was so much to tell; and he was a little surprised to find how soon the whole was told. He could not believe that he had told her everything, and he retraced his steps, repeated this and that, floundering more and more. For she lay so silent here beside him. . . . Till at last he was done, and there was no more that he could find to say, and he ended; and since still she did not move, he drew her close in his arms.

When his cheek touched hers, tears were there. Yet her voice when she spoke at last was clear and steady.

"I see," she said again. "Poor Miss Elcess! How unhappy she has been."

And a moment later, dreamily: "I can remember so clearly, little things. I remember that night of course, as though it were this night, Joe. But other, later things, too. How she used to watch the boys when she brought them in to me. She watched them with such searching, tortured eyes. I remember when she bathed them how she would turn their small bodies over and over on her knees, scanning every inch of them. I laughed at her once for this, and she stared at me pallidly, and she said it was just that she wanted to be sure all the little creases on their bodies were properly powdered and cared for. . . . And I can remember in the years since then, questions she asked me, and things she said, and the way she used to look at the boys, when she came here, and then look at you, or at me."

She uttered a low, sweet sound like a chuckle of tender mirth.

"She was trying to be sure we loved them both alike, Joe. She loved them both so jealously. You remember how she always praised Sandy, even when he was little, just because Tony was taller, and handsomer than he."

"I never noticed, particularly," he confessed. "I guess a man misses seeing a lot of things."

And he added in a sudden harsh agony: "I can't believe it, even now, Edith. I can't believe it's true. She's imagined it. Her—mind must be shaken, by pain, or illness or something. Edith, it can't be true."

She touched his brow with her cool palm. "My

dear, it's quite true," she assured him. "But what difference does it make? What difference does it make to us, Joe?"

"But it's incredible," he protested. "Someone would have seen, at the time; seen the difference between them."

"Not so easily," she assured him. "Babies are not much different, except that some are bigger than others. If they weighed the same. . . . And this wasn't one of those things anyone was likely to suspect, or challenge, Joe. It was so ridiculously easy and natural. It happened of itself. No, dearest Lad. No, it's quite true."

He was silent for a moment, said at last: "Edith, you're a wonder to me! Did you really know? How long have you known?"

She answered softly, half to herself: "I knew, yes. The way we do sometimes know things, with the back of our minds. Nothing ever happened to bring this into the front of my mind before; that's all. And—it didn't matter. They were my boys. I nurtured them and tended them and loved them; I put myself into them, till they were crammed full of me. They were mine!" She hesitated, on a sound like a sob; but after a moment she went on, steadily again:

"But Joe, my dear, when they didn't look alike, then I knew my dark dream was a true one."

"Twins don't have to look alike," he protested.

"I know," she agreed tenderly. "That would satisfy a man. You went to the doctors, and the books, and they told you that out of every three pairs of twins, only one pair was identical; and that contented you. So long as you knew that the lack of resemblance was scientifically possible, that was all you wished to know.

"You've always had such good, scientific explanations for things. When Tony and Sandy quarreled, you assured me that the books said twins who didn't look alike were apt to quarrel; and when they used to deny they were twins, you quoted such learned doctors who declared that dissimilar twins often tried to hide their twinship.

"Oh, you could always find scientific explanations, dear; but science never went very deep with me. Scientists are dusty folk, I think. And I never believe more than half they say, because as soon as one scientist proves something is true, another scientist comes along and shows the first one was mistaken.

"But my dear, mothers aren't very often mistaken in matters that concern their children. We usually know!"

He said no word, lay quiet there beside her; and after a little she continued thoughtfully:

"But it didn't make me unhappy, Joe. It needn't make you unhappy now. We've got them both, and they're fine boys, and that's all that matters, isn't it?" And when he did not at once reply, she added, as much to herself as to him: "Tony's made us proud of him so many times!"

He stirred suddenly. "Sandy's a substantial sort

of boy," he urged, as though this were to dissent from her praise of Tony.

Something in his tone perhaps perturbed her, for she did not immediately speak; but when she did, it was comfortingly.

"They needn't ever know about it," she pointed out.

"I hope not," he agreed. "That—worried me! They jar on each other, sometimes, as it is. If they knew this, there'd always be a deeper pit between them. Real friction, I'm afraid."

And he added, with a masculine eye to practical detail: "But—we might quietly take some legal steps, in case the question is ever raised. Adoption?"

"Who can ever raise a question?" she chided him, laughingly. "Don't be absurd, Joe."

"A matter of inheritance," he urged. "You can't be sure."

"Nonsense," she protested. "We're giving them their best inheritance, every day; giving them ourselves. The rest doesn't matter. But nothing's going to happen, anyway!"

"And of course, if we did anything of that sort, they might find it out," he doubtfully agreed.

"We'll just love them both very dearly, and that's all that matters," she told him.

He said after a moment: "I expected you to—take this hard, Edith. You're a wonderful creature. You're so wise, and fine, and strong and—everything. You know, my dear, I love you."

"Do you?" she echoed, smiling in the darkness.

"More each day."

"There are so many days in twenty years. Twenty-three years, now, isn't it. Almost twenty-four. What children we were, Lad!"

"I've been happy," he said.

"I've been happy too."

His cheek pressed hers strongly, and she lay in his arms; but after a moment she said: "We must be so good to them, Joe. Sandy needs love, especially. He doesn't know how to—compel it from people, as Tony does. But he wants it, only you have to understand, and give it to him."

"His college work has picked up this year," Caterson remarked. "I've been worried about him, sometimes. I don't want him to lead the class, or anything of that sort; but I want him to get by."

"Never worry about Sandy," she bade him gaily. "Only love him."

Outside, the stars shone; the casement windows were jewelled rectangles of deep night. A late travelling automobile passed in front of the house with a hiss of tires on asphalt, turned up a neighbor's drive; they heard the creak and click as the garage doors were closed. Somewhere two or three miles away a clock struck thrice, the slow strokes booming.

"Time we were asleep, my dear," she said.

"I'm not—sleepy," he confessed.

"I'm growing so."

"I'll get into my own bed," he decided. "So I won't disturb you." He kissed her. "Good night, Lady!"

Her arm tightened around his neck. "And it's all right, my dear," she whispered. "All right, remember. Believe me, Joe."

"All right if you say so," he promised, and kissed her long again.

A moment later, when they were settled in their own beds, she spoke dreamily.

"I'll go in and see her tomorrow, and tell her not to be unhappy about it, and comfort her."

"I doubt if you can see her tomorrow," he suggested. "Perhaps in a day or two."

"A day or two, yes," she agreed.

And for minutes then, neither of them spoke. Caterson was wide awake, staring at the windows. There was that in his thoughts which more and more tormented him; sleep was far away. His wife had given him full measure of comfort; but there was one comfort she could not give, one wound it seemed to him not even Edith could heal.

And there was one dark enigma, still unanswered. Unless she could answer it. She who was so wise. He was driven in the end to speak to her.

"Edith," he whispered. "Asleep?"

"Not quite, my dear," she confessed.

The question broke from him like a cry. "Edith, which boy is ours?"

A long silence lay beside him; a silence so long that it ached, and it burned. Mrs. Caterson did not answer him, and he thought she must have fallen asleep between her last word and his question, she lay so still.

But suddenly she moved, and sat up; he heard the stir of her coverlets. Then the light snapped on, and he saw her, leaning on one elbow, staring at him. Her eyes were wide and stricken with dark fears.

"Which one?" she echoed.

He scrambled to a sitting posture, leaned to catch her in his arms. "Miss Elcess didn't know!" he confessed. "She didn't know, Edith. I thought you must know."

She caught his arms in her hands. "She doesn't know?" she cried, and her tone was as fierce as a flame. "She gave me someone else's baby, and she doesn't know!"

"Edith," he begged. "Please. Don't!"

Her fists beat at him. "She took my baby," she ejaculated. "Now she's taken both my boys from me."

Even in that moment, while he strove to comfort her, he could know astonishment at her grief and rage. She had been able to face bravely the fact that her baby had died twenty years ago; but this lesser loss, this minor torture wrung from her keen outcries, half hysterical, and marked her countenance with deep lines of anguish and of pain.

"My dear," he whispered. "We have them both! They're ours!"

"But not to know, not to know!" she wailed.

"Dearest, dearest!" he urged. "We love them both alike."

She would have risen, would have leaped out of

bed. He had to restrain her forcibly. "I want to go to her," she protested. "I must, Joe. I must talk to her. We can compare notes, we can figure it out between us, Joe. Tonight. Before they operate on her. Joe, Joe, let me go."

"Dearest, she doesn't know," he urged.

"I want to go!"

"If you go," he argued, "it will make a tumult at the hospital. Make talk, Edith! Guesses, whispers. Wait till tomorrow, the day after!"

And he added: "If I thought she could tell us, I'd take you over right away. But dearest, she doesn't know."

"I have to talk to her," she repeated piteously.

But in the end he was able to persuade her to some composure.

"We'll remember something, between us, she and I," she whispered, reassuring herself, comforting herself. "And anyway, Joe, we have them both."

"And love them both!" he reminded her.

"Oh, we do love them so," she echoed. "But I can see her tomorrow, Joe? Or the day after. Promise me, surely. There'll be something we can find!"

So in the end she was persuaded; and with the quick spring of hope, it seemed to them both that what she said was true; that when she and Miss Elcess could talk together calmly, they must discover some point, forgotten till now, which would distinguish their true son.

For not to know the truth would be intolerable, a long anguish hardly to be borne. It seemed to Mrs.

Caterson in this dark moment that merely to con-
template that possibility was to despair. She could
lose a son long dead with only tender grief; but to
be unable to recognize a son alive was not to be
endured.

X

THEY slept at last, but briefly; for the night was drawn toward dawn before their eyes closed, and the risen sun aroused them. It is only youth which can at such hours sleep its fill, sleep till the reservoirs are replenished and the strength renewed. Caterson was the first to wake; and instantly remembering, he lay very still, not even turning on the pillow lest he disturb her here beside him. He could by a movement of his eyes mark where her fair head lay, half hidden by the coverlets; he could see the line of her body, curled like a child's.

But he made no sound, scarcely even blinking his eyes when the sun shone into them. Only he lifted the edge of the blanket as a bulwark between him and that blinding light, and closed his lids, and thus assumed once more the aspect of sleep without the reality.

Mrs. Caterson roused presently, and looked toward him; but his eyes were closed, and she in turn lay silent, that he might rest while he could. Yet she watched him tenderly, brooding over him as though he were son as well as husband. She watched him, and grew impatient for him to wake; while he lay wide awake with lowered lids, rigid as stone lest he awaken her.

Once she closed her eyes, and at the same moment he opened his; but his were closed again before she renewed her scrutiny. Eventually, however, their glances did encounter, and she smiled and said tenderly:

"Good morning, my dear."

"Morning, Lady," he returned. "Awake, are you? I hoped you'd sleep a while."

"I've been awake half an hour," she assured him. "Waiting for you to wake up."

He chuckled. "Pshaw, you were fairly snoring! I've been listening to you since half past seven."

She chuckled, for this was an old argument between them; and as he leaned across to kiss her, she whispered: "Everything's going to be all right, isn't it, dear? Nothing changed?"

"Nothing changed."

Her eyes trembled. "But I will know, Joe. I must know. I must talk to Ruth."

"Yes, Lady. Yes." He added soberly: "But— nothing's changed, anyway! Whatever happens!"

"But I couldn't bear it if we never did know, Joe."

He sat up in bed. "I'll telephone the hospital," he decided; and he went into her dressing room, to the phone. She lay a moment longer; but then, in an uncontrollable impatience, she rose and slipped her arms into the sleeves of her kimono, and her feet into the loops of her sandals, and went to stand beside him, listening, watching his countenance.

But the hospital could only tell him that Miss Elcess was in the operating room; and he replaced the receiver, his cheeks sagging with disappointment.

Mrs. Caterson nodded, in acceptance of this delay. "Go back to bed, Joe," she suggested. "I'll ring for breakfast, but you needn't get up for fifteen minutes." She pressed the button in the wall beside the telephone table. They were accustomed, when the boys were away, to breakfast on Sunday mornings in her dressing room; to spend here together an indolent and happy hour or two. So now he went back into the bedroom; and he heard presently the hiss of the shower, and a little later she opened the door to see whether he had fallen asleep again. His eyes met hers; and she said cheerfully:

"All right, my dear. You can get up now."

When a little later, in pyjamas and dressing gown, he came to join her, there was a fire on her hearth, and the table was laid just before the fire. While grapefruit engaged them, the maid appeared with a laden tray. Sunday morning breakfast was always the same; sweetbreads, kidneys, small crisp sausages. When the maid was gone, they were still silent for a while, and he watched the curve of her arm as she poured his coffee; and she watched to see whether his breakfast pleased him. By ancient rule, there were no newspapers at the breakfast table. She insisted on this, and he had become accustomed to submission. But this morning, ill at ease, anxious for distraction, he missed them, spoke of this lack.

"We can break the rule for once," she agreed smilingly. "I want to read about the game, myself."

He rose to press the bell. The maid would understand what was desired. Mrs. Caterson's household ran by smooth and orderly routine, responsive to appointed impulses. She was as systematic and efficient as her husband was casual.

After the table had been taken away, they sat for an hour or more together by the fire there, each in turn reading the varying accounts of the game; and each in turn now and then read a paragraph aloud. The *Herald* spoke of Tony as the finest open-field runner seen in the Stadium since Mahan; the reporter wrote:

"Brilliant last year, he was superhuman yesterday. Give him the ball and a broken field and he was like an artist at his chosen instrument."

The other papers were equally laudatory; and these two here before the fire read some paragraphs over and over, to themselves or to each other, and their eyes were swimming with pride.

"They're enough to turn the boy's head," Caterson said once, somewhat doubtfully. But she protested:

"Nonsense, Joe! Of course, Tony loves applause. He loves to be liked, and approved. But he's not a bit spoiled by it all, and never has been."

"That's right," he agreed. "The boy does carry it well."

"Of course he does!"

If there were any jarring note in the general approval of Tony, it was not emphasized. The episode of the opposing touchdown was treated rather casually than otherwise. The *Herald* said it resulted from "a freakish bound of a rolling ball, which brushed against Tony Caterson's leg, and which Hall promptly fell on just across the line. But for that bound, the punt would have gone for a touchback. It was a break of the game, and the only break in this game, which was won by superior speed and skill and power."

The *Post,* referring to the same incident, remarked:

"This was the only moment in the game when Tony Caterson seemed in doubt what to do. He apparently at first intended to run with the ball; then decided to let it roll across the line. Hall was coming down fast, to try to fall on it inside the ten yard line, so Caterson turned to block him off. The ball bounced against his leg, and it looked from the press stand as though he felt it touch him, and tried to pick it up and run with it. But it was out of reach, and he was too late, when he swung around again, to block Hall.

"It was said after the game that Caterson did not feel the ball hit him. He had been hit in the head on a preceding play, and was still somewhat shaken up, at the moment."

Mrs. Caterson, in a warm indignation, read this aloud to her husband.

"You'd think they thought Tony did feel the ball hit him, and lied about it!" she protested. "Joe, that's outrageous! I'd like to sue them, or something. Tony wouldn't lie!"

Caterson's eyes were momentarily shadowed. "Pshaw, my dear," he reminded her at last, smilingly. "Tony's a public man. Public men must expect to be misunderstood, and slandered too."

"If he said he didn't feel it, then he didn't!" she insisted; and Caterson agreed with a chuckle, and a nod.

"Listen to this," he urged, diverting her attention. "Here's something about Sandy, in the *Herald*. Says his defensive work broke up their attack. You remember the *Transcript* said the same thing last night."

"I'm ashamed of myself," Mrs. Caterson confessed. "But I couldn't tell Sandy from the other men in the line. They were all packed so close together." She laughed apologetically. "I always watch the man with the ball, I guess. They say you miss the best part of the game, that way."

"I noticed Sandy made a lot of tackles," Caterson remarked. "He didn't seem to stay in one place, like the other men. He'd jump out and run along behind our line, keeping opposite the man with the ball. I could tell him because one sleeve of his jersey was shorter than the other, torn away."

She nodded, and they sat for a while without speech, absorbed in the papers. She finished them before he did; and while he still read, she moved here and there, busy with small tasks, setting the room in order. Presently she began to dress, while he sat engrossed in the sporting pages. She was suddenly lonely for him; and to attract his attention to herself, she suggested:

"Telephone the hospital again, will you, Joe?"

His eye was caught by something in her countenance, by the shadows there, the lines newly drawn; and his own eyes clouded at what he saw. He lifted the telephone; and Mrs. Caterson, though she affected still to occupy herself, watched him attentively, came at last to listen by his side.

He spoke to Miss Foley. She advised him to call Doctor Bright, at the surgeon's home, and Caterson did so. Mrs. Caterson heard him explain his interest to the physician. " . . . saw her last night, to discuss—some matters she wished me to handle. Can you tell me her condition?"

And he listened then for a moment; and Mrs. Caterson saw the sudden bleak foreboding in his eyes.

"I see," he commented; and again: "Yes, I see." And after a moment:

"Well, if there is any time when she can talk, there's one point we neglected to clear up. Ten minutes or so, it might require."

And presently: "I see." His eyes met those of Mrs. Caterson. "We might come to the hospital and wait, perhaps, on the chance."

Then shook his head, as though in agreement with the negative of the physician. "Well, thank you, Doctor. You'll let me know? I'll be all day at home."

So he hung up the receiver. She held his arm, her eyes interrogating his.

"Doctor Bright operated," he recited in a monotone. "It wasn't quite clear to me. But—either she will live for a while and have some relief. Or—she will die. She is under opiates now, may not recover consciousness at all."

He saw her fingers clench, bite in her palm; and he caught her hands in his. "Please, Lady," he begged. "Steady, dearest. Even if she dies—there's nothing changed."

She shook her head, her eyes streaming. "I can't bear that, Joe. I can't bear it."

"They're both—our fine lads, my dear."

She nodded, and suddenly she was pressing close against him, in his arms, curiously small and soft and helpless. His arms enfolded her; but above her bowed head the man stared across the room with a blind gaze like that of one in torment, like that of one whose very senses are bemused by a stupor of despair.

When presently she freed herself, she was more composed. She crossed to her dressing table, touched her eyes with toilet water, turned to smile at him reassuringly.

"Sorry, Lad," she whispered. "It's not fair that you should carry a double load. I'll take my share."

"You always have," he assured her. "You've always borne your share and more, my dear."

She smiled again. "Sweet thing!" she told him; then added teasingly: "But I know why you're so good-natured. You know you won't have to go to church today! Infidel!"

He chuckled. "Right," he agreed. "I'm going to loaf! I'm not even going to put on my pants till dinner time! I propose to stay right here and luxuriate. Of course you'll go, though."

"Of course—not!" she assured him, and her color swiftly drained away. "Together, Lad. We stick together, now."

He stood a moment, head bowed. "I'd better dress," he decided. "After all."

And she understood. "Perhaps so. In case they do —telephone."

So they passed that day in waiting; in a patience enforced and almost unendurable. Once, toward mid-afternoon, he telephoned the hospital again. He had no satisfaction from that inquiry, yet did make sure that he should be instantly informed of any change in the condition of the sick woman. For the rest, these two sought bravely to affect an usual demeanor. They read, they dined, they returned to the living room again, they spoke of matters of no consequence; but their thoughts ran side by side. Already the first shock of this intelligence was passing; already they were full of many questions, each demanding to be answered, yet unanswerable now and perhaps forever. He remembered this trait and that one in Tony, and found its prototype in himself or in Mrs. Caterson; but he was as easily able to discover these resemblances of character and heart in Sandy as in the other boy. Tony had Mrs. Caterson's gaiety, and her charm; and he had too her sense of order. Another of his qualities, that desire to be liked, that desire to please, was closely akin to a characteristic which Caterson could recognize in himself. He too had in his day done this thing and that one, not so much to win praise as to avoid blame. . . . Yet this was almost the only trait which he and Tony held in common, while he and Sandy were as like as twins. Twins? The word, coming unheralded into his thoughts, struck him a sharp and poignant blow. He shuddered; and he looked toward where Mrs. Caterson sat, beyond the hearth, half expecting to see her flinching too.

She was, he discovered, weeping silently; she pretended to read, but he saw her wink in an effort to clear her eyes, saw her touch them with her finger tip and shake her head as though to banish the mists that clouded her vision. And a sense of personal guilt fell suddenly upon the man; a memory almost forgotten did raise its dark head to mock him. There was, he perceived with a grim resignation, a fateful similarity between that affair and this one; between that old beginning and this that had overwhelmed them now. Since the revelation of Miss Elcess, this old memory had been quickening; it roused like a giant waked from slumber, it leered at him like a malicious gnome. When he saw Edith, whom he loved, thus weeping, it was as though a whip were laid across his own shoulders.

But he submitted to the lash. There could be no escape for him. This flagellation he had long since learned he must endure, and must endure alone.

Through all that day they waited for the call from the hospital, and Mrs. Caterson dwelt in a maze of fearful hope, and he in a haze of pain. Late in the afternoon, a car rolled into the drive and stopped before the door. They heard it, and came swiftly to their feet; then Mrs. Caterson almost ran toward the hall, and he was on her heels. But they had taken no more than a step—all this in a second's space after the car stopped—when the door flung open and a gay young voice called:

"Hello, everybody!"

It was Nina. She came in, eyes shining, cheeks glowing, lips bright. She saw them check and stand; and she cried:

"My, it's getting cold! You didn't come to church! We missed you!" She chuckled. "That is to say, mother missed you. I was dead to the world." She stripped off her coat, and she seemed suddenly to realize that they were curiously rigid.

"What's the matter?" she asked, looking from one to the other. "Is anything wrong?"

Mrs. Caterson smiled reassuringly, shook her head. "My dear, no, of course not," she said, too vehemently.

"You were—so quiet!" Nina explained.

"Old folks seem quiet to young ones, I expect," Mrs. Caterson pointed out. "Come in to the fire, dear."

"Old nothing!" Nina retorted, laughing again. She linked her arm through Mr. Caterson's. "Been reading all about the game?" she challenged. "Aren't you proud of those boys of yours?"

He made some husky sound; and Mrs. Caterson said quickly: "Of course he is. He's done nothing but talk about them all day."

"Tony's All-American, sure," Nina declared. "And of course he'll be captain next year. I should think you'd swell up like . . ."

"Not poisoned pups, please," Mrs. Caterson protested laughingly.

"Balloons!" Nina assented. "Like balloons then."

"They burst so easily," the older woman argued, smiling. "And so do mushrooms, and most things that swell too rapidly. But of course we've been ever so proud of—the boys for years."

Only Caterson's ear remarked that faint pause, as she went on:

"Did you get them safe back to the hotel? And have a beautiful time afterward?"

Nina nodded happily. "Wonderful!" she agreed. "Tony was a scream. He made us all dance with him, right in the lobby, and kissed us good night." She chuckled faintly. "Even Sandy loosened up enough to dance with me."

"They're so fond of you, Nina," Mrs. Caterson assured her.

"Me too," the girl assented. "They're peaches!" She added quickly:

"But I can't stay but a minute. I'm running in to Barb Delevan's for tea. It's her going-away party. She's off to New York tonight. Isn't it a scream, her going on the stage? She'll be a hit, sure as anything. She's made for it. But what I came for, mother and dad want you tonight for supper and bridge afterward."

Mrs. Caterson hesitated, and Caterson said

quickly: "I'm expecting a phone call, Nina. Not to-night, I'm afraid."

"Have them call you at our house," she urged.

"I didn't sleep well last night," he evaded. "I expect we'll go to bed pretty early tonight."

She shook her head gaily. "Nonsense! You won't go to bed before ten o'clock! and if you don't come home by then, dad'll send you! Hurry up and promise, so I can go along. I can't stay here teasing you all afternoon!"

Mrs. Caterson looked at her husband hesitantly, and Nina cried in affectionate derision:

"You can brag about Tony to them, just as well as to each other, you know!"

Mrs. Caterson touched her husband's arm, warning him while she nodded her assent. "All right, Nina," she promised. "We've been in the house all day. It will do us good. We'll come!"

Nina whirled toward the door. "Lovely!" she cried. "I'll be home before you leave. Six o'clock, mother said."

They followed her, or rather Mrs. Caterson followed her, as far as the door. Caterson stayed doubt-fully by the fire. He was strangely shaken. He heard his wife say: "And give Miss Delevan my good wishes!" Then the outer door closed, and the car darted away, and Mrs. Caterson came back to him.

"She drives as fast as Tony does," he said.

His wife nodded. "They're—congenial in so many ways," she inattentively agreed.

XI

IT was toward half past four when Nina stopped at the house; it may have been a quarter of five before she hurried away. Mr. and Mrs. Caterson sat down again before the fire, and Caterson said doubtfully:

"I don't see how we can go, Edith! I—dread facing anyone. Even such old friends as these."

She smiled at him, shook her head chidingly. "My dear, we've the world to face," she reminded him. "And to face bravely, so that it may seem that there is nothing changed."

Caterson, silent for a space, confessed at last doubtfully: "I'm not much of an actor, not much at make-believe. Will and Mrs. Buckel will know something's worrying me. . . ."

She protested gaily: "Nonsense, my dear! You can pretend as well as anyone. You've never tried, that's all."

"I'll want to telephone the hospital," he remembered presently. "So they'll know where to find us." And she assented, suddenly white with fear. In the last moments before their departure, while she was adjusting her hat, he did thus telephone; and when he joined her afterward, and saw the question in her eyes, he shook his head.

"No change," he confessed. "But I gave them the Buckel's number."

Something evasive in his glance caught her attention. "She's worse?" she asked.

Reluctantly he nodded. "I'm afraid so, Lady. Yes, worse. Very bad."

They went out to the big limousine in silence, told Richards where to go; and on the way to the Buckel home they were for the most part silent. Caterson did remark:

"Well, the boys are back at college by now."

She made no comment upon this obvious fact, but later, when they swung in to the curb, she clung suddenly to his arm, whispered achingly:

"Joe, Joe, suppose we never know!"

And he could only grip her hand, turn his head away.

They went arm in arm, silently as fearful children, up the walk to the door; and Mr. and Mrs. Buckel came to meet them with cheerful greetings. "I just felt like a game of bridge," Mrs. Buckel volubly explained. "We haven't played since two weeks ago. I tell Will I don't want to get rusty at it. He laughs at me, but I always say you can't play bridge well unless you play a great deal. You do get rusty, don't you think so?"

"I'm afraid my bridge will always be rusty," Mrs. Caterson smilingly confessed, as Mr. Buckel took her coat and laid it aside.

"Why, you beat us badly, last time," Mrs. Buckel retorted. "But we'll get our revenge tonight. You can't always hold such cards as you held last time."

Buckel chuckled. "No alibis, Grace," he protested. "It's a game of skill, you know."

"Well, I always say I'll take the cards and you can have the skill," Mrs. Buckel said in cheerful defiance; and she added: "We won't start before supper. We're just having a pick-up supper, of course; beans, and ham, and scrambled eggs for you, Joe. But I've got the table all ready, and some brand new cards. . . ."

Caterson thought gratefully that she talked so much there was no need of speech from them. You knew all the things she might say; yet there was such a lack of sequence in her words that you had to pay attention, too. She put just sufficient burden on the mentality of her listeners so that they could not safely refuse her their attention. He began to be glad they had come, after all; and he was hungrier than he had expected to be, hungry with that weary appetite which results from mental rather than from physical fatigue. When they crossed presently to the dining room, he moved almost eagerly.

"Nina says they had a nice party last night," Mrs. Caterson suggested, when they were settled at the table; and Mrs. Buckel nodded readily.

"They have such good times," she agreed. "I think young people do have such good times, nowadays. I never take any stock in all the things you hear about the things they do. They're just happy children, I always say, and why not let them be so."

Mrs. Caterson smiled. "You certainly need never worry about Nina," she remarked.

"And boys like yours!" Mrs. Buckel echoed. "Isn't Tony the handsomest thing you ever saw? Joe, Sandy looks exactly like you. He's more like you every day. But Tony's really handsome!" She smiled at their shout of laughter. "Well you know what I mean," she urged. "Tony's beautiful, the way a woman is beautiful. He has all your loveliness, Edith. But of course, Sandy's nice and rugged looking."

Buckel chuckled. "You make it sound so inoffensive, Honey," he applauded. "Tact is always feminine!"

Caterson's eyes met those of his wife; and she spoke quickly, to cover and conceal his distress.

"Though I'm not sure all young people are as nice as Nina, and our boys," she suggested.

"Oh, of course not," Mrs. Buckel agreed. "But I always say it doesn't hurt a fine person to have contacts with the other sort. It's educational. Nina and Tony know hundreds of young people, and they're not all nice, I suppose. I don't care for Barbs Delevan at all, for instance. I think she's vicious. But Nina and Tony are completely unspoiled."

She caught Mrs. Caterson's eye and smiled, as though to mark some tacit and unspoken understanding between them. "Unpleasant things don't touch either of them," she repeated.

Buckel detected that interchange of glances, and he chuckled warningly. "Let them grow up, my dear," he urged. "I don't mind supporting Nina for a while yet. Child-marriages are dangerous, you know."

His wife cried: "Why, Will! I never said anything of the kind. Of course, if they do . . . I always say when a boy and a girl have known each other since they were children, if they do choose one another, it's almost sure to work out well."

"I've had a notion sometimes that Nina felt closer to Sandy than to Tony," Buckel suggested; but he saw the distress in Caterson's eyes, and without knowing the cause, yet sought to divert the conversation. He spoke of the game, and Tony's brilliancy, and Sandy's sound and useful play; and Mrs. Buckel asked some question about that incident which resulted in the opposing touchdown.

"What happened?" she demanded. "Didn't Tony feel the ball hit him? I heard Bob Curry ask him, at your house last night; but Sandy interrupted and said he and Tony didn't want to talk football. Tony didn't hear Bob, I think. He didn't answer, anyway. But he must have felt the ball hit him, mustn't he?"

Buckel said quickly: "It made no difference in the result, Grace." And when she was about to speak, he went on, with an effect of silencing her, referring to the game which would occur on the succeeding Saturday, and the chances of victory in that encounter. So the talk passed to safer ground.

Once the phone rang, and Caterson sat rigidly till the call proved to be for Buckel. Later they finished supper and returned to the living room, seated themselves at the card table. Buckel recommended a cigar; but Caterson preferred his pipe. Mrs. Buckel spread the cards, and Caterson cut high and dealt. He and Mrs. Caterson opposed the other two. They played together regularly, these four; the quarter cent stake was as eagerly contested as though it were of the most tremendous consequence.

Mrs. Buckel was a loquacious bridge player; and tonight she seemed even more talkative than usual. Caterson blessed her nimble tongue. It made so much easier the part he had to play. There was something soothing in her constant flow of conversation, and the game itself was sufficiently interesting to hold his attention. He became by and by engrossed in the play, forgot his other and more grave concerns; and Mrs. Caterson, watching him with eyes full of solicitude, saw contentedly his increasing absorption.

They divided the first two rubbers, and were in the third when the telephone in the hall rang again; and Buckel, who was at the moment dummy, rose to answer it. Caterson, playing the hand, spread his cards and claimed the remaining tricks as Buckel returned to say in faint surprise:

"For you, Joe."

And Caterson, suddenly remembering, went stiffly to the telephone. Mrs. Caterson dealt while he was gone, and her fingers were thick and clumsy, so that she spilled the cards, and Mrs. Buckel helped her pick them up again. Mrs. Caterson finished the deal somehow, and she tried not to look around as Caterson returned to the table. He said nothing, but when he sat down, she saw his eyes.

Nevertheless, the question must be asked. She wet her lips. "Who was it, Joe?"

He hesitated. "The hospital," he told her then, huskily. "She—died half an hour ago."

Mrs. Buckel cried: "Dead? Who is dead?"

Caterson was sorting his cards. He could not speak. But Mrs. Caterson said: "Miss Elcess, Grace. You know, the nurse we've always had. From the time the boys were born, or whenever we've needed a nurse for anything." Her tone was only normally sorrowful; and Caterson was full of wonder at the strength in her.

"Oh, too bad!" Mrs. Buckel protested. "What was it, Edith?"

"An operation," Mrs. Caterson explained. "A cancer, I think. She—let it go too long for any hope, they said." And she added: "We were so fond of her. She was like one of the family."

She looked at her husband, as though to prompt him; he glanced at his cards and passed. Mrs. Buckel started to ask another question, but Mr. Buckel urged:

"Your bid, Grace."

"Oh, is it my bid? Who dealt?" she asked.

"Joe," her husband told her. "He dealt and passed."

Caterson's eyes met Mrs. Caterson's and held

them long. He saw her lids half close as though she were faint with pain.

"H-m!" Mrs. Buckel muttered, studying her cards. "What's the score?"

"Game each."

"But didn't we win a game?" she exclaimed. "We won the first game, didn't we?"

"Yes. It's game and game."

"Oh, they've got a game, too?"

"We've each a game," Buckel explained, in amused patience. "We made game on spades; and they made a game in two jumps. Three diamonds, and then two no trumps. We have a total of seventy-six points, thirty-six below the line, and forty above. They have twenty-one and twenty below the line, and thirty above, or a total of seventy-one. And it's your bid!"

"Why it's almost exactly even isn't it!" she cried, in pleased delight. "My bid! Now let me see." She studied her cards gravely. "A heart," she said at last, and bought the contract.

On the third trick, Mrs. Caterson refused. Caterson said automatically: "No hearts, Edith?"

"No hearts," she replied.

But it developed later that she held a single heart. When it was belatedly played, Mrs. Buckel pounced upon it vigilantly; she claimed the revoke, and she cried delightedly:

"And we'll take two tricks penalty. That gives us game and rubber, and two rubbers out of three!"

Caterson abruptly rose, and he tried to laugh. "When Edith revokes on trumps, it's time to take her home to bed," he exclaimed.

She was, he saw, near the breaking point; and a little later, in the car, she collapsed limply, pitifully, in his arms.

XII

MRS. CATERSON kept her bed for days thereafter. She had always a certain physical fragility which was apparent not so much in her bright cheeks and clear eyes as in the exceeding and poignant beauty of her smile, and in her readiness for tears. She kept her bed for days, and they made pretext to their friends. They spoke of a grippy cold, contracted perhaps at the game on Saturday afternoon. Nina sent her a great box of cut flowers, and so did others too. But at first Mrs. Caterson saw no one except the household servants, the doctor, and her husband.

Caterson haunted her bedside. He would not leave her, even to go to the office; and when her insistence could no longer be overruled, he made pretense of going away, withdrawing to some other part of the house, staying always within easy call. That sense of personal guilt for this catastrophe more and more oppressed the man. He had at first refused to recognize it, until he perceived in this attitude on his own part a sort of moral cowardice which, long since recognized, he had fought all his life. In line with that long discipline, he now put aside all excuses for himself and accepted the burden of his responsibility;

and this state of mind grew more and more apparent in his countenance.

Mrs. Caterson, with a keen eye always to read her husband's glance, was quick to perceive his distress; yet she did not at first recognize the true character of this which so perturbed him. She thought it was simply his concern for her, and she sought in many little ways to reassure him. Tuesday morning, she spoke of getting up for breakfast, but he would not permit this, and himself met the maid at the door, and took from her the breakfast tray, and brought it to Mrs. Caterson's bed. She chided him then for worrying, sought to smile, promised him that she would be up by noon and would be her old self by evening.

"It's just that I have to get used to it, Joe," she told him wearily. "I'll be all right in a little while. You go on to the office, and when you come home tonight you won't know me for the same woman."

He told her fondly: "Then I shan't go to the office. I don't want to find any other woman here when I come home!"

And she laughed happily at his twisting of her words, yet still urged him to go. But he stayed. He was there when, toward half past nine, the postman made his first call of the day, bringing letters from the boys. It was their old habit to write home every Sunday evening, and they were in this matter singularly conscientious; so much so that if either of them failed to write on the appointed day, Mr. and Mrs. Caterson felt a quick concern lest something was amiss. When this morning the letters were brought to her bedside, Caterson took them up and began to sort them through; and she cried softly, with a quick pang of terror:

"Are the letters from the boys there, Joe? Are they all right?"

"Here's Sandy's," he assured her, an envelope in his hand. "Yes, and here's Tony's too, Lady. They're all right, my dear."

And she whispered apologetically: "I keep forgetting that they don't know anything about this. We mustn't ever tell them, Joe. Never as long as they live!"

"Shall I read them aloud?" he asked; and at her assent, he opened first the letter from Tony. Tony's letters were always more voluminous than Sandy's, were always filled with something of the boy's gay and friendly humor, his invincible charm. Now while Caterson read the letter aloud, Mrs. Caterson again and again smiled happily at some passage it contained. Tony wrote, in that surprisingly unformed and sprawling hand which always amused them so:

"Dearests: Twenty-three hours and twenty minutes ago —twenty-one minutes and twenty seconds, to be exact—I said goodnight to you. And it seems like twenty years already! What the devil am I going to do tomorrow night? That will be forty years, and that's a lifetime. Why don't you two pack up and come up here? You could stay at the Inn, and I could come over and do my studying there, and be with you all day except for classes and football practise. If it weren't for training table, I could eat with you; and if it weren't for training rules, I could sleep on the floor at the foot of your beds. Honest, you can't imagine how I miss you! And especially after I've just seen you. It's not so bad after a while, because I get so homesick I'm numb! But just at first it surely is tough!

"We got back here this morning; woke up on the siding, in the car. I had a good sleep on the train. I've got a sore muscle in my leg where I ran into somebody's toe, but Doc rubbed most of it out this afternoon. Otherwise, slick as a trout! They had quite a celebration for us, a big gang down to meet the train, and all that. I get a great kick out of it. I suppose I ought not to say so; but there's no modesty in my make-up. When five or six hundred fellows give me a long cheer, I eat it up, and I don't care who knows it. I wouldn't say so, of course, to anybody but you, but I know you get just as much thrill out of it as I do. And anything I get out of life, that I think you people would enjoy too, is going to be sent forward post haste—registered mail, special delivery, insured—to your address. And you can lay to that, my hearties!

"Of course there hasn't been any talk about anything but the game, since we got back here. I get a little tired of that sometimes. I suppose maybe you get stale after a while, towards the end of the season. What I'd like to do would be to go and see a good show or a movie, or something of that sort; or sit up till midnight and drink three or four bottles of ale, and have a long talk with you two dear ones. But instead of that, everybody wants to say something about the game, that first touchdown I scored, or some darn thing that I'm ready to forget. Of course Doc keeps us clear of it, as much as he can, but you've got to have a certain amount of it. Everybody up here is pretty well satisfied with the way it went. Only, a good many of the fellows bet that they wouldn't score, and about every other man I meet wants to know what happened on that punt. I tell 'em to ask the referee! As far as I know, the ball didn't touch me at all. But the referee isn't here, and I am, so of course they ask me. I'll be glad when the season's over. Next week, and then the western trip, will finish it. There's snow on the ground up here now—about two inches this morning when we got off the train—but it's melting fast. But I always get a little tired of football when the ground begins to be slippery. You keep falling down without being tackled. Your feet won't stay under you.

"I'm going to do a lot of winter sports this winter, more than I've ever done before. I get a great kick out of being out-of-doors, and I've got a pretty easy schedule this year, so I'll have more time than I usually do.

"Well, I don't think there's anything more to say, except the old stuff; how much I love you both, and how I miss you when I'm away from you, and how I never can see enough of you when I'm with you. I think when I get through college I'll get you, mother, to give me a job as a butler. Then I can stay at home with you all the time, and bring you your coffee in the morning, and your tea in the afternoon, and your slippers at night! That's my idea of a real career! I don't know any other one where I'd be as happy. Honest folks, you haven't any notion how much I do love you both!

"G'by,

"TONY."

Caterson finished reading, and Mrs. Caterson's bosom rose in a long inhalation, as though she had been holding her breath.

"He's a sweet thing, isn't he?" she murmured happily; and Caterson nodded, though some faint shadow dwelt in his eyes. She saw this, and she asked at hazard: "You think that touchdown is bothering him, Joe? He ought not to worry about that. It wasn't his fault, was it?"

Caterson said: "You have to expect youth to

worry over little things, Lady. Little things seem big ones when you're young, you know."

"I know," she agreed. "But it makes me furious to have anybody blame him. Why he practically won the game, all by himself!"

"Here's Sandy's," he suggested, to divert her; and, as he drew the single sheet out of the envelope: "Short and to the point, as usual. Sandy's not articulate on paper, is he?" She nodded, abstractedly, and he read:

"Dear Father and Mother: Well, we got home all right. I slept pretty good on the train, and I feel fine today. You don't need to worry about me. I wish we had had longer out at the house, and I wish there hadn't been such a crowd there. You both looked well, and I guess you are. Mother looked well. Sometimes she looks tired, but I thought she looked mighty well. Well, I've got to get to work. I've got a math quiz tomorrow. I hope you both keep well.

"Your son,

"SANDY."

Mrs. Caterson laughed, with a quick catch in her throat.

"Isn't he amusing?" she protested. "His letters sound like those of a boy ten years old."

Caterson nodded. "It's curious, too," he remarked. "Because his handwriting is regular, and well formed, and mature. Tony's is just a scrawl."

She murmured, repeating the closing words of this letter: " 'Your son, Sandy.' " And her eyes were suddenly brimming, so that Caterson cried protestingly:

"Please, Lady! I shouldn't have read that." His own lips twisted with the pain which tormented him, and she said, reassuringly:

"I'm not unhappy, Joe. But, you know, I'm—I think I'm a little tired."

"You didn't sleep well," he reminded her. "You need to sleep, that's what. I'll tell you, I'll leave you alone for a while. I'll be in the next room, if you want me."

"You go on to town," she urged. "I'll rest so much better if you go in town. With you staying at home, it keeps me feeling that I ought to get up, so you can go. Do go! Will you, Joe?"

He promised, in the end, to run into the office for a little while, and with this pledge he left her. But he could not bear actually to leave the house; so, since she might be watching for his departure, he took his car and drove out by the drive and around the block, returning furtively by the rear of the house. And he stayed below stairs all that morning, trying to read, yet instantly attentive to any sound from her room.

Toward lunch, he went out to get his car, and openly returned to the house again; and some such routine became, during the succeeding days, established between them. Mrs. Caterson was not long wholly deceived, yet she pretended to be, since thus she gave him comfort. As her strength somewhat returned, she saw his need of comforting; and she watched him more and more intently, puzzled by something in his demeanor she could not at once define.

Toward the end of the week, she saw occasionally those closest friends who came to call on her. Nina spent one afternoon with her, and the girl's gay and affectionate friendliness served as a tonic. Yet, since Nina talked most of all of the boys and of their affairs, this hour they had together was to some extent an ordeal too, and a test of Mrs. Caterson's ability to endure.

Nina asked: "Have you heard from them?" And Mrs. Caterson read Tony's letter to the girl, her voice keen with pride at the tenderness and affection with which it overflowed. "He's a sweet thing, isn't he?" Nina exclaimed, when Mrs. Caterson was done.

The older woman smiled. "Yes, my dear, he is," she agreed. "Although I expect he'd writhe with shame, to hear us say so."

"Oh, of course," Nina laughingly assented. "He'd writhe, but he'd love it, just the same! Tony loves to be praised. You know that as well as I."

Mrs. Caterson nodded. "You notice how distressed he is," she suggested. "About that play, last Saturday, when they scored that touchdown? That's so typical of Tony!"

Nina hesitated for an instant. "Isn't it?" she echoed. "But he ought not to worry about that. Nobody remembers things like that very long."

"He says the ball didn't touch him," Mrs. Caterson pointed out, wishing to be reassured.

And Nina stoutly asserted: "Of course it didn't! Or if it did, he didn't feel it. Everybody knows that."

When she departed, by and by, she met Mr. Caterson downstairs, and said cheerfully: "Her cold's better, isn't?"

Caterson, for a moment, did not remember that Mrs. Caterson was supposed to have a cold. The man moved nowadays in an increasing abstraction, absorbed in his own thoughts, tormented by his own problem. Nina saw his hesitation, and touched his arm reassuringly.

"You mustn't worry about her!" she urged. "She'll be all right in a day or two."

He agreed, nodding doubtfully.

"Will you go up to this week's game?" Nina asked, and Caterson shook his head.

"No, we're not going," he replied. "We have tickets, and reservations at the Inn; but they've had some snow up there, and it's a hard, cold trip if you drive, and tiresome on the train. I don't think she can stand it. Are you going?"

"Father and I will drive up," she explained. "Mother doesn't get much out of football, you know, but I wouldn't miss it for the world."

"Give our love to the boys," he bade her. "I'm writing them we're not coming, but you can tell them we're all right, tell them you saw their mother."

And she promised to do so, as she took herself away.

During the succeeding days, Mrs. Caterson's strength—and more than that, her courage—returned. This recovery of hers was perhaps helped, rather than hindered, by her increasing appreciation of the fact that her husband was supporting some burden of his own, the nature of which she could not comprehend. He was, she thought, losing weight. His appetite had failed. Also, his eyes bore a red weariness which testified to short rations of sleep. She watched him more and more acutely, yet at first without questioning.

Saturday afternoon they got the returns from the game by radio, and again the name of Tony Caterson was repeated endlessly, and always with credit. Also, in this play-by-play recital, the phrase, "Caterson made the tackle," came with an astonishing frequency. Mrs. Caterson did not at once appreciate the fact that this must be Sandy, rather than Tony; but when it did at last occur to her, she asked a question, and Caterson said:

"Yes. Yes, Tony's playing back. But these tackles are all right up at the line, for short gains or none at all. Yes, Sandy must be making them."

She watched his eyes for the elation this knowledge should have set there, but his countenance was sombre and almost grim. So she remembered this, her nearer, problem; this question of what it was that so perplexed her husband. And she became, thereafter, less and less attentive to the game.

That night she asked him:

"Joe, is anything worrying you? Anything I don't know about?"

His denials silenced without convincing her; and

a day or two later, she opened the subject again, more pressingly. But again he reassured her, this time so earnestly that she was almost convinced. Yet, an hour after, the shadow rested in his eyes again.

But in the course of the next few days, when she had been for some time about the house as usual, she became satisfied that there dwelt in his heart some ugly spectre which must be dragged into the light before it could be dissipated. Caterson, on this particular morning, had gone to the office; but when he departed, she thought he looked almost ill, and before he came home that night she had made up her mind to force at last the issue.

Yet she waited her time. They had dinner alone together, and she was gay and charming as she used to be. They read aloud for a while in the evening, one of those books which their habit was to share, and still she held her tongue. Not till they had gone upstairs did she speak. When he went to his dressing room, she called to him:

"Joe!" And at his answering word: "Put on your dressing gown and your slippers, and come into my sitting room. I want to talk with you. I'm lighting a fire."

It was a moment before he replied; then he said, evasively: "Why Lady, don't you think we ought to get to bed?"

"We'll sit a little while first," she insisted, gaily. "Don't argue, my dear. Just do as you're told." He did not reply, and she called, challengingly yet tenderly too: "Joe, did you hear?"

"All right," he agreed. "All right, Edith. I'll be in."

And a few moments later, while she still sat at her dressing table, slowly brushing her hair, he appeared in the doorway. When she saw his countenance, she perceived that he knew what was coming, that he had somehow mustered a store of resolution for this hour.

XIII

CATERSON came into his wife's room and he stood for a moment in the door, uncertainly; then he sat down in the big chair by the fire that was always ready for him there.

"A cold night," he said uneasily. "The fire is pleasant."

She laid her brush aside; she swung about to face him, and while her white fingers twisted the rope of her hair into a braid, she eyed him smilingly.

"Joe, my dear," she said. "You and I need to talk together. What is it you want to tell me?"

He did not immediately answer. He looked once toward her, then his eyes fastened on the fire. He said at last stoutly:

"Nothing, Lady."

"Something is—eating at your heart, Lad," she urged. "It will be easier for the sharing."

"You've—enough to bear," he protested. "This is mine. My own."

"What is it?" she persisted. She finished braiding her hair; she crossed to the chaise lounge and took a great cushion and dropped it at his feet. She sat down there, her shoulders against his knee, her feet twisted under her, and she reached up over her shoulder with her right hand and found his hand and held it, her fingers twining into his.

"I'm well now, Joe," she told him. "Strong enough for—anything. And—knowing will be easier than guessing, my dear."

He sat like stone; and she waited for a long time, till he should be ready to speak. But when he did not speak, she asked at last:

"You're—blaming yourself, somehow, for—this. Is that it, Joe?"

So a word was wrung from him. "There's an ugly fitness about it," he confessed. "It seems to—complete the pattern. But my dear, why should it fall on you as well as me?"

The question was like a cry, but she answered steadily:

"Nothing that hurts one of us can fail to hurt the other, Joe. We're too much one person."

"I could stand it if it were just me," he protested. "It's the feeling that I've—somehow—brought this all on you."

"My dear," she said pleadingly. "You're hurting me rather badly."

And so he came to the telling. When he was once begun she had no further need to prompt him; he seemed to forget she was there against his knee. Only his hand tightened on hers, with a strange ferocity, as though he would cling to her against all odds. For the rest, he spoke evenly, in a hushed and monotonous tone, like a man dreaming; for indeed this that he had to tell was like an old dream, long lost to all reality.

That which he related had happened in his youth,

during that year of field work which intervened between the beginning and the conclusion of his technical training. He was employed in a construction camp in the western mountains, where a great dam took shape across a deep canyon, to herd back miles of water and conserve it for the frugal uses of the farm lands far below. Caterson had never been in the west before, nor in the mountains. The long days of blazing sun, the skies bright with snowy clouds from which here and there sharp showers descended, the nights clear as the heart of a diamond and like a diamond shot with sparkling stars, and the air like wine bewitched and intoxicated him. He moved in a continual wonder and delight.

He roomed, he explained, in a boarding house kept by a woman named Benddy. She was a harridan, a sloven, a termagant and a terror. There was a husband in the background; a treacherous, rat-like man who was craven where his wife was concerned, insolently bold to others. He lived in ways devious and dark, seizing upon the weaknesses of those about him so that he might fatten on them, as a leech fastens on an open wound to draw the blood therefrom.

"I was afraid of him," Caterson confessed. "With the sort of fear a snake provokes. I knew I could crush him, destroy him; but there was something obscene in the man. The thought of hitting him with your fist was hateful!"

And he was afraid, too, he admitted, of the

woman. She had the shameless courage which women sometimes acquire; she would shout a man's name after him down the canyon in a way that for a young man was worse than a whiplash, for there is a modesty in youth which shrinks from being made in any wise conspicuous.

But these two individuals had a daughter, and her name was Mary Benddy. "I don't know, now, what she was like," Caterson admitted, added honestly: "But I liked her then." He could not even remember whether she were pretty or no. He seldom saw her by day, or in the boarding house, but sometimes on starlit nights they met outside, at first by accident and then by choice; for to her as well as to the boy, these were nights of beauty, tremendous and intoxicating.

Afterward, Caterson came back east to finish his technical course. But another young man, a year behind him at the Institute, went to work on the dam; and from this young man Caterson had by and by news of Mary Benddy. She had borne a child, and died; and she died with sealed lips, grimly opposing to the end the frantic persistence of her father and her mother, and their vengeful questionings.

"She had never told me," Caterson said now, huskily. "But—I think I knew. Even without admitting the knowledge to myself, I knew. But after she was dead, it was too late to help her; and I was afraid of Benddy, and of the woman."

So, he sorrowfully confessed, he had held his tongue.

Later, during that final year of his work at the Institute, he heard that the baby was a girl, and that Mrs. Benddy was by her new responsibilities vastly changed, tending the child with a keen and slavish affection. She had banished Benddy, it appeared, for good and all; she clove to the baby, and it worked its alchemy in her.

Caterson's voice droned on, and Mrs. Caterson sat without stirring. Her face was hidden from him, so his task was easier.

"I might have gone out there, that next summer," he concluded at last. "But—I was afraid to go, and too weak to fight down that fear. Two years later, I did go. But Mrs. Benddy had disappeared by that time, with the baby, and no one knew where she had gone. And for years—even after we were married, Edith—I tried to find her."

She nodded, without speaking.

"But I never did," he said, and after a long space of silence he cried:

"Oh, I've no right to tell you this! It's something I ought to carry alone. I never meant to tell you. For years, I expected something to happen. I expected a—blow that did not fall. And when it didn't fall for so long, I began to feel safe, immune, secure. I thought—fate, or whatever it may be—had forgotten."

He laughed bitterly. "See what a fool I was! How this fits in now! First our own girl baby died, and that was bad enough; but now, one of the boys I counted my sons is a foundling! And I'm not to know which one, not to know the true from the false." He stirred like a horse under the spur.

"And you've to bear it with me," he protested. "That's the unfair part, Edith. That's what I can't endure!"

Again he waited, but for a long time she did not speak; yet her very silence held him silent, till at length she stirred, and she said tenderly:

"My dear, I think I've always known. That trick of yours of watching the faces of young girls in crowds. Yes, always known."

"Known?" he protested.

"Known in the way I knew about the boys," she explained. "Subconsciously, without ever putting a name to the knowledge." Her hand pressed his, and after a moment she asked softly: "Was she sweet, Joe? I think she must have been," she confessed.

"It's hard to remember, now. It's been just—a sort of sick dream to me for so long."

The fire on the hearth before them was burning down. The flames which had danced brightly for a while were shrinking and fading, but the embers held a deep, warm glow.

"I like her for one thing," she said, half to herself. "For her loyalty, her silence. If she had told them, it might have ruined you, my dear." And a moment later, she asked: "You never got any trace?"

"Mrs. Benddy was supposed to have gone to Seattle," he explained. "But I had a dozen men working there for three months; found nothing, found just nothing." And he added, in a tortured tone: "I've had to imagine what might have happened to her. That's been the hardest part."

"But they said Mrs. Benddy was changed," she reminded him, reassuringly. "They said she was nicer afterward. She must have been a strong woman, Joe; something fine in her. I think she'd take good care of the little girl."

He sat brooding for a long time, finding some comfort in this thought; and she was wise enough to wait till he should be ready to speak, wise enough not to intrude upon him in this hour. Also, during this interval when neither spoke, she learned to still the ache in her own heart. She might be wise, but she was human too, and wholly feminine, and this had left its wound. Yet, because she did not reproach him, he began, as a man will, to forget how he must have hurt her; and when he spoke at last, it was of abstract things. He said slowly:

"There's a native cowardice in me, Edith. In—moral issues. I can face physical threats all right; but in more vital matters, it's always my instinct to dodge, and shirk, and to evade. Just as I've dodged now, by telling this to you. Making you share it with me, for the sake of easing my own load."

Her fingers held his warmly. "Dear Lad, I know," she repeated. "I've seen you, so many times, confronted by such choices. Seen you hesitate; and seen you—always—choose the finer, braver way. You've fought that cowardice always, Joe, and beaten it.

That battle has made you what you are. You're my dear man, of whom I am always proud!"

"It's inside me, like a rat!" he cried. "That sneaking cowardice!"

"Yes, but penned there," she insisted. "Baffled and checked and governed always. Everyone has some weak point in his armor, my dear. It's the ones who defend that breach successfully who in the end come to receive the victors' crowns. It's fighting down such enemies that make men strong."

"I'd have taken some open step to find her," he pleaded. "But I couldn't bear to distress you."

He felt her stir as she smiled. "Yes," she agreed. "That, too. I wonder how many men are cowards just on that account. Because they can not bear to distress the folk who love them most dearly. Or they may be fine for that same reason, to avoid making us women sorrowful. Tony has that trait, Joe; that longing to be loved, that desire to please, that craving for affection, and for praise. It may be an anchor for him, too, in some stormy time."

He said thoughtfully: "You know, Lady, it's a tribute to you. I mean, my attitude in this. I knew you would be—fine and understanding! It never occurred to me that you might quite reasonably be furious, bitter, hurt beyond repair. You're a—tremendous woman, dear."

She smiled up at him at last, her eyes shining. "I've had you long enough to value you, Lad," she told him. "I'm not likely to let you be torn away."

"You make it mighty easy for me," he confessed. "Easier than I deserve. Not to know what became of her was bad enough, severe enough. But for this to fall on you seemed like a double punishment."

She turned, on her knees, facing him; she was strong enough now to let him see her eyes.

"Not—punishment," she urged tenderly. "You've been—unhappy because you could not care for that other baby. That was your punishment, perhaps. But you've a—fatherless child to care for now, Joe. Don't you see—this is your opportunity! It's a sign you've been forgiven. Don't you see?"

Her arms encircled him, held him comfortingly.

"But not to know!" he cried despairingly. "Edith, that's going to be—terrible! When one boy does well, we'll be wondering whether we've a right to be proud; and when one does ill, we'll be cowardly enough to think he is no blood of ours!"

She hushed him, her palm across his lips. "Nonsense!" she protested steadily. "Old things are done, my dear. This is all old, to be forgotten. We've not to make a choice between these two boys. They have been ours, and they will always be! Whether they're good or bad!"

"As they've always been?"

"Exactly," she insisted. "Joe, we've got to hold fast to that. Nothing must be changed. We want to keep our life always as it has been these twenty years!"

XIV

DURING the succeeding days they sought to adopt a policy of silence in this matter which engrossed their every thought. They spoke of Tony and Sandy as often as they had before; but they spoke of what the boys were doing, not of what they were. They practised a benevolent hypocrisy, each seeking to deceive the other, to lull the other into a false security.

Yet their hidden thoughts shouted aloud in the most casual phrase. When the weekly letters came, Mrs. Caterson opened Sandy's first; and this was a departure. Hitherto, quite unconsciously, she had seized on Tony's letters, because they were always filled with the gay tenderness she craved. Caterson did not comment on this variation of old routine, but he marked it, and understood her desire now thus to hold the balance even; to conceal what preference she might feel for either of the boys.

They conned this lesson well, yet always without speech upon the matter. If Tony's letter made them laugh, they reread Sandy's, and discovered a quaint humor in its almost formal phrases, and laughed as they had laughed at Tony's jests. If Mrs. Caterson wrote Tony, she was careful to say she had done so, in order that Caterson might address his letter to the other boy; and each of them took pains to alternate between the youngsters, writing each in turn.

When Nina came to the house, as she liked to do in the afternoon, if she spoke of Tony, Mrs. Caterson was sure to praise Sandy too; and if Nina referred to Sandy, Mrs. Caterson jealously included Tony in the conversation. Thus, in even the smallest matters, they sought to hold the balance true.

But a few days after the western trip and the team's last game of the season, that occurred which shattered all their shams; which left them face to face with a dark and threatening reality. Caterson, at home and ready for dinner, was sitting in Mrs. Caterson's dressing room, waiting while she dressed, and looking casually through the pages of the *Transcript*. While he read the paper, he answered her questions about his day; a conference with this man; an encounter at luncheon with that one; a remark by Tedlock on the tremendous increase in the firm's business for the year.

He came to the sporting page, and his eye ran down the columns inattentively. She was saying: "We must have the Tedlock's to dinner soon," when he exclaimed:

"Hello! Lady, Tony got the captaincy!"

She whirled around delightedly. "Did he?" she echoed. "Of course he did! I knew he would! But isn't that fine?"

Then she saw the color drain from his cheeks as his eyes fastened on the paragraph before him; and she cried:

"Joe! What is it? What's the matter, Joe?"

"It's—Sandy!" he stammered. "There must be a mistake. I only saw the headline, at first. 'Caterson Elected Captain.' But it says here it was Sandy!"

She flew to his side. "Let me see!" she insisted. "That's absurd, Joe!" Her white lips formed the words. " 'Alexander Caterson, guard on this year's team.' " She fell back, and her hand pressed against her mouth, as though to hold back a cry.

"But Joe!" she faltered. "What does it mean?"

"Why—good for Sandy!" he said stumblingly. "Good for Sandy, I say!" he urged.

"Of course!" she echoed. "Oh, of course, I'm proud of Sandy. But Joe, please . . ." Her voice failed; yet she managed chokingly to stammer.

"Joe, what does it mean, my dear?"

He shook his head. He knew too surely what it must mean to be able to answer her.

XV

NEITHER Tony nor Sandy came home for Thanksgiving. Mr. and Mrs. Caterson had expected them; and after Sandy's astonishing election to the captaincy that had seemed Tony's certain prize, they dreaded seeing the boys, dreaded the inevitable discussion of that surprising action by the team. Thus the word that neither would come home was at once a disappointment and a reprieve.

Sandy wrote: "Jim Madder wants me to go home with him. He lives down on Long Island, right next to Roosevelt Field, and I'll have a chance to look at all sorts of motors on the planes there. I guess you won't mind if I go. Tony'll be there with you, anyway."

But by the same mail came Tony's letter. Barbs Delevan's show was opening in New York. "So we've got to rally 'round and give the little girl a hand," Tony explained. "Nina's going to be in New York, and Audrey, and Dan Lind, and Bob, I expect. It looks like a big night. Barbs is going to stop the show, if noise will do it. They open Wednesday night, and I'm getting away a day early so as to be there. You'll have Sandy to keep you company!"

And in the next paragraph, almost casually: "I guess you saw in the papers that Sandy's elected captain for next year. It was him or me, but he eats up responsibility, and I don't like it; so I dumped the load on him. It's all in the family, anyway."

Mrs. Caterson felt a quick dismay at that last phrase, and the unanswerable question it provoked; and Caterson said doubtfully:

"Well, we'll miss them!"

She nodded. "Joe, do you notice that neither one of them knows the other isn't coming home?" she asked wistfully. "They're not very close to one another, are they?"

"They're all right, Lady," he urged. "Don't make too much of too little." And he added: "Tony evidently wanted Sandy to be captain."

She smiled at his masculine credulity, but made no other reply. This was a matter concerning which the fewer words the better. There are some wounds which attention can only irritate, some hurts too deep to heal.

Neither admitted to the other the guilty relief which each in fact felt because the boys were not coming home. But when Nina called, the day before she left for New York, and learned that they would be alone, she offered them quick sympathy.

"I thought Sandy would be here," she protested. "Tony wrote me he was going to New York, but he said Sandy would be here!"

Mrs. Caterson smiled reassuringly. "It would only be for a day or two, anyway," she pointed out. "And short visits are just an aggravation. We'll look forward to Christmas, to two real weeks with them."

"Of course," Nina cheerfully assented. "And if Sandy's over there, we'll be sure to see him."

Mrs. Caterson nodded her agreement with this prediction, and later she spoke of this probability to her husband, finding comfort in the thought that the boys would be together. But when Nina, after her return, came in one afternoon for tea, she told Mrs. Caterson that they had not seen Sandy at all.

"I suppose he was too busy poking into valves and spark plugs and things," she hazarded. "If you let Sandy stick his nose into an engine, he'll keep it there till a piston hits him in the eye or something." And she laughed in swift amusement. "He and Tony would make one fine chauffeur between them," she suggested. "Tony to do the driving and Sandy to keep the car in tune."

And she went on, cheerfully chattering of this and that, while Mrs. Caterson listened smilingly. The first night of the show, Nina said, had been fun. "Barbs has just a small part," she explained. "She's a sort of infant terrible; a kid sister who makes wise remarks at the wrong times. But she did it wonderfully; and every time she got a laugh, we clapped and clapped, till the ushers almost put us out. She's going to be a star, before very long, I think. She's got something that does get across. She looks just the same on the stage as off it; that sort of challenging impudence, so that you wonder what she'll do next, and you want to poke her in order to find out. And she makes you laugh, and like her too. Even the women liked her. You could see that, all around us in the audience."

Mrs. Caterson thought Nina's praise had an exaggerated warmth, but she was too wise to ask questions. She only said:

"And you saw her afterward, of course?"

Nina nodded cheerfully. "Yes indeed. We all went up to Gay Tavern. Audrey Deal took us; or at least Audrey knew the man there. So we had the best of everything, and danced for hours."

"I had never met Audrey till that night she was here," Mrs. Caterson remarked. "She—has something disquieting about her, don't you think, Nina?"

"That's just her line!" Nina said reassuringly. "She talks in that sullen, insolent way, and she pretends to be so bored; but really Audrey's all sound common sense at the bottom. She's the most level-headed girl I know."

"Miss Delevan was happy in her success?" Mrs. Caterson inquired.

"She must have been," Nina assented. "Though you never can tell about Barbs." She hesitated. "You know—Barbs and I've known each other for years. We all thought she was just doing this for the fun of it. But she told me . . ." She hesitated. "I suppose it's a secret," she admitted. "You see, her mother. . . . She's one of these women you see so often in hotels, very beautifully dressed. Well, I thought Mr. Delevan was dead; but it turns out they've been divorced for years, and Mrs. Delevan had some perfectly tremendous alimony, but now Mr. Delevan has lost all his money in the stock market. And Mrs. Delevan hasn't saved anything at all. So Barbs said it was up to her to marry a millionaire, or else start in and earn her own living. That's why she's gone on the stage."

Mrs. Caterson was silent for a moment, digesting this; her eyes shadowed, as though she glimpsed some peril remote and intangible. "Poor child," she said doubtfully. "So she's chosen to go to work, instead of marrying. That shows a certain soundness in her, doesn't it?"

Nina hesitated. "I think perhaps she's—combining both," she admitted. "After all, being on the stage does serve as an introduction. But I shouldn't say that," she corrected hurriedly. "I like Barbs, really. She's not so hard as she pretends."

"Of course not," the older woman agreed.

"And she's sure to be a success if she wants to be," Nina insisted. "Really, Mrs. Caterson, she was wonderful."

"Was Tony all right?" the older woman asked. "His letter didn't come today. I suppose it will be in the morning mail."

"Oh, Tony was on high!" Nina assured her laughingly. "I never saw him so—full of fun. We were kept busy, trying to keep up with him, till the rest of us were exhausted; but he never did seem to get tired. We were all fagged out long before he and Barbs were ready to call it a day." And she added instantly, as though to amend a mis-statement: "He was as nice to me as he always is. Tony has a genius for being nice to people."

Mrs. Caterson said affectionately: "It hardly requires genius to be nice to you, Nina."

"You sweet thing!" Nina retorted. "But he was a dear!"

Mrs. Caterson watched the girl attentively. "I'm always a little worried about Tony," she confessed. "His high spirits are apt to lead him into some—extravagance, something he might afterward regret."

"Oh, a man who's been in training for two or three months is bound to be—like a boy out of school, on his first party afterward," Nina pointed out. "And of course he hadn't had any chance to let go, till he got down there."

There was, Mrs. Caterson thought, a reticence in the girl's eyes; something withheld. "Even one cocktail always did—exhilarate him," she remarked.

"That just makes him more delightful," Nina reassured her. "Nobody minds Tony, anyway." She hesitated, faintly. "He is so—loveable, Mrs. Caterson. And he likes everyone. I suppose that's why everyone likes him!"

"He can be so generous," Mrs. Caterson suggested proudly. "He wrote us that he helped elect Sandy captain. He pretended that he didn't want it himself; but of course I know he did."

"He was sweet about it," Nina agreed. "Of course, we spoke of it; and Barbs did hint that his nose was out of joint. But Tony just laughed at her. He said he wasn't even a candidate; he said they elected

Sandy unanimously. He said Sandy deserved it, too; and he said a man in the line made the best captain, anyway, because he didn't have to worry about other things. . . ."

"Sandy hasn't even mentioned it, in his letters," Mrs. Caterson remarked. "That's typical of him, isn't it?"

"Sandy's a dear," Nina warmly assented. She was on her feet. "He'll be a good captain, too." And she added laughingly as Mrs. Caterson walked arm in arm with her into the hall: "Of course, it should have been Tony! But it's all in the family!"

The older woman recognized Tony's phrase, and winced a little. In the family? But was it, after all; or in what family? The unanswerable question must torment her, now and always.

But she only said: "You're a dear to come in. I like having you, Nina."

Nina kissed her swiftly. "I love coming," she replied. "Goodby!" And Mrs. Caterson stayed in the door to watch her swift departure.

She returned then to the living room, her steps lagging imperceptibly, her eyes dark with thought. She had received from Nina one of those intangible impressions which women are so quick to catch, and she disliked, suddenly, Barbs Delevan.

And she felt sure that Nina had thought, even though she did not voice, some criticism of Tony too. The girl had praised Barbs too warmly; and she had defended Tony—whom no one had accused.

Mrs. Caterson did not report these impressions of

hers to her husband. There were matters more immediate to perplex and to disturb them both; for in the
letters from the boys after their return to college
there appeared again and again sure evidence that
between the two a gap was widening. Sandy, for one
thing, never referred to his election to the captaincy;
and his very silence was eloquent. He knew that the
election must have been a surprise to them; he must
have guessed, Mrs. Caterson guiltily decided, that
they were disappointed as well as surprised. He must
believe that they would have preferred the honor to
go to Tony; and as the Christmas holidays approached, Mrs. Caterson, troubled by this understanding, spoke of it to her husband.

He agreed, unhappily. "Maybe so!" he admitted.
"Sandy—isn't blind! He knows we love him; but he
knows too that Tony is the one who has always made
us proud."

"We must be particularly nice to Sandy, while
they're at home," she urged.

"I've congratulated him, in my letters," he remarked, reassuringly.

"Oh, so have I," she agreed. "But I don't mean
that, so much." She smiled. "I suppose I was thinking that I'd cuddle him, and kiss him, and things like
that. Of course, you can't do as much as I can, in
such ways, Joe. Sandy's never been demonstrative,"
she added. "But I think it's time he began." She
laughed softly. "I hope my caresses don't embarrass
him too much," she confessed.

"Well, don't be too public with them," he advised;

and she looked at him suddenly, with a twist of pain in her eyes.

"You two are so alike," she murmured, half to herself. "You and Sandy, Joe!"

He knew her thought; and he sought by a jest to make her smile. "Well, Tony's a good lad, too," he said in mock condescension; and she did laugh aloud, and exclaimed:

"Conceited!"

They discussed what they might do to make Christmas happiest for the boys. Caterson had decided to increase their allowances. He had always been sufficiently generous.

"But they'll have incomes to handle, by and by," he remarked. "And they ought to be learning how."

His intent, he explained, was to establish trust funds which would provide for each one of them some four or five thousand dollars a year. "And a lump sum when they graduate," he continued. "They'll probably lose it in the market; but that experience will pay them dividends in the end." He expanded the scheme, and she listened inattentively. Matters financial had never seemed to her important. She had managed a small income as efficiently as she now dispensed a larger sum. When he was done, she spoke of a dance which she proposed to give for the boys on the twenty-third, of a theatre party or two, of a watch party for New Year's Eve.

But though they talked readily enough of these matters, neither of them referred to the problem which did in fact possess their minds. This would be the first time they had seen the boys since Miss Elcess, dying, had revealed the dark secret so long concealed. They had been able to hide from the eyes of their friends this hideous new thing in their lives; but they had not yet been compelled to face the boys.

To do so would be hard. To see Tony and Sandy day by day, to love this one and that one, to approve this word or action, or perhaps to disapprove.

And to confront in the very flesh that inscrutable enigma which must henceforward haunt their lives.

They mustered their courage for that ordeal now.

XVI

THE first evening after the boys returned they spent at home together. Mrs. Caterson drove in with Richards to meet their train; but she stayed in the limousine while Richards went to the platform to find them and fetch them back to her. While she waited there, after Richards had gone, she trembled with unadmitted fears; and when by and by she saw them coming, her eyes swam.

It was Tony she saw first; she caught a glimpse of him as he came swiftly through the doors from the trainshed, and then she could see nothing more. But a moment later he had scrambled eagerly into the car to catch her in his arms in the way she loved; he was kissing her eyes, and laughing at her tears, and whispering happily:

"Child, child, behave! Here are lots of young men to kiss your hand."

And when she was able to laugh back at him, he released her, and she saw half a dozen of his friends standing by the car, watching smilingly. Tony introduced them in a swift confusion of names; and someone said:

"Tony was bound we'd come and meet you, Mrs. Caterson. He brags about you all the time!"

"I don't brag, I understate the truth," Tony protested. "See for yourselves! No trouble to show goods. Hall-marked, fourteen-carat, triple A, pre-war stuff boys. Isn't she?"

They were uncomfortable, and she saw their un-easy stirrings as they sought to escape, but Tony held them with this word and that, planning for the days ahead. Luncheon, a game of squash, a dance. . . . Till Mrs. Caterson urged:

"But they'll want to find their own mothers, Tony dear. Let them go!"

She thought he bade them goodby regretfully, as though he dreaded being alone with her; and her heart ached for him. Then for the first time, with a pang of guilt, she remembered Sandy, and looked this way and that to find him. He was helping Richards stow the bags in the front seat, and he caught her eye and grinned a welcome; but not till the others were gone did he get in beside her and dutifully kiss her cheek.

She held him close and warmly, laughing at his awkwardness. "Sandy, Sandy," she whispered. "Am I as bad as that?"

Then Tony, at her other side, reached past her to push his brother laughingly away. "Here, Cap-tain," he exclaimed. "Let a man kiss her that knows how!"

But Mrs. Caterson, even as his lips touched hers, was stiff with pain. There had been something so derisive in that appellation. Captain! The sore was still open, then.

They were to pick up Caterson at the office; and

they did so, Sandy alighting to fetch his father down. Mrs. Caterson had Tony alone for a while; and they were both abashed by this isolation, till Tony rose to the moment and began to talk rapidly and surely of nothing at all. She had no opening for all the questions she longed to put to him before Sandy and his father presently appeared.

She thought, as these two crossed the sidewalk to the car, how like they were! Their square, blocky, awkward bodies; the way their heads were set upon their shoulders; their heavy, swinging hands. . . .

On the way home, Tony jeered at the infirmities of this ancient limousine. He embroidered the theme with a thousand variations, each one more amusing than the last; and if there was something forced and desperate in this monologue of his, the others were each so grateful at being spared the necessity of speech that they did not interrupt. At home, Richards took their bags upstairs to the room they had always shared; and Mrs. Caterson warned them:

"You've just time to brush your hair before dinner."

Tony called cheerfully to his brother: "You go ahead, Sandy. I want to look around a minute."

She was grateful that he had used, this time, the familiar name. Sandy, without comment, did as Tony suggested; and not till he came downstairs again did Tony go up in his turn.

Then dinner was announced, but they had to wait for Tony; and while they waited, Mrs. Caterson made Sandy sit beside her on the couch, and she put

her arm about him. But he was so stiff and unre-
sponsive that she could only laugh at him, content
herself with holding his hand.

"Poor Sandy," she laughed teasingly. "Red as a
beet because your own mother kisses you. Don't you
like it?"

"Sure, I like it," he assured her, grinning uncomfortably.

"You dissemble your love!" she protested.

But he said seriously, suddenly meeting her eyes:
"I guess I can't ever dissemble it enough to fool
you, mother." And she felt a swift delight, and she
brushed her eyes with her hand.

"No, son," she confessed. "I've known your father
too long. You bashful Catersons!"

And instantly paled at her own incautious word,
and looked up to meet her husband's tormented eyes.

Then Tony came running downstairs and took her
on his arm, and Sandy and his father followed them
to the dining room. Mrs. Caterson, facing her husband across the table, saw the terror which he sought
to hide; and she summoned her resources, and she
and Tony between them kept the talk alive. Only
now and then a momentary silence fell and endured
for seconds that seemed to her eternity. She was
tremendously relieved when she could rise, when they
could turn back to the other room.

There was a long hour there. Tony, she saw more
clearly now, was desperately ill at ease. Though the
room was not overwarm, there were beads upon his
brow. He spoke of the New York Thanksgiving,

and Mrs. Caterson told him she had heard about it from Nina. He looked at her, she thought, with a sharp apprehension, as though he feared what she might have heard. A little later, he glanced at his watch, and rose and moved restlessly about the room; he scanned the records on the phonograph, put one on to play.

There was, Mrs. Caterson understood, a spectre here that must be laid; and she mustered at last her courage. It were better to materialize the ghost, to confront it and so banish it forever. She said suddenly:

"Sandy, you've never even mentioned being captain, in your letters."

Tony sat down abruptly in the nearest chair; and Sandy, after a moment shook his head.

"Guess I'm not much on letter writing," he confessed. "You'd hear about it, anyway."

"We were mighty proud of you," Mrs. Caterson assured him. "It's quite an honor, isn't it!"

Tony cried laughingly: "Honor! Child, you'd be surprised! Sandy'll be the biggest man on the campus next year." There was only the faintest derision in his tones. "But it hasn't spoiled him. Nothing high hat about Sandy at all." He chuckled gaily. "Why, he acts ashamed of it. First time I called him 'Captain' he blushed like a girl!"

There was a dreadful silence, and Mrs. Caterson regretted her temerity. She said desperately:

"Of course, we knew it would be one of you. Maybe that's just our foolish pride in you both, but we knew." She appealed to her husband. "Didn't we, Joe?"

"Tony—withdrew his name, to let me have it," Sandy told them, blurting out the words.

But Tony laughingly contradicted him. "I hadn't a chance," he declared. "I could have made a fight, but they wanted him. And an argument might make trouble in the team next year. Sandy'll make a good captain. He'll get gray-haired over it, probably." He grinned cheerfully. "But he wanted it, and he got it, and he can't blame me!"

No one made immediate comment, and Tony added hurriedly:

"It's all in the family, anyway!"

Mrs. Caterson, with an involuntary gesture, pressed her hand to her lips to hold back a cry of pain. Tony saw her, and for a moment his face twisted; then he got swiftly to his feet.

"There, Child, we couldn't both have it," he assured her gaily. "Can't have two captains, you know. Now it's time little girls were in bed. You trot along upstairs. I'm going over to say hello to Nina. See you at breakfast, all."

"She's expecting you," Mrs. Caterson agreed. "Sandy—you're not going?"

"I've got a book to finish tonight," Sandy said slowly.

Tony grinned. " 'How to Play Football' in twelve lessons," he told them laughingly. "Sandy's taking his responsibilities hard, you see." He moved toward the door. "Good night, all."

And a moment later, after he had found his hat and coat, he came swiftly back to kiss his mother again.

"Please, Child," he whispered. "It's all right. I'll win some other crown for you, by and by."

After he was gone, the three left behind found little else to say to one another. Only Sandy confessed at last: "Tony took it hard. I didn't want it, honestly!" His eyes pleaded with them. "But—the team wanted me."

Mrs. Caterson cried reassuringly: "Sandy dear, Tony doesn't really mind."

"Well, I guess you expected he'd get it," he confessed.

And in the face of his honest understanding, they were both dumb. She could only cross and kiss him tenderly. "Good night," she whispered. "I'll leave you with your father, dear. I am a little tired, ready for bed."

She went upstairs. But when an hour later Caterson joined her, she asked desperately: "Is he all right, Joe?"

"All right? Oh, sure, yes."

"Joe, Joe," she cried in terrified appeal. "We mustn't let it go on so. Joe, it was terrible. Terrible! What are we going to do?"

"Sleep, Lady," he told her gently. "You're wrought up, tonight. Things will look better in the morning."

"I was in a panic for a moment. And when Tony said—that, I wanted to scream."

"It will be easier by and by!" he insisted.

But long after she had at last fallen fitfully asleep, he lay wakeful; he might comfort her, but his own heart was full of fears.

XVII

MRS. CATERSON had planned a watch party for New Year's Eve. When she told Tony, he applauded delightedly; but when he found she meant to have the party at home, he was dubious. "It'll be a rowdy time, Child," he protested laughingly. "You know this gang, when they get started. Better send us in town somewhere, save wear and tear on the furniture."

But she was laughingly insistent. "For one thing, I want you at home that night," she told him. "And besides, Sandy wouldn't go, if we had it in town. It's hard enough to persuade him to be festive, anyway. He's such a sobersides."

He grinned. "Responsibility sits on him," he suggested; and she caught the grim hurt in his tone, and felt a pang of regret for the disappointment he had known.

But in this matter of the party, she held her ground; so the occasion went as she had planned, and easily enough. The big living room and the hall furnished dancing space a-plenty; and those who for the moment or the evening did not care to dance could escape from the whirl and press of the dancers by drifting into the breakfast room, or into Mr. Caterson's study, or turning to the billiard room downstairs. There was even a table or two of bridge, in Mrs. Caterson's sitting room on the second floor, for such folk as Mr. and Mrs. Buckel, who soon wearied of dancing. The Christmas greenery was still in place; and if here and there it had begun to fade, flowers were massed to cover its deficiencies. In the hour after dinner and before the first guests arrived, Mrs. Caterson, surveying her arrangements, found them good; and Caterson and Tony assured her she was right in this appraisal.

She asked Sandy his opinion; he said awkwardly: "Why sure, mother! Anything you run is always run right."

"If it weren't, you'd never know the difference," she told him laughingly. "You'd never notice anything less conspicuous than a smoking chimney, or a leaky water pipe, or a furnace out of order."

"You've got us used to expecting things to be perfect," he insisted. "Make a mistake once in a while! Then we'll appreciate how slick you are."

She kissed him affectionately. "That's a very pretty speech, Sandy," she assured him. "Thank you kindly, sir." Then the orchestra arrived, and she went to direct the musicians. Tony departed to mix a punch. Sandy and his father drifted into Caterson's study; and Sandy examined, as he liked to do, the steamship model there, admiring its accuracies, discussing this point and that one with the older man. Caterson watched him thoughtfully. He found himself reflecting that Sandy's mind in such matters worked exactly like his own. . . .

But presently the tide of guests began to rise to a flood; and thereafter for a while there dwelt in these wide rooms a gay confusion. Mrs. Caterson meant to stay near the door, but when the first strains of music sounded, Tony swept her away to dance with him.

"The first dance is always the best one," he told her tenderly. "I'll take the first with my sweetheart, let the last fall where it may."

She protested: "But I ought to stay to greet people!" Yet there was no resolution in her dissent. She found always a keen delight in dancing with Tony; just now she was so happy that she closed her eyes, swaying in his arms, and he kissed her. She cried: "Tony! Don't do that!"

But he laughed at her. "When a lady closes her eyes," he argued, "What else can a fellow do?"

She caught sight of Mr. and Mrs. Buckel in the hall, and escaped from him; and Tony went with her to greet them, and seized upon Nina, cloak and all, and whirled her once around the room before she managed to free herself. She fled upstairs, laughing back at him; but he was already dancing with Audrey Deal, and then with this one and with that, as other folk arrived.

Sandy was not so ready as Tony in such matters as these. Mrs. Caterson had by and by to warn him, chidingly. "You must dance with everyone here, son, you know," she whispered. "I know it's hard, my dear. But you'd better be about it."

And Sandy went grimly at this duty of his, his

blocky figure moving indomitably to and fro about the floor. Other, lighter-footed folk dodged him or bumped into him; he remained unmoved. Only he managed always to receive the impact on his own shoulders, thus to protect his partner; and he never stepped on her feet. To avoid doing so, he kept his own feet solidly planted on the floor, moving them with a stern, trudging shuffle. Sandy might not be able to achieve virtuosity; but he was innocent of the more obvious terpsichorean crimes.

After a while, Mr. and Mrs. Caterson and some other older folk began to withdraw from the whirl. A bridge game got under way, upstairs. The billiard balls began to click softly on the table in the basement. There was a constant circle, forever changing, about the punch table. Sandy took Audrey Deal in to see his father's steamship model; he lifted the glass cover and let her examine it first hand. Then Tony came and seized on her, and Sandy resumed again his duties. At intervals, the orchestra stopped for a breathing space; but these pauses were brief. For the most part the dancers chose their own times to rest. Cushions began to be strewed on the stairs; and when Mrs. Caterson came down by and by to see that all went well, she had to pick her way between half a dozen couples sitting there.

Tony played host gracefully; he overlooked no one, seizing upon a new partner when he chose, dismissing her as readily when he turned to another. Sandy had more difficulty. He could ask a girl to dance, but he did not always know how to be rid of her; and Tony and the other men made a jest between them, so that no one relieved Sandy of these partners of his. Thus he danced for twenty minutes with Audrey Deal, and it was in desperation that at last he took her in to see the steamship model, where Tony came to his rescue; and Nell Dyson, his next partner, remained his partner for half an hour, till the girl herself cried laughingly:

"Now Sandy, you've done your duty by me! Run along and find someone else."

And he looked at her with the dumb gratitude of a dog. . . .

For the first hour, everyone was dancing; but after that the floor was not so crowded. Duty done, obligation gave way to inclination, and Tony turned to Nina.

"I've saved you," he whispered. "Last and best!"

"But you danced with me first of all," she reminded him.

"That didn't count," he assured her. "That was just like the old hymn, you know, about the 'foretaste of joys divine.' "

" 'Divine?' " she echoed. "I wonder if they do dance in heaven."

"Of course," he insisted. "Else why the harps? Or if you will have it, sweet, anyone who dances with you is in heaven, ipso facto."

She laughed at him. "Then let's dance instead of talking," she suggested; and for a while they moved in silence, the spell of the music fast upon them, the compelling beat of it welding them together like the hammer on the anvil. Till he was flushed, his eyes shining, and she was very quiet in his arms. Her eyes half closed, and he bent to kiss her as he had kissed his mother; but she drew a little away from him.

"Forfeit!" he urged. "You fell asleep!"

She shook her head; and with that sudden audacity which was native to Tony, he swept her through the hall and into his father's study. There were others there; he bowed, said gravely: "Pardon the intrusion," and danced into the hall again. The punch bowl was in the dining room; the breakfast room was crowded; they could hear the click of billiard balls downstairs.

"All right, then," he exclaimed. "So be it!"

And he swung her into the butler's pantry, between the dining room and the kitchen.

She protested, laughing quickly: "Why Tony!"

He looked into the kitchen, spoke to a serving maid. "Julia," he said smilingly, "Miss Buckel and I are in conference, not to be disturbed." And so turned back to Nina again. There were cups sticky with punch in the sink and along the drain boards. Nina asked in swift amusement:

"Are we going to wash dishes?"

He faced her, suddenly serious. "I've some dirty dishes to wash, Nina," he told her gently." You're a sweet thing! I was—unkind to you, in New York. I want you to know I'm sorry; always will be sorry. I appreciate the way you've—treated me since."

Her eyes fell, then rose to meet his frankly. "You weren't yourself, Tony," she agreed honestly.

"I've kicked myself ever since."

She smiled. "That's hard to do, even for you, boy."

"Please," he begged. "Don't make a joke about it. It's not a joke to me."

"All right," she agreed. "What shall I do, scold you?"

"You don't need to," he assured her. "I've said to myself worse than you can ever say. I just want to get the books clear. I was tight, Honey. First time I'd really broken training. And you were so darned sweet!"

She hesitated, said honestly: "I know. I understand. That didn't hurt me so much. I'm feminine enough to be—a little flattered, as well as hurt, perhaps. But the other hurt me, Tony. I'm being honest, too."

"Barbs?" he asked.

"Yes," she told him, her color flooding.

"I know," he admitted ruefully. "That was a part of it, though, Nina. I was sore at myself, so I wanted to hurt you. That's human, isn't it?"

She hesitated, shook her head then and smiled at him once more. "It's all right, Tony," she said reassuringly. "I've understood, all the time, I think. It hurt me, but I've got some common sense. And as long as you're sorry, too."

"Forgiven?" he challenged.

"Forgiven," she assured him.

He bent with a quick, charming gesture and kissed

her hand; and she smiled at his bowed head. "You're a nice boy, Tony," she confessed.

He drew erect again, spoke with a quick animation. "There's more to it than this, Nina," he said eagerly. "Something I want to tell you. Something that happened to me the other day that—changed my point of view in many things." He touched his chest, in faint mockery. "Behold an adult, Nina," he bade her. "I've suddenly grown up."

She puzzled for a moment, thought she understood him, said gravely: "There is that, about big disappointments, sometimes; if you're big enough!"

"Disappointments?" he echoed, and his brows suddenly twisted, and then he laughed. "Oh, you mean Sandy being elected captain." There were black shadows in his eyes. "That pretty near broke me," he admitted honestly. "They blamed me for that touchdown. But Nina, the ball didn't hit me. That damned referee. . . ."

She heard him with head a little bowed, not meeting his eyes; touched his hand at last to interrupt him. "Then what did you mean, Tony? I thought that was it. I'm sorry. I didn't mean to hurt you, my dear."

In the dining room there was a sudden clamor of voices about the punch bowl. Tony caught her hand.

"We'll have to hurry," he remembered. "Here it is, Nina. Father's made a trust fund for me. For both of us, Sandy and me. I'll have an income of about forty-five hundred, and ten thousand next year when I graduate. He and mother believe in getting married early. That's why he's doing it, I think."

He hesitated, held suddenly both her hands in his. "That's what it means to me, Nina. I expected to have to wait till I'd dug my toes in, got a start somewhere. Three or four years. Nina, I want you. You know I'm in love with you. I have been, for fifteen years, I guess. That's what I want; what it means to me. What do you say, Nina?"

She was looking at her hands, at his which held them. His fingers were long and slender, yet his hands were strong. He saw her glance, and he bent suddenly to kiss her hands again, and twisted his head so that he could look up into her eyes, and laughed appealingly.

"What do you say, Nina?" he repeated; then straightened again as she lifted her head. "I'm dead earnest, Honey," he told her. "You know that. Please?"

She smiled in sudden amusement at her own thought. "I gather that you'd like me to marry you, Mister," she said in fond mockery.

"Right!"

She freed her hands, put them behind her. "Just what is it you propose, Tony?" she asked, suddenly grave.

"A year from now," he said, his voice husky with feeling. "I'm not a fool, Nina. I want to finish college; and I'd never be able to look at a book with you waiting to be loved. A year from June. We can

upstairs and into the circle around the hearth, where the blaze leaped high.

Nell Dyson, rifling Mrs. Caterson's pigeonholes, had discovered there a new date pad, for the year about to begin; she produced it now triumphantly.

"And here's one for next year!" she cried. "Let's burn up the New Year too! The more the merrier!"

Tony caught it from her. "Right," he agreed. "Throw it on the fire!"

But Nina snatched the calendar away from him, held it fast to her heart.

"No, no," she protested. "Not the New Year, Tony! There'll be so many things we want to do, or ought to do, or must do in the New Year. No, my dear!"

And her eyes held his warmly, as the great clock in the hall began to chime.

XVIII

WHEN the boys went back to college, Mr. and Mrs. Caterson drove them to the train, saw them aboard the car, and then turned back together to where Richards waited with the limousine.

And Caterson thought that now that they were gone, something had gone out of Mrs. Caterson. She was suddenly weary, and smaller than she had been a moment before; her cheeks which had been full and firm were faintly lined. It was always thus with her when these two who were her life departed from her for a little while.

So long as Richards was working his way through the worst traffic, Caterson said nothing; nor did she utter any word. She was content to sit beside him, her hand touching his, her thoughts absorbed with these loved ones just departed. But he watched her; and when by and by he saw her eyes fill, he could not longer hold his tongue. He gripped her hand more firmly; said in a cheerful tone:

"Well, it's been a gay, happy time, Edith. You're a fine mother to those boys."

"I tried to make it nice for them," she agreed. "They won't be coming home to us many more times, Joe."

"They'll always be coming home," he protested.

"You've put so much of yourself into them; that will pull them back to you as long as they live."

She nodded. "How are they, do you think?" she asked.

"Why, all right," he declared. "I think they're fine."

"Tony is—pitiful, isn't he?" she suggested; and he stared at her in honest bewilderment.

"Pitiful?" he echoed. "Why, Lady, that's the last word I'd ever put on Tony."

"Oh, he tries to hide it," she agreed. "He fools some people, perhaps. He may even fool you, my dear." Her smile forgave Caterson his blindness. "But he can't fool his old mother."

"You mean this business of the captaincy?" he asked lamely.

She nodded. "It's the first big shock he's ever had to stand," she suggested. "The first big disappointment. He's been so used to success, Joe. If it were Sandy, now, it wouldn't get under his skin at all. He'll always be able to support failure with philosophy."

"So will Tony," he protested. "Tony's got a backbone, Lady."

"But his heart's near broken," she whispered. "Oh, it will mend, by and by; but the thing seems so big to him now. You can see it in his tones, in that desperate gaiety he wears."

"Tony always was the life of the party," he urged.

"Yes, but now he's fighting to be," she amended; and she added: "Oh, I hope Tony always does get what he wants. He doesn't want so very much. Just for people to like him, and approve of him. He doesn't mind being whipped in a good, honest fight, if he can lose gracefully. But this struck close home, Joe. It meant the men on the team didn't like him, don't you see?" She made a sick gesture. "If people don't love Tony, it will ruin him, my dear."

He said desperately: "Everybody does love him. Nobody can help it."

She smiled in proud memory. "He proposed to Nina, while he was at home," she reported. "He told me about it, so delightedly."

"Did she take him?" Caterson asked, in some doubt. "He's got a year in college still ahead of him."

Mrs. Caterson shook her head. "She bade him wait till he graduates," she explained. "But—she told Tony that if now were a year from June, she'd —marry him. Didn't you see how much happier he's been, since New Year's?"

"I didn't notice," he confessed. "She's sensible, isn't she?"

"She's a blessed girl," Mrs. Caterson agreed.

There was silence again while Richards stolidly pursued the homeward way; but by and by Caterson remarked:

"Sandy and Audrey Deal struck up quite a friendship. Did you notice?"

"I certainly did," she agreed. "Wasn't it funny? She's not at all the sort of girl you'd expect to appeal to Sandy."

"He was keen about her," Caterson insisted. "Told me he liked her very much." He smiled faintly. "Sandy is going to have a lot of surprises for us, as the years go on, I expect, Edith." She was still thinking of Tony, and did not reply; till he added: "This new responsibility, the captaincy, has changed him already."

She smiled happily. "Wasn't he—cunning about it? A boy suddenly trying to be grown up and responsible."

"That's one thing about Sandy," he remarked. "He never evaded a responsibility in his life, once he recognized it. He's plugging on the theory of football, now; reading up on it and so on. He'll make a good captain."

"Of course he will," she cried. "I only meant that I'm sorry Tony couldn't have it, because he'd have been so happy about it, Joe."

He touched her hand, smiled to himself. "I was thinking last night," he remarked. "I'd been talking to Sandy. He—opened up, more than he usually does. You remember in one of the Musketeer romances where Colbert is talking to D'Artagnan. D'Artagnan had always fought him, and despised him; and Colbert said in effect that power would make a difference in him. He told D'Artagnan that hereafter there would be a new Colbert, more gracious, more benign, more loveable; and made so by his new power. You remember it?"

"Vaguely," she agreed. "I haven't read those books for years."

"Tony might be D'Artagnan," Caterson suggested. "And Sandy might well be Colbert."

She was silent for a moment, considering this; then she shuddered, laughingly. "I don't think I ever came to love M. Colbert," she confessed. "And I was wild about D'Artagnan!"

But her own words seemed to chill and frighten her; he saw the color drain from her cheek, and her hand clung to his till they stopped before their own door.

XIX

TONY decided to go abroad that summer. Half a dozen of his fellows were going; and though Mr. and Mrs. Caterson had at the parting that pang of dreadful apprehension which is the lot of parents, they bore smiling faces to the wharf to see him sail. Nina was with them; and when Tony kissed her goodby, he whispered:

"A year from now, my dear. A year from now!"

She stood on the stringpiece of the wharf waving her handkerchief long after his face was lost in the blur of other faces along the rail.

Sandy decided to work on a farm in New Hampshire through the summer. "It means just that much less time wasted getting in condition in the fall," he pointed out, to his mother's mild demur. "Pitching hay will keep me in shape. And I'll be able to run down and see you and father once in a while."

So Mr. and Mrs. Caterson were alone in the big summer place on the North Shore. The Buckels and Nina were nearby, and the tennis court behind the Caterson cottage was busy all summer long, thronged with young folk who came whirling up in their cars for three or four sets before the morning swim, or drove over for an afternoon on the court and tea with Mrs. Caterson. Nina came often; and thrice

Sandy came down for a week-end; and once Mr. and Mrs. Caterson drove into the mountains and picked Sandy up on the way, to join them for the week of their tour.

For the rest, they had long letters from Tony, full of affection, packed with the details of his journeyings, rich and satisfying. He went first to England, then to the Continent, then back to London again. Nina came over one day and Mrs. Caterson read aloud to her Tony's latest letter; and Nina listened smilingly.

"I had one from him, by the same steamer," she confessed. "But it wasn't nearly as nice as yours."

"Tony's letters are always charming," Mrs. Caterson agreed. "So exactly like him."

Nina said casually: "Barbs Delevan's show is opening soon in London. She's rehearsing over there now, Nell Dyson heard the other day. I expect Tony will see her."

"He hasn't spoken of her," Mrs. Caterson returned. "Is she still doing well?"

"Oh, I think so," Nina declared. "Yes, Barbs is very successful, Nell says. I don't hear from her directly."

"It will be nice for him to have someone he knows, there," Mrs. Caterson commented. "Of course, the boys with him are all congenial. But they like to have girls to play around with, I suppose. Another cup, Nina?"

But Nina had to hurry away.

Tony landed in New York early in September;

and he made haste to join his father and mother. Sandy had by this time finished his summer's job and come home; and he was there when Tony arrived. Tony stopped in town to get his own car and drove down to the shore; he swept up the circling drive at his usual breakneck speed, and Mrs. Caterson flew to catch him in her arms. She hugged him hard, kissed him roundly, pushed him to arm's length so that she might scrutinize him again, and hugged him tight once more.

"But you look tired, Tony," she protested. "I don't suppose you've had a proper night's sleep all the time you were gone."

Tony laughed at her cheerfully. "Don't you ever go to Europe to sleep, Child. There's too much to see and do." He gripped his father's hand, turned casually to Sandy. "And you, Captain!" he remarked, in that tone of light derision which could color Sandy's cheek so hotly.

"You're overweight," Sandy accusingly commented.

"I'll take that off in a week."

"Soft, aren't you?" Sandy insisted.

Tony said in faint irritation: "Discipline doesn't begin yet, Captain. Wait till we get out on the field." And he added a question, eyeing Sandy's blocky figure. "How's the farm?"

Sandy nodded. "I put on some weight, but it's solid," he replied.

"You look muscle bound," Tony suggested, grinning maliciously; and he linked his arm in his mother's as they turned toward the house together. She had watched this interchange between the two, helpless to interfere; and she seized on Tony now with many gay questions, not so much because she was driven by curiosity, as from a desperate desire to prevent any open outbreak between him and Sandy.

Tony had many things to tell, and told them well; and always it was "we" did this, and "we" did that, so that his mother said finally:

"You were a congenial group, weren't you?"

Tony chuckled. "Absolutely!" he agreed. "Oh, of course, there's one grouch in every party." He looked toward his brother. "Lob Dudley, Sandy," he explained. "He never wanted to do what the rest of us wanted to do; but he wouldn't go off and play by himself either. He'd stick around and watch us disapprovingly." He grinned. "You know his line, Sandy."

Caterson asked curiously: "Isn't he the boy who used to sub for you at right half, Tony?"

"Sure," Tony assented. "He's one of these saps who take football seriously." He looked at Sandy in a cheerful mockery, and Sandy grinned and Tony swept on into some new recital, and won them all to swift mirth again.

It was Mrs. Caterson who asked, when after a time the talk began to lag, whether Tony had seen Barbs Delevan abroad. "We heard that her show was rehearsing for a London opening," she explained; and Tony nodded cheerfully.

"Saw her once or twice," he agreed. "She was busy

as a paperhanger, though." He chuckled, caught Sandy's eye again. "Lob Dudley fell for her," he remarked. "Can you tie that?" And he explained to his mother: "Lob's sober as a judge, and you know Barbs!"

He may have seen in Mrs. Caterson's glance some mild disapproval of this implied criticism of Miss Delevan, for he added quickly:

"I don't mean to say Barbs isn't fine. He's not her kind, that's all."

But before she could ask a further question, a swarm of young folk came whirling up the drive, and Mr. and Mrs. Caterson had to surrender Tony to them for a while. During the few days remaining before he and Sandy went back to college—they were returning a week early, for preliminary practise— the older folk had little of their company; but this is a deprivation to which parents grow accustomed. They enjoyed watching the continual activity of youth as it swept and spun about them; and they spoke together now and then of the boys, yet always guardedly. Tacitly and without specific arrangement, they sought to give the deep wound in their hearts a chance to heal; they ignored it, pretended it did not exist, affected to find their lives unchanged. And even when, as happened not infrequently, the slumbering hostility between the boys threatened to wake, Mr. and Mrs. Caterson usually pretended neither to hear nor to see.

Once Mrs. Caterson did say, in an effort to find comfort:

"I suppose all brothers have their arguments."

And Caterson stoutly retorted: "Of course! I wouldn't give a hoot for them if they didn't, my dear."

Yet the night after the two went back to college, Mrs. Caterson could not sleep till Caterson got into her bed and took her head on his shoulder. He lay for hours in an aching rigidity lest he disturb her there.

XX

THEY did not see any of the games that fall, for Mrs. Caterson was not so well. There were in her shadowed eyes and in the color of her cheeks and in the deepening hollows of her throat suggestions of an increasing fragility; and these indications became more marked after the newspapers printed the fact that Tony and Sandy were twins.

The story first appeared as a news dispatch under a college date line, in the morning *Post*. Tedlock called it to Caterson's attention at the office, asked whether Caterson had seen it, pressed into the other man's hand a paper folded with this item uppermost.

The story was no more than a paragraph. Its substance was that Tony and Sandy were twins, that no one in college had known this fact, and that there was no resemblance between them "except in the circumstance that they are both stellar athletes, and that they were rivals for the captaincy last fall."

Caterson read the few lines and his lips tightened; and Tedlock said sympathetically:

"I understood the boys themselves didn't want it known."

Caterson nodded. "That feeling dates back to the time they were children," he explained. "We've always ignored it, in the family. Very few people do know it." He frowned thoughtfully. "I can't help wondering—how this came out, now."

Tedlock said reassuringly: "Well, it will blow over in a day or two." And he turned to other matters. But Caterson was all that day abstracted and distressed; for Mrs. Caterson, he knew, would be by this incident increasingly disturbed.

When he reached home, it was to find that someone had told her about the story in the paper; but between them they erected a pretense that the matter was of no consequence. They did not discuss the possible effect of the disclosure upon the boys, nor did Tony mention what had happened, in his next letter. But Sandy, with that blundering honesty which was a part of his character, did refer to it.

"I guess you saw it," he wrote. "I've been trying to figure how it got out. Lob Dudley's room mate is the *Post* correspondent up here, and Barbs Delevan might have told Lob, last summer in London. She probably heard it from some of the girls around home, years ago. And Lob and Tony don't hit it off very well; so if Lob knew, he might tell, just to start something. I think that must have been the way it happened, because there weren't but a few fellows here that we'd ever told, and they wouldn't tell. It doesn't matter, of course, only Tony always sort of wanted to keep it dark, and he's sore as a boil at Lob about it. Of course his being sore just makes the rest of them kid us all the more."

When they had read the letter, Caterson remarked: "I suppose Dudley resents the fact that he can't beat Tony out for half back." And he added, thinking aloud: "But—Miss Delevan must have a malicious streak in her, if it was she who told. Or some grudge against Tony . . ."

Mrs. Caterson made no comment, but there was a groping understanding in her eyes.

The story flared up again, a fortnight later, to occupy a full page in the feature section of the Sunday *Post*. There were photographs of Tony and of Sandy, their descriptions were compared, there was even some discussion of their contrasting traits of character; and to this material was added an extended interview with a leading doctor on the general subject of twins, and the similarity or dissimilarity between them.

Caterson, when he first saw this story, was desperately dismayed; but it seemed to him wise to accept it in a matter of fact way, affect to find it merely interesting. He even started to read it aloud to Mrs. Caterson, who that Sunday morning lay late abed. He thought that to be able to discuss the matter would be in some degree a cloak for their mutual distress! But Mrs. Caterson checked him.

"I'll read it by and by," she suggested. "I think —just now, dear—I'll sleep a little more."

So he went into the other room and closed her door; and he sat down and his eye once more scanned the columns. Two kinds of twins, fraternal and identical. . . . Identical twins always of the same sex. . . . Fraternal twins no more alike than ordinary brothers and sisters. . . . Twins who are

decidedly unlike seldom discuss their twinship. . . .
Fraternal twins probably twice as numerous as identical. . . . Twins not identical seldom show any
close spiritual attraction or keen attachment, as
identical twins so often do. . . .

This was all sufficiently familiar. These things he
had read or heard so many times before. But at
the foot of the column there was a paragraph
which struck him into sudden terror. For the
reporter had written:

"The popular impression that twins are apt to
die young has scientific fact behind it. Statistics
show that of all twins born, over 400 out of every
1,000 die before they are a year old. In one study
of 317 pairs of twins, 150 pairs survived, 90 pairs
died, and of the other 77 pairs, one died and one
survived."

Caterson read this paragraph a second time, not
because the facts set down were new to him, but
because there seemed no reason why the paragraph
should be here at all. It was to begin with, almost
entirely irrelevant; and that very fact made it the
more disturbing. It seemed to Caterson to suggest
that someone knew or guessed this dark secret
which oppressed him. The innocent paragraph was
like a hideous threat; and he felt the beads of perspiration start upon his brow. He did not discuss
the point with Mrs. Caterson, trying to persuade
himself that it had not occurred to her; but he saw
the increasing sadness in her eyes.

They gave only a perfunctory attention to the triumphs and the defeats of the current football season. The newspapers after one game remarked that Tony seemed sluggish and unsure. Sandy was credited with his usual sound defensive play. Later Tony strained a ligament in his knee; and though he played in every game, his old speed like that of a leaping flame was gone. When the boys came home for the week-end at Thanksgiving, it was plain to them both that Sandy was disappointed with the record of his team; and Tony seemed indifferent to his own failure to shine as he had in former years. Mrs. Caterson ventured some word about his knee, and its effect upon his play, but he only said casually:

"Oh, I guess I'm growing up, Child. Football doesn't seem as important to me as it did a year or two ago. I'm a grave old Senior now, you know!"

Sandy had some talk with his father about the team, for there was an increasing confidence between these two, a tightening bond; and Caterson, after the boys were gone, reported the conversation to Mrs. Caterson.

"He said the failures were his fault," he explained. "That is to say, he blamed himself indirectly. He feels that he did not make an inspiring captain. I gathered that the captain of a football team should be a plumed knight, or something of the sort; a combination of a stroke of lightning, a crusader, and an orator. Sandy's sense wasn't wholly clear to me, but that was the general idea."

"And of course, Sandy isn't any of those things," she agreed.

"He's a plugger, a plodder," he returned. "He said as much to me. And he remarked that Tony would have made a better captain."

Her eyes clouded. "Yes, I think so," she at last assented; and she added wistfully: "Better for the team, and—better for Tony, too. That's the hard part of it, for me."

This seemed to him so true that he could find no honest word to comfort her.

When the boys came home at Christmas, Mrs. Caterson had a lingering cold which kept her much of the time abed, so they were very quiet over the holidays. Only once or twice groups of young folk did come to the house. Nina, and Nell Dyson, and Audrey Deal; Bob Curry, and Dan Lind. The familiar faces. Mrs. Caterson was usually up and about during the afternoons; she gave them tea, and smiled happily at their gaiety. Audrey was home from Vassar for the holidays; she reported that Barbs was a hit in London, that the play was like to go on forever. Dan Lind suggested that they all run over to see her, return by the next boat. Tony, somewhat to Mrs. Caterson's surprise, took no part in the absurd elaboration of this fantastic idea; and when she asked him afterward, with a faint solicitude, whether he were tired, or ill, he laughed at her in swift astonishment.

"I noticed you were quiet," she explained.

"Getting old, Child! Getting old!" he assured

her. "Don't you realize I'm about to go out and face the cold, cold world!"

"The cold world will warm up mighty quick to you," she promised; and they laughed together at her fond approval.

He and Nina were as constantly together as in the past, and as happily. Sandy, she saw with a faint surprise, liked Audrey Deal. She never found it easy to question Sandy; but he confided, she knew, in his father. She asked Caterson one night while they were preparing for sleep whether what she imagined was true; and he nodded, chuckling.

"Audrey has run motorboats all her life, up at the Lake," he explained. "She knows a lot about engines, and Sandy means to make internal combustion engines his job, he says. He's plugging on them all the time. And he finds her ready to listen, and intelligent enough to ask proper questions, or even to answer them."

Mrs. Caterson smiled thoughtfully. "Nina told me once that Audrey's level-headed," she agreed. "Trust Sandy to discover it, under her veneer."

By and by the boys went back to college; and at spring vacation they were home again, away again. But before they departed, Sandy came to his father, awkwardly.

"Mother all right, is she, father?" he asked. "She doesn't look well to me."

"Why, she's had a cold," Caterson confessed. "A little run down, perhaps; that's all."

"Had a doctor?" Sandy persisted; and he added

apologetically: "You see, you're with her all the time, and you might not notice. She—seems thin, looks—tired."

Caterson was troubled. "I think she's all right, Sandy," he repeated. "But I'll keep an eye on her, son."

"Women are funny," Sandy suggested. "Audrey wrote me the other day that Barbs Delevan has had a nervous breakdown, or something; had to go away to Switzerland for a while. And Barbs is hard as nails. You will watch out for mother, won't you? If Barbs can crack, anyone can."

And Caterson promised to do so. Toward the first of June, when Commencement was only some three weeks away, he persuaded Mrs. Caterson to see Doctor Savage. She laughed at his fears, yet in the end consented to do as he desired.

The physician's verdict Caterson found hideously disturbing. "Nothing wrong with your wife," Doctor Savage told him, after a series of examinations. "That is to say, nothing wrong with her physical machine. I've been over her with a fine tooth comb. Let me ask you a question or two. Have you any business worries?"

"None," Caterson assured him.

"Your health good?"

"Perfect." Caterson was pale and still.

"H-m! I believe in frankness. Have you given her cause for any worry? I mean anything. Another woman? Even in Mrs. Caterson's imagination?"

Caterson's eyes clouded with a guilty memory; but after a moment he shook his head. He knew Mrs. Caterson too well to accept this as an explanation. He said in a proud certainty: "It's not that, you can be sure."

The physician nodded. "I thought not," he assented. He considered for a moment. "She doesn't need a doctor," he remarked at last. "But—I'll tell you what's the matter with her. We'll say she's bleeding internally, my friend."

Caterson weighed this gravely. "You mean—spiritually, I assume?"

"Yes. Something. Any idea what it is?" Caterson did not immediately reply; and the other man rose. "No matter. If you need my help, call on me. I think she'll be all right, by and by. These wounds usually heal in time. But—that's my diagnosis now."

Caterson hesitated. "You think she's fit to go up to the boys' Commencement, all right?"

"She wants to go? Loves them? Proud of them?"

"Yes."

"Go, by all means," the doctor agreed. "It ought to be good for her."

And as the time approached, it seemed to Caterson that this prediction proved itself true. Mrs. Caterson, either by virtue of her happy anticipations, or because June was fine and summer was near, did improve. They looked forward to the days that lay ahead; and he remarked that she spoke of the boys more frequently, and more freely.

"They've done so well in college," she explained. "We're going to be so proud of them, up there, Joe."

"Fit to bust," he stoutly agreed.

"Sandy's class marshal," she reminded him. "Just think of it, Lad. Our stodgy, plugging, uncouth little old Sandy leading his class."

"He's improved his marks, too," he pointed out. "Sandy picks up momentum every year, Edith. I'm beginning to be more and more impressed with that young man."

She said laughingly, as though it were a jest: "Why, I believe you like him as well as you do Tony!" But this jest of hers for a moment silenced both of them. There lay in it more truth than wit. It occurred to them in this moment's stillness now, that there had been years when Tony made them proud and happy, while Sandy brought them only doubts and fears. This new equality between the two boys served to emphasize that ancient difference.

"Yes," Caterson assented. "Yes, Sandy's come along!"

Their eyes met and held for a moment; then she drew him near, drew his arms around her. She clung to him with something passionate in her close embrace, as a man drowning clings to a chance caught spar. And he held her tenderly.

They would drive up through the hills to college but Tony came home beforehand, for a day or two with them and with Nina. Nina was to be his Commencement guest; and he meant to take her up in his car, while his father and mother would go with Richards in the limousine.

Mrs. Caterson thought Tony looked badly; tired, perhaps, from the long year. But when she suggested this, he protested: "You're the one who's run down, Child!" And when she tried to question him, he put her inquiries aside, swept her away at last for a drive along the shore road.

"We'll put the top down and I'll let the wind whip some roses into your cheeks," he cried. "Come along!"

She went with him, happily; she even stifled her protests when he pressed the accelerator down and the needle crept up to fifty, and sixty, and above. They drove for miles, before they turned homeward again; and he laughed down at her there beside him; and sometimes he watched the road and she watched his countenance. Beneath the smooth contours of his cheeks and the clean line of his brow she saw, or seemed to see, a new rigidity; the beginning of the stiff strength of a man. And she wept that she must say goodby to this boy son of hers, and she laughed to greet the man who was about to emerge from his boyhood, and she prayed that he might encounter no too grievous sorrows, no trials too severe.

The thought provoked her to a question.

"Tony?" she asked; and he slowed down a little to give her his attention. She hesitated, laughing in faint confusion. "It's none of my business, son," she confessed. "But have you said anything more to Nina?"

She thought a faint shadow lay for a moment in his eyes, before he looked at the road again; but he laughed, cheerfully enough, as he shook his head.

"No," he told her. "No. Time isn't up yet, you see; not till after Commencement. That's nominated in the bond, Child."

"Of course," she assented. "I'd forgotten." And she added, teasingly: "Promise to tell me, first of all?"

"You'll know as soon as I do," he assured her fondly; but his cheek was rigid, and there was no further word between them for a while.

As they drew nearer home, he slowed to a more moderate speed. The road ran close along the shore, following the crest of the low rocky bluffs above the beaches, emerging now and then on a shouldering point of land so that the sea lay cleanly blue below them and away to the far line where it met the sky. The highway, crowded with other cars, meandered tortuously; and sometimes it was only just above the level of the tide, and again it ran high above the water across some rocky headland.

At one such spot, Tony checked the car and pulled to the side of the road and stopped. The sea, long ocean surges rolling in, pounded ponderously on a welter of shards and boulders far below them. From the road, the rocky cliff descended sharply; and between them and that declivity, there was only a low uneven wall of loose stones. A cottage was set on the higher ground above them; and below them, on jutting ledge, there was a sort of summer house where a person might rest and look abroad across the sweep of sea.

As they came to a stop, an old man in a limp Panama hat, blue coat and flannel trousers, who had been sitting there, ascended to the road level and crossed in front of them and went on to his cottage up the hill. They paid him no particular attention. Mrs. Caterson wondered why Tony had stopped, and she looked at him and saw that his eyes were fixed on the rugged precipice below them. Faintly at a loss, she suggested softly:

"It is lovely, isn't it?" She was watching the bright sails against the blue. "I like to stop here, too, when the day is fair."

Tony moved sharply, laughed uneasily. "Hah, yes," he agreed. "But I wasn't noticing the view! I was thinking what a fall you'd take, if your car went over the wall."

She touched his arm: "Please, Tony. Don't. Drive on."

"Sorry," he assented, and he meshed the gears. Added with a reassuring chuckle: "Don't worry, Child! I'll take care not to try it out, you know!"

Yet his word had chilled her to the heart with a dreadful, formless fear. It took all his tender badinage to win her back at last to smiles again.

XXI

JUNE in the New Hampshire hills is a season of delight. There is a breathless sort of languor in the air. The fields are bright with new grass, and the trees are lacy with half formed, still unfolding leaves. The sun is warm while the air is cool, so that you may choose sun or shade as you prefer. It is warm enough for an easy indolence, cool enough for brisk activity; and the air is clear as sparkling wine.

On the night after Mr. and Mrs. Caterson arrived at the Inn, they sat for a long time in the window of their room, listening. On such still nights, sounds carry far and sweetly. From the direction of the Gymnasium they could hear the subdued murmur of an orchestra, at times almost inaudible, at other moments in the frail pattern of some persuasive melody. Voices rose from the little group along the street below their window; they heard the throaty chuckles of young men, and the laughter of the girls whom they amused, like the tones of crystal bells. From the campus paths sounded the shuffle of passing feet; or some youngster crossed alone, and whistled for company. Regularly, the clock chimed and sounded out the hour; and there were moments when it seemed possible to hear the stirring wind in the pine trees toward the river, or the rumble of the rapids below the dam two or three miles down stream. The night tingled with small sounds, each one enticing and provocative; it was hard to be thus indoors, and Mrs. Caterson said as much, regretfully.

Caterson, sitting beside her in the darkness, chuckled.

"We have to stay here, Lady," he pointed out. "The boys have tucked us in for the night, you see. We're supposed to be fast asleep, as staid old folk should be."

"I don't feel old," she protested. "I'd like to go out and walk barefooted on the campus sod, and have you whisper things to me, and coquet with you so tenderly . . ."

"Well," he suggested drily. "I expect the same idea has occurred to others, tonight. Perhaps it's even being done!"

She laughed in warm understanding. "But barefoot? Shocking!" she protested.

They had arrived in the late afternoon, after a leisurely drive. Tony and Nina, leaving home at the same time, were here almost two hours ahead of them; but these young folk had departed on some new adventure long before the big limousine trundled up to the Inn. Sandy was there to greet them, even though he had to hurry away almost at once. He was just now a young man bowed by responsibilities; and they were amused at the seriousness of his countenance. He had, he confessed, invited Audrey Deal as his Commencement guest; and Mrs.

Caterson smiled toward her husband when she heard this intelligence.

Later, they all had dinner together. Then they went for a walk around the campus, returned to the Inn again; and the young folk stayed dutifully for a while, till Mrs. Caterson tactfully suggested that she was tired, ready for bed, and so let them go. But that evening, and again next day when with either Tony or Sandy, and sometimes with both of them for escorts, they moved to and fro about the town, Mr. and Mrs. Caterson watched with a keen delight the attention these boys of theirs attracted. She saw inconspicuous undergraduates point out her sons to their companions, with a whispered explanation; she saw the youthful reverence in the resulting keen inspections. And Mrs. Caterson trembled with delight, and Caterson, in more sober fashion, was as pleased as she.

To Tony, she thought, these comrades of his gave a jovial friendship; their greetings were loud and cheerful; they slapped him on the back, spoke to him heartily. Everyone seemed to know him and to like him. Sandy was met with no such general familiarity; there was a reserve in the attitude of those who spoke to him. When she and Caterson compared notes by and by, they sought to appraise this difference. They were forever thus comparing the boys, driven by an instinct too strong to be resisted; they had for a while fought against this, yielded to it now because they were, after all, too full of pride in both the boys to seek to choose between them.

"They love Tony," Mrs. Caterson pointed out.
"You can see it in the way they speak to him. It's
more a sort of respectful deference that they pay to
Sandy."

"Tony evidently knows everybody," Caterson
agreed. "Or at least, everyone knows him." If he had
suspected now and then a superficiality in the cordial
familiarity with which these other boys spoke to
Tony, he did not choose to suggest this to her.

"Sandy's so serious," she commented, amused.
"He acts as though the world were on his shoulders.
I'm afraid Audrey's not having a particularly lively
time."

Caterson chuckled. "Oh, she's not neglected.
There are always boys around her, and Sandy turns
to her when he wants a word about engines to relax
his mind."

"Tony and Nina seem very happy," Mrs. Caterson suggested, half to herself.

"Tony's—stimulated by all this," he agreed. "I'd
almost wager that he's running a fever. Sandy takes
it stolidly. . . ."

"He's you all over, Joe," she urged, and their
eyes met, as in such moments they were apt to do,
as though her words had startled them. They were
thereafter silent for a while.

They met in the course of the three or four days
of the Commencement season, many young folk;
boys and girls. For the most part these names and
faces merged in an indistinguishable confusion; but
one name struck them, and one personality. Lob

Dudley. Mr. and Mrs. Caterson and Tony and Nina were crossing the long diagonal of the campus when they encountered this young man; and Tony hailed him with a lifted hand.

"Hi, fellow!" he shouted.

The other hesitated doubtfully. "Hello yourself," he retorted in a wary tone, and looked at Tony's companions, and asked, with half-averted eyes: "See Brick Black anywhere?"

"Wait a minute," Tony urged. "I want you to meet my folks. This lovely kid is my mother; and this is my father, and you know Nina Buckel."

Dudley shook hands with each in turn, and Mrs. Caterson spoke to him cordially enough; but when he had gone on, she slipped her arm through Tony's. "I don't like him very much," she confessed.

"He's all wet," he agreed. "But I wanted to show you off."

"But isn't he the one who—doesn't like you? She saw the assent in his tightening lips. "I shouldn't think you'd even pretend to be nice to him!" she protested, and when Tony did not reply she added resentfully: "He's stupid! You can see that. His eyes come out of the same hole!"

"Oh, he's dumb as an owl!" Tony cheerfully assented. "But the poor devil worked for three years to beat me out at half back, and never did manage it. You can't blame him for being sore." And he added: "You ought to see his folks! Rich as Rockefeller, but gosh, they're hopeless! That's why I

wanted him to see you, see what a real father and
mother can be."

Caterson was a step or two behind with Nina, but
he paid no heed to what the girl was saying. This
glimpse of Lob Dudley had revived old fears in him.
He remembered that newspaper paragraph which
recited the high mortality that attends twin births;
and he wondered whether Dudley had prompted it.
How much did this stupid young man know? And
was he possessed by a malevolence that equalled his
stupidity? He wiped his brow, suddenly wet and
cold; but after a moment Nina compelled his attention, and he forgot his fears.

They had during these moments of steady, thrill-
ing pride other hours when their happiness was
almost too poignant to be borne. Sandy, very white
and serious, at the head of the long gowned proces-
sion; his broad, battered countenance set like stone
beneath his mortar board. Tony dominating by his
charm and wit every group in which he found himself. The award to Sandy of the Forbes medal, given
each year to the Senior who had made the most
progress during his college course. Tony moving to
and fro day by day in a sort of triumphal progress,
greeted by every man he met. . . . If it occurred
to them that Sandy's were the more substantial triumphs, neither commented on this fact. They were
in these days so full of happiness in watching both
the boys that they did not attempt to hold any balance between them. . . . These were both their sons
in heart, let the fact be what it chose.

Yet the fact dwelt always with them, never long forgot, tormenting, inescapable.

They had once or twice an hour or two alone with the boys; and in one such moment they fell into some discussion of the fruits of college. It interested Caterson to elicit from each his individual estimate. Tony, not surprisingly, dwelt upon the association value of these four years.

"You know so many fellows," he pointed out. "Make friends who will always be your friends. That isn't just sentiment, either. A lot of the men in our class will some day be successful lawyers, and doctors, and bankers and so on. There's a definite cash value in such friendships, you know." He caught Sandy's eye, and laughed.

"Sandy here won't agree with me," he conceded. "He hasn't gone in for that sort of thing, so much. Most of them know him, but he doesn't know very many of them." And he added, in a derision not wholly good-natured: "Of course the faculty pinned a medal on him, to testify that he's come a long way, in four years. But what a long way he had to come!"

Caterson spoke quickly. "How about it, Sandy?" he asked. "How does college strike you?"

Sandy hesitated. Words came not easily to this young man; yet he tried now to speak, to make his meaning clear.

"I don't see it the way Tony does," he confessed. "Seems to me the only things a man can get anywhere are what he can stow away inside of him

Things outside are just a nuisance. You have to be always taking care of them, or they'll get lost."

"What things inside?" Mrs. Caterson prompted. "What do you mean, Sandy? Your studies?"

Sandy grinned doubtfully. "No, I guess not. I don't think very much of that will stick to me. No, I mean—well, self discipline, say; and responsibility. Prexy talks about the duty of leadership." He flushed to the ears at Tony's dry chuckle.

"There's something in it, though!" he persisted. "And I think tradition is a lot of it, too. There isn't much of that in this country, but a college man has a tradition back of him. He acquires up here a lot of spiritual ancestors, and some of them were fine men. He might get into the habit of building on what they started. I guess to lean on old things, old sound foundations, is to be steady, maybe, and strong."

There was a momentary silence; then Tony laughed aloud, but Mrs. Caterson did not smile. She knew a sudden certainty, indescribably sweet, that she had for a moment caught a glimpse of something in Sandy, deep and permanent and sound; and this perception illumined with a swift radiance the boy's rude exterior. She was nearer to Sandy in this instant than she had ever been before.

Yet it was like Tony, she told herself eagerly, to make a jest where his feelings lay too deep for words. Tony's exuberance was as much a mask for his deeper thoughts as was Sandy's slow stolidity.

When the day of departure presently arrived, they separated. Sandy would drive over to the Lake with

Audrey Deal and stay there a day or two, and his mother, at the last moment, said to him teasingly: "You're growing rather fond of Audrey, aren't you?"

"Yes," Sandy confessed. "Yes, I am. I like her better than any girl I know, except Nina."

"Nina?" she echoed, in faint surprise. "Oh, of course Nina's fine!" she agreed. "Well, run along with Audrey, son. And have a good time."

He nodded shyly as he kissed her goodby.

Richards brought the limousine around, and Mr. and Mrs. Caterson got under way. Tony and Nina would be starting presently. "We'll pass you on the road," Tony promised. "You'll see a cloud of dust, and that's us, my dears."

Mrs. Caterson thought there was something taut and vibrant in his tone; and when they were alone, she said to her husband:

"They'll come home engaged, those two, Joe."

"Tony and Nina?"

"She told him a year ago that he was to ask her now," she reminded him. "And he's going to, on the way home. I could see that in his eyes."

He chuckled. "You women!" he chided; and he added after a moment: "I gave the boys each their check, this morning."

"Ten thousand? I wonder what they'll do with it."

Caterson smiled. "Tony'll margin a thousand shares of something," he predicted. "And Sandy'll buy Government bonds."

"It will be fun to see," she agreed.

Half way home, Tony and Nina did whirl past them; and Nina waved her hand, and Tony pressed the horn as they went by. Mrs. Caterson watched the roadster whip out of sight ahead of them with swimming eyes, dreaming happily. When late in the afternoon they approached the cottage on the shore —the house in town was already closed for the summer—she said:

"I don't suppose we'll see Tony tonight at all."

But when they alighted, Tony was there to greet them cheerfully.

"Just in time," he cried. "I've mixed your favorite cocktail, mother. Water and orange juice and a dash of sugar, Child! Father, you'll have one of mine, won't you? Dinner's due in half an hour?"

Mrs. Caterson, watching his eyes, tried to guess whether he had spoken to Nina, what the girl's word had been. But there was a screen across Tony's glance; it told her nothing. Her question still unanswered, she went to rid herself of the traces of the journey, and presently came down again to find Tony and her husband together on the wide veranda toward the sea.

When dinner was announced, a moment afterward, she linked her arm in Tony's. "You got home safely, son?" she remarked, urged by a curiosity beyond her control.

"Safe as a church!" he assured her. "And by the way, Mr. and Mrs. Buckel may come over this evening for some bridge, they said. I stopped there for a while, when I left Nina."

Her heart quickened its beat, but his eyes were still inscrutable. He was, she thought, somewhat flushed, and she took this as a happy augury; but when after dinner she had a chance to ask him directly the question she could not restrain, he laughed and shook his head.

"Don't be absurd, Child!" he protested. "When I propose to a girl, it's not going to be in a car. I want at least one free hand to drive."

She smiled with him. "Forgive me!" she begged. "None of my business, is it, Tony?"

"You'll know," he promised. "I'll run to the telephone and call you the minute the deed is done. Don't fret yourself. You'll know."

And she was with this content. But when later in the evening Mr. and Mrs. Buckel and Nina did arrive, and the old folk sat down to bridge while Nina and Tony whirled away to some youthful rendezvous along the shore, Mrs. Caterson's thoughts went with them, so that she was inattentive to the game. When she and Mr. Caterson were by and by abed, Tony had not yet returned; he must, she thought, have in the morning some fine word for her.

He did not rise in time for breakfast; did not come downstairs till Caterson had departed for the city. When he did, she was waiting for him; but he spoke evasively of other matters. She managed to control her tongue, but not her eyes, till he said at last, in a faint irritation:

"No, Child! If you must know. I'm waiting for

the proper time. There was always a gang around, last night!"

"I didn't ask a single question," she protested, laughing ruefully.

He grinned. "You didn't have to," he assured her. "There were question marks sticking out like hooks all over you."

She made some amused and indignant protest at the picture his words evoked; but during the succeeding days she managed patience. Yet as these days did pass, patience turned slowly to concern. Watching Tony with that attentive scrutiny not easily to be deceived, it seemed to her that he dreaded the issue, that he put off the moment which would determine matters. She watched Nina, too; and she thought there was a hurt in the girl's clear eyes. And she was more and more uneasy for Tony's sake. Sensing in him some conflict whose nature she could not determine, she suffered more than he.

Sandy came home, and it was a relief to turn to his matter of fact good nature. He at least would cause her no concern; and with the thought, she came to perceive that imperceptibly the roles the two boys played in her life had changed. There had been years when she worried about Sandy, while Tony caused her only pride; but their parts now began to be reversed. She knew, suddenly, that Sandy's future was as sure as it would be slow; but what the future held for Tony, no one yet could estimate.

Sometimes when the boys were both away from

home in the evening, she could not sleep; and on one such night, early in July, she slipped out of bed and into the next room, to a window that overlooked the road and the slopes beyond toward the shore. She had no formed intention of waiting for her sons' return, but her thoughts began to run, and time sped, and by and by she saw a car approaching, and under the last street light recognized it as Tony's roadster.

She watched it eagerly, and then with a sudden misgiving; for the car came on so slowly. It turned into the drive at a crawl, and it came to a stop just below the window where she sat.

She saw then that Tony was at the wheel, Sandy by his side; and Tony stilled the engine, and she heard him say thickly:

"Matter with that? Told you I c'd drive."

"All right," Sandy agreed. "If you're sober enough to drive, you can listen to me for a minute."

"Say I'm drunk?" Tony angrily demanded.

"Any time I think you're drunk, I won't bring you home," Sandy told him. "You know how mother'd feel, if she saw you. You're not drunk; but you've had too much. And Tony, you've got to watch your step."

"What if I don't? Eh? What if I stum'le now'n then?"

"I'll tell father," Sandy warned him. "He won't stand for it."

"Tattle tales, eh?"

"I'll do any blasted thing," Sandy agreed. "Anything that will keep you straight, keep you from hurting mother. And you can make up your mind to it."

"You ought to turn your collar 'round," Tony derisively suggested. "Hire a pulpit, somewhere."

"You heard me," the other insisted. "And Tony, mind, won't you? You know what mother thinks of you, and that just makes it easier for you to hurt her. If it was me, she wouldn't mind so much!"

There was no complaint in his tones; nothing but an honest recognition of fact. Yet at his word, Mrs. Caterson's hand pressed her throat, and for a moment her senses swam, and she could neither hear nor see. When her eyes cleared again, the boys and the car were gone. Some one was moving about, belowstairs. She heard the closing of the garage door at the end of the drive, and then Sandy came back alone, and entered the house by the door just below her window.

Long after all was quiet once more, Mrs. Caterson crept pitifully back to bed. She was not wholly surprised when next day Tony laughingly told her that Nina wished him still to wait a while.

"Wants to wait till I've settled what I mean to do," he explained. "Thinks I ought to take a year, first, in Business School."

Mrs. Caterson only nodded, unable to reply.

XXII

THERE are some griefs too deep for words; some anxieties so poignant that to voice them only makes them hurt the more. Mrs. Caterson did not speak to her husband about this interchange between the boys which she had overheard. She wished to do so, yet could not summon the necessary resolution; so she waited, half expecting that as the days passed the pain would ease and make speech easier.

Yet in the end she never spoke at all; for though she did not again see Tony muddled by liquor, there was in his bearing during these weeks something increasingly disturbing. He was as tender to her as he had always been, and as vivacious in any company; but it seemed to his mother that there dwelt a sort of defiance in his very gaiety, as though he would by laughter hide a shameful hurt from all the world. There abides in women an understanding sympathy which enables them to apprehend the fact that their menfolk are troubled; but it does not always enable them to guess the source of this disquiet. Mrs. Caterson knew Tony was unhappy; she supposed it was because Nina had put him off with a new delay. And she tried not to feel hardly toward the girl who had hurt the boy she loved.

She did not relate this suspicion to her husband.

As her own anxieties became more persistent, so did her instinct seek to shield them from the world; and also, she would not trouble Mr. Caterson more than she must. He, as men will, took the surface of life as fair evidence of what went forward underneath the surface; because his days ran calmly, because Mrs. Caterson did not discuss with him this torturing conundrum which had been propounded to them, he thought that it no longer saddened her. Her silence seemed to him evidence that she was forgetting; and since his own unhappiness could only, in the last analysis, result from hers, it began to ease. Also, he remarked nothing unusual in Tony's actions during these summer weeks; so Caterson began to resume his normal composure, and the wound in his heart to heal.

Now and then some small incident, like a whirlpool momentarily appearing on the smooth surface of a deep stream, suggested the turbulence below. Thus one day Mrs. Caterson drove to town with him. He was used to take an early train; but on this occasion she meant to do some shopping, and ordered the limousine, and suggested that Caterson ride in with her.

The day was fine; one of those moist, cool mornings which sometimes occur along the shore even in July. There was a mist on the seaward horizon which the sun had not yet wholly burned away; and dew lay across the lawns, and the foliage was very green. They took the shore road, which wound at times along the water's edge; and so by and by they approached that precipitous and rocky shoulder where the way curved high above the water. As the big limousine lumbered up the grade and reached the spot above the little summer house, Caterson called to the chauffeur:

"Oh Richards, stop a minute. Edith, this view is better than breakfast!"

But Mrs. Caterson leaned forward to cry almost desperately to the chauffeur:

"No, Richards; no! Don't stop. Go on!"

Richards nodded, and obediently did so; and she relaxed limply, with closed eyes, head against the seat behind her, clinging with both hands to her husband's arm.

He said uncertainly: "Sorry, Lady! I thought you liked that view."

She tried to laugh. "It's all right, Joe," she assured him. "I used to. But—I've taken a dislike to the spot. It's so steep, down to the water. I prefer to hurry by."

Caterson chuckled. "Nerves, Edith? Richards drives carefully."

"A wheel might break, or something," she persisted. "Humor me, Joe."

"Of course," he agreed. But later—they had talked of other things—he asked casually: "How're you feeling lately, Edith? All right?"

She smiled. "Now don't worry about me just because I was fussy, Lad," she told him. "It's just that I'm getting old, perhaps. Of course I'm all right, my dear."

"Seems to me you look better than you did in the spring."

"Of course I do," she repeated, so that he was reassured.

There were other such occasions, when momentarily the storms that harried her disturbed the serene countenance she presented to the world. But for the most part their lives went smoothly. It was seldom that they referred directly to the matter which must always engross them. Sometimes their unspoken thoughts came near to utterance; but at such moments they drew back in swift shrinking from the dangerous ground. Thus when one night they drove over to the Buckel cottage for an evening of bridge, she remarked:

"You drive as fast as Tony, Joe."

And he answered evasively: "That reminds me! Mr. Tedlock was saying today that the Ganymede people are bringing out a new model this fall."

Or when Sandy bought an old motorboat and dismantled the engine and proceeded to dissect it in order to study the relation of each working part, Mr. and Mrs. Caterson, wandering arm in arm about the lawns, discovered him thus occupied, and watched him for a moment smilingly; and when they turned away, Caterson commented:

"Sandy goes to the root of a thing, doesn't he? No short cuts for him. I never could take short cuts, either."

And she flung an arm toward the sea below them and cried: "Look, Joe, there goes the Masterson yacht. We must have a boat some summer, Lad."

Each one of these occasions left them momentarily shaken; but they perfected in time a sort of conspiracy of silence, mutually avoiding any word that suggested a comparison between the boys, or a likeness between the boys and themselves. They were happy in the fact that Tony and Sandy this summer were at home; they had much of the company of their sons, and they clung to it as a last fine feast of the old companionship before the young men departed into the outer world.

Tony meant to go to the Business School in the fall, and Sandy to the Institute. Internal combustion engines more and more engaged his interest; he studied at first hand every one that came under his eye, and he considered attending an aviation ground school and was only dissuaded when Mrs. Caterson begged for more of his time. He had, it appeared, a natural bent for research and experiment; but Tony's leaning was toward the financial world. Soon after Commencement, he had margined some stock with his father's check; and there was during the summer a steadily rising market, so that he drank success like a heady wine. He used to speak jestingly of his manipulations, and one day he told Mrs. Caterson that he would come home some fine afternoon a millionaire.

"Or a pauper, Tony," she suggested smilingly. "No one ever made money in the end by speculating, son. But never mind. You're not too old to learn."

He kissed her teasingly. "All right, Child," he protested. "You've no confidence in your son. But wait till I bring you home a limousine full of pearl necklaces. Then you'll be sorry you treated your Tony so. . . ."

She shook her head. "Sorry, but not sorry I treated you so," she warned him cheerfully. "I'll be sorry you won. I want you to lose, for your own good, you see."

"Hurts you more than it does me?" he suggested in swift amusement. "Well, of course, I can tear up my profits, if that will content you. Anything, Child; anything to oblige."

Mrs. Caterson thought sometimes that Tony made a jest of too many things. His trick of badinage served as an armor against her when she wished to come close to him, to establish a closer sympathy between them. It was hard to bring him to speak seriously of anything. He called her "Child," and she thought sometimes that he treated her like a child, in fact; but she did not say this to him, for she was too wise to irritate him by what must be empty chiding. Yet she thought, in small ways, to lead him into confidences.

She had no success at all. Tony was always tender, always demonstratively affectionate; but there was a light impatience in him, something fevered and hectic, a restlessness easily perceptible and hard to overcome. He was seldom long at home; he rose late, drove to town, came back for tennis or a swim or a round of golf, departed to dine or to dance, and came home long after Mr. and Mrs. Caterson were abed. Mrs. Caterson solaced herself for a while with the consideration that he must be spending much time with Nina; but she discovered by and by that this was not the case. A chance word now and then from the girl or from Sandy revealed the fact that these two had in fact been together at some time when she supposed Nina had been with Tony. Nina was developing a certain reticence; her old gay friendliness and frankness began to give way to reserve. But Sandy was guileless enough so that without his realizing the fact, his mother drew from him many things it did not occur to him to conceal.

Toward the end of the summer, Mrs. Caterson and Nina did come at last to something like a straightforward discussion of that which was in both their minds. Linda Crater and Nina had come over for tennis with Tony and Sandy. Linda was a slender, fair young woman with an astonishing capacity for liquor, and she smoked innumerable cigarettes, so that Mrs. Caterson disapproved of her; but Tony this day paid her an almost extravagant attention. They were partners against the other two, and he exerted himself to make up for Linda's deficiencies, covering the whole court, poaching ruthlessly, striving for the victory which he failed in the end to achieve. And when the match was done, with a laughing impatience which failed to conceal his resentment at defeat, he whisked Linda away to the beach, while Sandy went up to change, and Nina was left to drink a cup of tea with Mrs. Caterson.

"You didn't want to swim, dear," the older woman suggested, hoping for some word which would explain why Tony had failed to propose that Nina go with them; and Nina, understanding, said reassuringly:

"No, I haven't been swimming much in the afternoon, this summer. The beach is always jammed. A mixed crowd."

She hesitated, added quickly: "I mean, outsiders of course." And Mrs. Caterson understood that the girl did not wish to appear to criticize Tony. She nodded, her gratitude in her eyes; and after a moment she said thoughtfully:

"Tony's on the go so much this summer we hardly see him. It would wear me out to keep pace with him, I'm afraid."

"It's a—lively summer," Nina agreed. "So many people here this year. I never saw so much going on."

"Even Sandy gets swept into the whirl sometimes," Mrs. Caterson remarked, smiling whimsically. "And it takes quite a whirlpool to engulf Sandy. His feet are anchored pretty solidly, most of the time."

Nina chuckled, her shoulders dancing with that old trick she had, and Mrs. Caterson felt a quick pleasure. It was long since she had seen Nina laugh so heartily.

"Sandy was funny Friday night," the girl confessed. "The dance at the country club, you know. I think he changed his collar a dozen times. He must have brought a private haberdasher with him. After almost every dance he'd disappear, and come back so clean and shiny, with his hair slicked down; and ten minutes later he'd be limp as a rag again."

"Mr. Caterson always took extra collars, when we used to dance," the older woman thoughtfully commented, and she added quickly: "But Sandy never will learn to dance, I'm afraid."

"He does very well," Nina insisted. "You'd be surprised, sometimes!"

"Tony dances beautifully, I think," Mrs. Caterson suggested, and Nina nodded readily enough.

"Divinely," she assented. "Almost too well! You're a rag when he's done with you."

"You and he dance so well together," the older woman insisted. "I've always liked watching you." And at Nina's momentary hesitation, she added: "Of course, you've always been so much together; you're used to one another, I suppose. That must make a difference."

Nina stirred and rose. "I ought to trot along," she said uneasily.

And Mrs. Caterson took her courage in her two hands. "Tony told me you decided that you and he must—wait a longer while, dear," she remarked; and Nina stood pale and still, her eyes troubled.

"Yes," she confessed at last. "Yes, Mrs. Caterson. I thought he ought to—find the road he means to take, first, you see."

Mrs. Caterson filled again her empty cup. "Tea, dear?" Nina shook her head, but she did sit down again. "I'm rather sorry," the older woman admitted, smiling apologetically. "I think Tony feeds on success, and happiness, and approval. Don't you, Nina? Nothing succeeds like success, they say. That isn't always true, perhaps; but I have always felt that success was good for Tony."

"This—isn't failure," Nina demurred.

"I had a feeling," Mrs. Caterson remarked, "that he foresaw something of the sort, dear. In June, when we went up to Commencement, I kept teasing him with questions." She smiled into her tea cup. "Kept asking him whether he'd spoken to you. Tony tells me everything, you see. Or at least he used to. It seemed to me he—dreaded the issue, a little. Perhaps he felt you weren't ready to give him the —answer he wanted so much."

Nina's eyes were shadowed. She said at last, with a faint, apologetic smile: "I felt that, too. As though he were dreading asking me." Color flooded throat and cheeks. "As though he had to do it, because he'd promised to, but he didn't really want to. That piqued me, I suppose."

"My dear, he adores you," Mrs. Caterson urged warmly, fighting for this boy she loved. "You know that, Nina!"

The girl made a little gesture, a faint grimace. "You know, he never did—ask me to marry him," she admitted soberly. "He just—led up to it, in a cautious sort of way. And I——" She laughed uneasily. "I was a little sorry for him, but I was provoked, too, of course. Any girl would be, don't you think? At any rate, I told him he need not feel bound to ask me, need not feel that he must. I told him to wait till he was sure what he wanted to do."

Mrs. Caterson nodded. "I can't blame you, of course, Nina," she admitted, and she smiled appealingly. "But you know how I love Tony, and want his happiness." She hesitated. "I saw his—doubts," she confessed. "But—afterward, dear, he changed. You've seen that?"

"I think so," Nina agreed. "I think at first he was afraid I'd carry him off and marry him; and then he was mad at me because I didn't!" Her cheeks were bright, her eyes shining.

"That's the man in him, Nina," the older woman urged. "You hurt his vanity!"

Nina moved one hand in a sign of assent. "And he hurt mine, I expect," she acknowledged.

Mrs. Caterson smiled. "There," she exclaimed. "You'll forgive one another by and by!" She caught the girl's eyes. "But there isn't any reason why you should—avoid me, Nina. We've always been good friends, and always will be."

"I'm fond of Tony," Nina said uncertainly. "He's so loveable, in so many ways. And I—didn't want to hurt you, you see." She added, almost unconsciously: "I've talked it over with Sandy. He said you'd understand; said Tony understood, too. He told me I ought not to mind." She smiled faintly. "But it has been a little awkward, hasn't it, sometimes." And she added, before the other could reply:

"I know Tony resents it. He's shown me so."

"Going off this way to swim with Linda?" Mrs. Caterson asked wisely. But her thoughts were straying, pondering something she had detected in the girl's tone when she spoke of Sandy; and there was a cold hand on her heart, a dreadful fear.

Nina answered honestly. "Yes. That, and other little things. So many of them, as though he wanted to hurt me, all the time." She smiled unhappily. "He does hurt, too. Tony can."

"Tony needs love, and approval, and—success," said Tony's mother. "I—know his weaknesses, you see." She smiled. "Forgive an old woman, Nina," she urged. "This is none of my business, I'm afraid; and it's courteous of you to refrain from telling me so. I'm very fond of you, dear, and always will be, no matter what happens. You won't forget that, will you?"

Nina's eyes suddenly were brimming, and this was a strange thing to see; for there was always a steady, friendly strength in the girl, and she was not given to tears. But now her eyes filled; and then swiftly she laughed, and rose and crossed to kiss the older woman, to whisper:

"Sweet thing! I love you."

"And I you," said Mrs. Caterson.

Nina whirled away. Her car was down by the tennis court; she ran toward it, leaped into the seat.

As she swung into the drive she lifted her hand, and smiled goodby. It was easy to see her smile; it was too far to see her tears.

After the girl was gone, Mrs. Caterson sat for a long time without stirring. She felt astonishingly frail and weary and old.

A few days later they moved back to town. Tony and Sandy would live at home this winter, but they had agreed that they needed separate rooms, and this required some readjustment of the household arrangements, which Mrs. Caterson supervised. Sandy began his work at the Institute with a sober diligence, but Tony took his classes at Business School more lightly.

"I can teach them more than they can teach me," he boasted laughingly. He had during the summer built his original ten thousand dollars into almost five times that amount—on paper—and he spoke of this success now.

"That's four hundred percent in less than three months," he pointed out, and made amusingly grandiloquent calculations of what the result would be if this rate of profit should continue.

"I'll have a quarter of a million in six months," he predicted. "And a million and a quarter in nine months, and six million and a quarter in a year. . . . Hm, let me see? That's three billion, four hundred million in a couple of years. I suppose I might as well retire, then. . . . Say two and a half billion, to allow for accidents. I want to be conservative, you see."

They could not help laughing at him; he had always this capacity to make them smile.

By the end of September, the winter's routine began to possess them all. The boys were usually at home for dinner, and Sandy seldom went abroad in the evening. Mrs. Caterson looked forward to long, happy hours with both of them. She planned this and that; a dinner, a dance, Symphony, the football games, the theatre. . . .

Early in October, the Sunday *Herald* carried in its theatrical pages a story about Barbs Delevan. She had adopted a baby in Switzerland; she and the baby would land in New York on a boat due within a day or two; she was to star in a new play that would go into rehearsal immediately upon her return. Caterson discovered the story while they were at breakfast Sunday morning, and he read parts of it aloud. The boys were there, at the table in Mrs. Caterson's sitting room. Sandy thought the baby part was press agent stuff; and Tony, in vociferous amusement, asserted it was just the thing you might expect from Barbs.

Only Mrs. Caterson made no comment at all. She was, she said after breakfast, rather tired; and she went back to bed for a while.

XXIII

TONY and Sandy had shared since they passed the nursery age a room in the north wing of the big house. When they were boys, the place was always full of a pleasant disorder, littered with the innumerable treasures of youth; and as they grew older, their increasing maturity was mirrored in the character of this litter. Mrs. Caterson used to like to go to this room, when the boys were away from home, and sit quietly and feast her eyes upon the innumerable unimportant objects which were each to one or the other of the youngsters so incredibly valuable. To do so was like watching them at play; was like having them here in the flesh before her eyes. The imprint of each one of them was strong upon the spot.

But now that college was behind them, they had agreed that they preferred separate quarters; and Mrs. Caterson rearranged one of the guest rooms for Sandy's use. Also that young man commandeered what had been designed as a play room in the basement, and presently installed there a work-bench and an extensive array of machine tools. He brought in odd bits of metal, parts of old engines, outworn carburetors, pitted valves, piston rings; and he dis appeared downstairs every evening, and he might be heard there sometimes till late at night, filing and drilling and hammering. Once or twice Mrs. Caterson went down to see what he was about, but the place itself was black with grease, and so was Sandy, so she laughed and fled; and after a while she no longer came to visit him there.

Caterson used to descend, sometimes, and find a spot reasonably free from grime, and sit and watch Sandy at his work; but they seldom had much to say to one another. Sandy was preoccupied, and Caterson understood and respected this preoccupation.

Mrs. Caterson asked her husband, once or twice, what Sandy was doing; and when Caterson could not tell her in specific terms, she suggested:

"Just tinkering and puttering? That's so like Sandy."

"Not quite that," he objected. "Sandy doesn't do many things aimlessly, you know. I think he knows where he's going, even though he doesn't make very swift progress along the way."

"I wish he'd come upstairs once in a while," she confessed. "He's as hard to move as if he were bolted down." And she added: "He has your trick of sticking to his knitting, Joe."

Caterson nodded his agreement. They had unconsciously resumed the habit of watching the boys, discovering in each one's simplest action some resemblance to themselves. Thus they opened old wounds; but those old wounds had never wholly healed, and— the pain served as counter irritant, helping them to forget another terror which began more and more keenly to oppress them now.

For it was clear to each of them that Tony, the beloved son, was treading ways which were casual and heedless, if they were nothing worse. Mrs. Caterson had never told her husband of that night when Sandy brought Tony home befuddled, nor did she again encounter Tony in that condition. But she, and Caterson too, saw now and then signs which were unmistakable. They might be awakened by one of Tony's belated homecomings, long after midnight; they might hear his stumbling feet upon the stair; they could not fail to remark his burning eyes when he came downstairs in the morning. Yet they did not speak of these things, each seeking to hide from the other not only the grief they felt, but a sort of guilt, too.

For it was inevitable, as Caterson had long ago foreseen, that when either of the boys did that which seemed to them unworthy, the two should ask themselves:

"Is he indeed ours? Is not this the stranger, the foundling child?"

Two years ago, when the conundrum was first propounded, they had sought to avoid choosing between the boys even in their thoughts; yet to each one it had been secretly intolerable to suppose that Tony was not their own flesh and blood. Their doubts of him now seemed a betrayal, a treachery too dark to be confessed.

So they beclouded their own shamed hurt by talk

ing emptily of this trait and that one, of Sandy's physical resemblance to Caterson, of Tony's likeness to his mother, of Sandy's grim persistence and Tony's tender charm. . . . Thus they avoided admitting, even to themselves, the treason to Tony of which their hearts were guilty.

Yet on the surface his life went gaily enough. He had always a quick, sweet word for Mrs. Caterson; he knew how to meet Caterson in a manly equality. If he was sometimes late in coming home, he rose serenely. He appeared to give to his class work a diligent interest, and during the fall his attendance at Business School was only interrupted for a hurried two-day trip to New York. He drove over with Bob Curry, and they went in Tony's car, Tony at the wheel. Bob confessed to Mrs. Caterson, when they came home, that there were moments when he could only shut his eyes and pray; and Mrs. Caterson smiled, though her lips were white. Tony had always driven at a reckless speed, from which he could never be dissuaded.

A day or two after Tony came back, she asked him casually at breakfast whether he had seen Barbs Delevan.

"I phoned her," Tony replied. "She was all tied up with rehearsals." He hesitated, added with his familiar levity: "Picture of the brave little working woman!"

"Did you see the baby?" Mrs. Caterson inquired, while she poured him a fresh cup of coffee.

He shook his head, laughing at her. "Over the

telephone, Child?" he protested. "Television isn't working yet, you know."

"Of course," she agreed, in smiling apology. "I'd forgotten. You only telephoned!"

The autumn months gave way to winter, and their days ran in ancient channels. Now and then they played bridge with Mr. and Mrs. Buckel; they went occasionally to the theatre; Nina dropped in once in a while for tea, or to go down to watch Sandy putter at his intricate devices in the cellar. Even though the boys were at home, the family routine was a quiet one. Mrs. Caterson half expected, half longed for the usual whirl of festivities over the holidays; but though Audrey Deal was in town, and Linda Crater and other familiar ones, the fortnight was quiet enough. Tony was spending a good deal of time at a broker's office in town; he was, he told his mother in laughing braggadocio, manipulating an extensive pool in rails, and it required all his time. She thought sometimes it drained his strength, too; for he seemed tired.

She attributed to this preoccupation on Tony's part the fact that the house was not infested with young people as it had been in former years, and she remarked as much to Nina one day.

"Tony's settling down, I suppose," she said. "He doesn't keep the house full of excitement as he used. His mind's on business all the time."

Nina hesitated, nodded vaguely. "And Sandy's not much of a social magnet, down cellar every evening," she laughingly suggested. "Nobody's likely to come to watch him file an old piece of iron."

"Except you, dear," Mrs. Caterson pointed out. "You come!"

"Oh, of course, except me," Nina readily admitted. "But I'm used to the grubby old thing!"

And: "Of course," the older woman assented, ever so casually. After Nina was gone, she sat for a long time with her thoughts. By the shadow in her eyes, they were disquieting.

She was disturbed anew, a little later, when after the mid-year examinations at Business School, Tony confessed that his marks were poor; but he laughed at his own deficiencies, insisted they were of no importance.

"I'm giving more time to the practical side of finance," he assured them. "Let the professors have their theory."

But Tony had always ranked high in his studies at college, theory or no.

Sandy, on the other hand, was in his classes doing very well indeed.

XXIV

TONY and Sandy, when they encountered one another here and there about the house during this winter, met with a casual word and parted as casually. If there was no affection in their attitude, neither was there any marked hostility. The question of their like or their dislike for one another was never forced upon the attention of Mr. and Mrs. Caterson.

But Sandy did not trespass on Tony's domain, nor Tony on his brother's sanctuary. So when, one spring evening while Tony and the two older folk were sitting on the terrace by the front door, Tony rose and said casually that he meant to go downstairs and see how Sandy was getting along, Mr. and Mrs. Caterson were at once surprised and faintly concerned. They tried, after he had left them, to hazard a guess at the reason for his going; persuaded themselves at last that the incident had no significance, that it was simply a part of Tony's native friendliness. When after half an hour or so Tony returned with some amusing jest at Sandy's absorption, they laughed with him; but they still wondered what had happened between the brothers, in Sandy's work room belowstairs.

What had happened was this. Tony descended

through the billiard room and went along the corridor to the door of Sandy's shop; and he paused
there to listen. Within the closed door he could hear
the whirring of a lathe, the bite of steel on steel.
He knocked and had no immediate reply; he hesitated; and in the end he thrust the door slowly open
and stood indolently, one shoulder leaning against
the jamb, waiting for Sandy to discover him. Sandy
was very much engrossed, but Tony presently lighted
a cigarette, and Sandy—his attention perhaps attracted by the odor of the smoke—turned his head
and saw his brother there.

This apparition was so entirely without precedent
that Sandy was startled. Instinctively he shut off the
lathe and swung around; he said doubtfully:

"Hullo!"

Tony grinned. "Don't stop the wheels of industry
on my account," he protested. "What's that gadget
you're working on?"

Sandy hesitated, coloring with faint embarrass-
ment. "Oh, just a sort of a do-funny."

Tony strolled across to the bench to examine the
curiously shaped bit of metal upon which his brother
had been engaged. Other parts along the bench gave
him a clue. "A carburetor?" he persisted.

Sandy wiped his hands on his overalls. "Why,"
he confessed uncertainly, "I've got a sort of notion
to superheat the mixture on the way through the
manifold. Thought it might cut down gas consump-
tion."

Tony nodded. "They've got something of the kind

already, haven't they?" he inquired; and Sandy, quickening with pleasure at having an audience, undertook to explain his idea. He began to pick up the disunited parts of his device and assemble them, pointing out as he did so what he meant to do. Tony, watching him, thought his blunt fingers were surprisingly deft and sure. He paid no particular heed to what Sandy was saying; yet he seemed to do so, and Sandy was flattered and happy.

"I've got an old engine on the block over there for tests," Sandy explained. "I've run it for a given number of hours with three or four other types of carburetor, and when I've finished this, I'll be able to check it against the other figures. I think it might do some good."

"Don't see why not," Tony assured him cordially. "Yes sir, I wouldn't wonder if you'd got hold of something." He clapped Sandy on the shoulder. "You'd be the one to do it, too," he applauded. "I'll bank on you!"

"Of course, I'll have to make tests at different R P M's," Sandy eagerly continued. "And I want to figure out some way to put a load on the engine, too, see if that makes a difference. And try different temperatures, and so on."

"You ought to be able to sell it, if you get hold of something," Tony remarked.

"I haven't got that far yet," Sandy admitted. "I guess I'm more interested in working it out than I am in selling it."

Tony nodded. "You would be," he assented, grinning in amused derision. "Money never did mean much to you, did it?"

Sandy chuckled. "Why—not as long as I had all I wanted," he confessed.

The other hesitated; but Sandy had turned back to the bench, and he did not see Tony's faint confusion. Tony asked casually: "Bothering you, am I?"

"No, I'm about ready to put this together, now," Sandy explained. "Sit down. Here." He brought a newspaper from the end of the bench, spread it on a box against the wall. "Sit on that, and you won't get your clothes greasy."

"That's all right," Tony assured him. "Don't worry about me." But he did sit down; and after a moment he reverted to Sandy's remark of a moment before. "All the money you want, eh? Haven't got more than you want, have you?"

Sandy looked around at him in quick attention, and for a moment there was silence between them. Then he asked: "Need some, do you?" And in quick solicitude: "Anything wrong?"

Tony chuckled. "Wrong? No! I just thought if you had some money loose you might want me to invest it for you."

Sandy put aside his tinkering. He wiped his hands on his overalls. "Why—it's all invested, Tony," he said slowly. "But I guess you know that if you need it, you can have it."

Tony waved his hand. "I'm offering you a chance to make a killing," he protested. "I'm not asking for charity."

"Well, I mean, if you ever did want anything."

Tony slapped his knee. "Here's the situation, Sandy," he explained. "I'm in a big thing. Got all my own funds tied up in it. That's how good I think it is. But it's so big it's a shame not to get into it. Come along in with me."

"What sort of—thing?" Sandy asked.

"Investment."

"You can't make such very big profits in investments," Sandy protested; and Tony laughed.

"Found that out, have you?" he chuckled.

Sandy colored. "Why, I've done all right," he corrected. "I'd saved some on our old allowance, and bought some stuff; and I invested the ten thousand father gave us when we graduated, and some I've saved since. I've got about five thousand profit on a capital of nineteen thousand, Tony. That's pretty good, even with a market like this one."

Tony stared at him for a moment, and his color rose, and he laughed sharply. "Good!" he cried. "That's the stuff! Take your profits, old man. This market's going to bust inside the month."

Sandy considered the matter, his eyes downcast, leaning motionless against the bench. "Short, are you, Tony?" he asked at last.

"The elevator's going down," Tony predicted, his tone rising. He leaned forward alertly. "Here's the story, Sandy! You don't need to take any risk, if you don't want to. Just give me a check. I'll handle it. As much as you want to put in, or as little. I'll guarantee you against loss, and split the profits. That safe enough for you, old boy?"

"I thought you were long," Sandy muttered, half to himself.

"I took a big profit in January," Tony explained. "I saw that the thing was going to turn. I waited till it looked like the right time, and then sold."

"When?"

"Oh, off and on for six weeks, now," Tony said easily.

"Market's been going up," Sandy protested. "You're pinched, aren't you?"

Tony's eyes clouded; he demanded, in a sudden defensive irritation: "Do you want to come in, or don't you?"

Sandy said in a carefully even tone: "Father disapproves of short selling, doesn't he? He says it's dangerous business, for a beginner, anyway."

But Tony leaped to his feet, his face suddenly black with fury. "Damn it, no lectures!" he exclaimed. "What are you going to do, tattle? Tattle and be damned, if you want to. You tried that last summer. Keep it up if you like. But don't preach to me!"

Sandy answered steadily: "I'll go to father any time I think it's a good thing for you, Tony. Hard names won't stop me. I told you that before."

Tony swung toward the door. "All right!" he exploded. "Every one to his taste!"

In another moment he would have been gone; but Sandy added: "But I'll help you all I can myself, first. You know that, too."

And Tony checked, and half-sullenly he turned. "I don't want to be rescued if I have to listen to a sermon," he said morosely. "Let's have it! What are you going to do?"

"How much do you want?" Sandy asked.

"The more you put in, the more you'll take out," Tony told him easily.

"I see," Sandy commented. "All right, I'll arrange it tomorrow. You can have it the day after, Tony." He hesitated. "I deal through Mr. Champernoon," he remarked. "You know him."

" 'Liberty Bonds our specialty,' " Tony derisively suggested.

"If you ever want advice, he's pretty sound," Sandy urged, and after a moment he asked: "Will —twenty thousand be enough for a while? I want to keep a little leeway."

Tony, in spite of himself, was suddenly pale with relief; his eyes filled, with that quick trick so characteristic of Mrs. Caterson. He took a stride forward, thrust out his hand. "Good kid!" he said awkwardly.

"Grease on my hands," Sandy doubtfully suggested, looking at his grimy paw. "But—who cares about that? Eh, Tony!"

And he grasped the other's hand strongly. They stood a moment thus, and Sandy grinned happily. Then Tony, with another word of thanks, turned away.

He stopped in the lavatory on the first floor to wash his hand.

XXV

IN May, Tony decided to give up Business School and begin his active business career. He spoke of the matter to his father; and Caterson at first dissented.

"I might as well," Tony urged cheerfully. "The exams in June will do me up, anyway." He laughed at his own frailties. "Guess four years of studying was all I could handle, father." And he added more seriously: "And—I want to get to work. I'm beginning to feel old, you see."

Caterson smiled in quick amusement. "What did you plan to do?" he asked. "Can I give you a lift, any suggestion?"

"Stocks and bonds," Tony promptly explained. "That's the stuff for me." His eyes were wistful. "I'd like to be a man like Mr. Tedlock," he said, in swift, endearing confession. "That's my dream, I think. To handle big sums wisely and carefully and shrewdly, and all that."

"Mr. Tedlock's not a—bond salesman," Caterson suggested.

"What else is he?" Tony argued. "He finances your operations, doesn't he? Runs a line of credit for you. That's the same thing as selling bonds. Only where I'll sell a thousand dollar security, he'll sell your note for a million. Anyway, that's what I want to do."

His father nodded. "That's one way of putting it," he agreed, and lighted his pipe afresh. "Had you any opening in mind, Tony?"

"I can get into Havely's office," Tony assured him. "I've traded with them. They know me."

"They're—all right," Caterson guardedly remarked. "I don't wish to criticize them. But I doubt if the house has any sure future, Tony. Possibly Mr. Champernoon might have an opening for you, if you care to have me talk with him?"

Tony cried delightedly. "Do I? That's the finest house in town, of course. They've a tradition behind them! I didn't suppose they ever took in youngsters."

Caterson pressed his finger tips together, his eyes reflective.

"I went to old Mr. Champernoon almost thirty years ago, with my first thousand dollars," he explained, and after a moment, he chuckled. "We've always kept that thousand in a separate account," he told the younger man. "Reinvested the income, and so on. It amounts to over twenty thousand now. It's been amusing to watch the vicissitudes it has undergone, through good times and bad. You spoke of tradition. That account is one of the Champernoon traditions."

And he added: "I'll speak to Champernoon, if you like. Of course, the old man's been dead these ten years; but young Champernoon is sound, too."

"Gorry, that would be great," Tony assured him. "Do, will you?" His eyes shone with gratitude.

Caterson spoke to his wife about this talk with Tony. "I'm—sorry, in a way," he confessed. "Sorry he doesn't want to finish the course."

"I think I'm glad," she countered. "I'll be glad to see him settled down in business." And she added a moment later, wistfully: "And married, too. . . ."

"He and Nina," Caterson remarked, as though this were understood; but Mrs. Caterson did not reply.

Caterson lunched next day with Champernoon. The broker was a man in his middle thirties, lean and taut as a fine hound; and he heard Caterson's suggestion with quick interest. Caterson had referred to Tony only as "my son," and when he was done, Champernoon remarked:

"He has an account with us, of course. A pretty sound youngster, isn't he?"

Caterson shook his head. "That's probably Sandy," he corrected. "I'm speaking of Tony." He chuckled. "Sandy has no financial ambitions," he explained. "He's much more interested in carburetors than in bonds, just now."

Champernoon hesitated, checked the remark which was on the tip of his tongue. If Caterson underrated his son's capacity, it was not for Champernoon to enlighten him. Sandy's account was, after all, the boy's own concern.

"Tony, eh?" he echoed, in a tone not quite so

cordial. "Oh, of course, I know him, too. Great half back, wasn't he?"

"Tony's a—colorful youngster," Caterson assented. "Singularly loveable. Makes friends readily. I should think he ought to be a good man for you."

"I saw him play, two years ago last fall," Champernoon remarked. "What an open field runner he was! Keep in shape, does he?"

Caterson smiled. "Not what you would call strict training, perhaps. He's been at loose ends, since college. He tried Business School, but theory hasn't attracted him. I think he needs to be driven a bit, before he settles down." He hesitated, and the other, his eyes like mirrors that concealed what lay behind them, said casually:

"He had tough luck on a punt, that day, I remember."

Caterson sat very still, finding no reply; and after a moment Champernoon added:

"But then, the boys on a football team are just youngsters, after all. They're pretty hot, and tired, and excited, in the heat of the game. I've played football myself."

Caterson nodded. Champernoon had been the outstanding end of his Senior year.

"Well, send him in to see me," the broker suggested. Their luncheon was done. "We'll see what he can do!"

And Caterson, rising as the other rose, smiled in quick relief and gratitude. He reported the conversation that night to Tony, and Tony said eagerly:

"I'll go in tomorrow afternoon!"

Mrs. Caterson asked her husband, after they were abed, what Mr. Champernoon's attitude had been. "Wasn't he pleased?" she demanded. She detected in Caterson's replies some faint evasion; but though she cross-examined him, she elicited nothing to explain this mystery, and in the end she contented herself. Tony, at least, was launched on his career.

Next day, toward late afternoon, she began to expect the young man's triumphant home coming; and she waited with an increasing impatience that turned at last to apprehension. He had not yet arrived when Caterson appeared, but her husband was able to reassure her. He had talked with Champernoon over the telephone, and Tony would go to work on the Monday following.

"But where is Tony?" Mrs. Caterson protested. "Why hasn't he come home?"

Caterson shook his head. "He'll be along," he predicted. "Probably stopped to tell some of his friends."

Tony did not arrive in time for dinner, but Sandy did; and Sandy had news for them. He told it diffidently and yet proudly too.

"I saw a Ganymede Motors engineer today," he explained. "Showed him the records of my tests, and so on. They're going to check up on it, but he says if it's what I think it is, they want it."

His eyes were shining, his homely countenance somehow transfigured; and Mrs. Caterson swept him close in her arms, while Caterson more soberly questioned and applauded.

"Sure of your figures, are you, son?" he asked.

"Yes, sir," Sandy told him steadily.

"Why, then, it's as good as done, eh? How about patents? Want me to take them out for you?"

Sandy shook his head. "I didn't want to bother you," he explained. "The Ganymede people will take care of that. I'm to get a thousand dollars, and royalties if they use it, and so on." He grinned. "I'm probably foolish to leave it that way," he remarked. "They say big corporations buy things and put them on the shelf for years. But if this isn't good enough so they want to use it, I don't want them to."

Caterson caught his wife's eyes in a swift glance of approval. "Well," he said judicially: "I don't think you'll find them unfair with you."

Sandy grinned, and he went up to his room, and came down presently for dinner. Afterward he disappeared belowstairs; but he said before he left them that Nina would be over presently.

"I promised to show her how it works," he explained. "Send her down, will you, when she comes."

Mrs. Caterson nodded. "Of course, Sandy," she assured him cheerfully. But when she and Mr. Caterson turned into the living room, she clung a moment to her husband's arm, so that he asked solicitously:

"Tired, Lady?"

"No indeed," she protested; and to distract his attention from herself she added: "This is Sandy's big hour, isn't it!"

"The boy's got something in him, I guess," Caterson agreed, his gruff tone accenting rather than serving to conceal his pride, so that she laughed softly by his side.

A car by and by swung into the drive, and they expected Tony; but it proved to be Nina. She left her roadster at the door, and came in for a word with them before she turned to run down the basement stairs, leaving them there before the fire. Mrs. Caterson was sewing buttons on some of Sandy's shirts, while her husband read aloud; but after a while she put her sewing aside. He saw the movement, asked again:

"Tired? Want to go to bed?"

She shook her head. "No, dear. Go on. I just want to rest my eyes."

And she sat thereafter like one asleep, her lids lowered, while his voice droned on.

It was nearly half past nine when Tony did at last come home. Mrs. Caterson heard the quick rush of his car, and she exclaimed: "There's Tony now!" Caterson lowered his book, and Mrs. Caterson went swiftly toward the front hall to greet the boy. He caught her in his arms with that familiar gesture, and he cried:

"Hullo, Child!" Then looked past her into the living room. "Nina here? Saw her car outside. Where is she?"

"Down with Sandy," she confessed. "Is her car in your way?"

"No, no," he laughed, and kissed her swiftly.

"Well, my good woman! Heard the news? Your talented son has entered the market place." He caught his father's eye. "Tell her, did you?" he called.

Caterson nodded, in a vague disquiet. Tony, obviously, had stopped somewhere to celebrate his new estate. His eyes were burning and his cheek was red; and when he and Mrs. Caterson came into the living room, Caterson caught the unsavory taint upon his breath. Mrs. Caterson must have remarked it, too; but she was smiling, sharing to the full in Tony's happiness which she would not mar.

He began to tell them about his interview with Champernoon, tilting on his heels before the fire, talking full pace, enlivening the narrative with every whimsical device. Mrs. Caterson sat facing him, and Caterson too; so their backs were toward the door when Sandy and Nina appeared there and came slowly into the room.

But Tony saw them, and his eyes lighted. "Hullo, Nina!" he cried, and leaped toward her. "Just in time for the celebration! I've gone into trade, my good girl! A big kiss for luck, eh?"

Mrs. Caterson turned and saw him sweep Nina into his arms; and then she saw him, without having kissed her, thrust the girl to arm's length again.

"But here, what's this?" he protested with mock severity. "A smudge on your nose! What is it?" There was a moment's confused silence while her color rose; then: "Grease, by Gorry!" Tony ejaculated, in a new tone, and he stared across Nina's shoulder at his brother, and slowly he released his grip upon Nina's arms. After a moment he chuckled unpleasantly.

Nina was like a crimson flame, her cheek blazing. She scrubbed at her nose with her handkerchief, and she laughingly protested:

"Sandy, why didn't you tell me?"

"There's a smudge on his nose, too," said Tony grimly.

"I didn't even notice it, Nina," Sandy confessed.

For a moment no one spoke. Mrs. Caterson was trembling, helpless; but Caterson cried, jocosely:

"What have you two been up to, Sandy? Eh? Circumstantial evidence, Nina, seems to me!"

Nina scrubbed her nose again, and she looked at Sandy, prompting him; and Sandy, obeying that glance, turned to face his father and mother. He hesitated, beaming with a happy triumph; and he said at last:

"Why, yes sir. Yes mother. I guess it is."

Tony stood leaning against the wall by the door, his hands in his pockets, his eyes morose and angry. Nina looked toward him with something like an appeal in her glance; but he said nothing, and after a moment she came to where Sandy stood, and slipped her hand through his arm. Then Mrs. Caterson, summoning back her strength and courage, rose, and Nina turned to meet her, smiling wistfully; and Mrs. Caterson pressed the girl close in her arms.

"You know I'm glad," she whispered. "Happy as can be."

"Sweet thing!" Nina told her gratefully.

Still Tony had not moved; and Mrs. Caterson, her word at once a plea and a command, called to him: "Tony? Aren't we glad?"

Tony stirred at that. His chuckle was sardonic.

"Oh, sure!" he agreed. "It's all the same to me. Anything to keep her in the family!"

The phrase stung Mrs. Caterson like a lash. Nina's hand flew to her throat, and even Mr. Caterson seemed visibly to flinch. But no one of them stirred. It was left for Sandy to challenge the dark spectre invoked by Tony's word. His broad and rugged countenance, which had been suffused with happiness, set suddenly in grave, stern lines; and he swung to face his brother across the room, their eyes opposing.

XXVI

THIS was for Mrs. Caterson one of those moments like an evil dream. Her perceptions pitilessly clear, she understood all the cross currents that were in conflict here, yet was herself helpless to intervene; she was no more than a spectator, torn and terrified by what she saw, yet bound by a still paralysis. She could foresee, without being able to avert the catastrophe that was impending.

Tony had come home in a triumphant elation over his new estate as a man of business; he had worn, too, a more tangible intoxication. And at this moment when the heights must have seemed to be waiting for his ascending feet, Sandy had matched his brother's triumph with a greater one. Mrs. Caterson knew Tony so well; she knew how he did always feed on success, how failures shattered him. And she watched him now with stricken eyes, foreseeing that like a great tree when the axe is laid at its root, he must shudder under the blow.

His outward composure did not deceive her. He leaned so indolently against the wall, yonder by the door; he watched them all with a sardonic humor in his eyes; his words were tinged only with a mirthful mockery. But her eyes pierced this mask he wore, and she knew that his soul was bruised and raw and quivering. When Sandy swung toward him now, Mrs. Caterson wished to cry out, to bid Sandy be still; she was afire with a fierce pity for Tony in his defeat, a burning loyalty and tenderness for him. She could have hated Sandy, because he had succeeded where Tony had so sadly failed. These were both her boys, whom she loved; but Tony needed her, and toward Tony in this moment all her tenderness was turned. She wrapped it like a protecting cloak around him; her eyes, by their glance, seemed to enfold him, as though to draw him close against her bosom comfortingly.

All these winds blew through her heart in no more than the time it required, after Tony's word, for Sandy to turn and confront his brother. Mrs. Caterson sank into her chair again, and Caterson, from the further angle of the hearth, watched these two young men, and Nina swung at Sandy's side.

Sandy said steadily: "Tony, what's in your mind?"

Tony lifted his eyebrows in affected bewilderment. "In my mind?" he echoed.

Sandy frowned in a slow confusion. "I can see that you're sore," he explained. "But—why? Whatever it is, let's have a look at it."

Before Tony could reply, Nina suddenly assumed direction of the situation. She touched Sandy's arm, and when he looked down at her, she smiled reassuringly. "Sandy, dear," she said gravely, "I think this is between Tony and me." Then, to the other man: "Tony, I want to talk to you." She hesitated, looking back across the room. "Can we go into your study, Mr. Caterson?"

Their defenses all were down, now; they no longer pretended that this moment was merely the happy announcement of the betrothal of a beloved son. Sandy, bluntly challenging his brother's attitude, had forced the issue, and Nina's word had made it definite and plain. They would meet it squarely. Caterson, after a glance toward his wife, nodded his consent to the girl's request.

"Of course, Nina," he assured her.

She moved toward Tony, and Tony slowly colored. He said, almost stammering: "What's it all about, Nina? What's the matter, anyway? I didn't say anything."

She smiled faintly. "Let's not dodge, Tony," she urged. "Let's get it all straight, lay this ghost! Please, my dear. So it can't ever come to haunt us again. Will you come with me?"

He moved irritably. "Oh—all right!" he blurted. "But there's nothing to talk about."

Yet he followed her, with a shambling affectation of indifference, into Caterson's study along the hall. His head was swimming. He was not drunk; but the liquor he had taken combined with the storm of emotions which now tormented him to produce a sort of stupor, so that his eyes were heavy, almost glazed. He faced her across the broad desk in the study; and he tried to light a casual cigarette, and flipped the match away, and met her glance uneasily.

Nina was pale, yet there was courage in her. She

said quietly: "Tony, my dear! You're hurting your mother and father, and Sandy; and you're hurting me."

He shook his head. "I wouldn't hurt you!" he protested.

She colored slowly. "Two years ago, you asked me to marry you, Tony," she reminded him. "I've always been so fond of you. I told you so then, and I tell you so now. I almost loved you, perhaps, Tony. And I told you to ask me again, after you graduated."

"Well, didn't I?" he challenged.

Nina nodded honestly. "Not in so many words, perhaps," she suggested. "But—near enough. But —Tony, dear, you didn't want to ask me then."

He made a swift protesting movement; but the word he might have spoken died on his lips. He colored with sudden confusion, and his eyes fell.

"You didn't want to ask me, dear," she repeated. "And—I didn't want you to. We don't need to discuss—reasons; but we both know that, don't we?"

Tony stared at her for a long moment, and he licked his lips, suddenly dry as though with terror. Nina insisted gravely:

"That's the honest truth, isn't it?"

He made, in the end, no denial. For a moment they stood thus, the desk between them; and since her own eyes were downcast, watching her still hands, her finger tips resting on the dark mahogany, he studied her, searchingly. Till she lifted her head to meet his glance again.

"So—Tony," she insisted. "You've no grievance, and I've no grievance. Have we? No true grievance. The thing hasn't had to be put in words; neither of us wanted it that way. But we both knew, dear."

He said, with a sudden flash of that quality which always made folk love him:

"Yes, Nina. You're—fine! I'm sorry. You've always been fine and square with me; and I've treated you rotten."

She smiled wistfully. "I understood. You wished to hurt me, because you—still liked me pretty well. But Tony, you mustn't hurt these others, now, and you mustn't hurt Sandy, and you mustn't hurt me, any more, please. You can, when you want to. But —please, Tony."

He asked, after a moment: "Love him, do you? Sure?"

"Yes, Tony." Her eyes were warm.

"Why?" he persisted; and suddenly he added: "I don't mean to—make fun of him. But Sandy's never struck me as having any great pulling power." His eyes clouded. "I guess he has, though," he confessed. "They elected him captain." His face twisted. "Gorry, but that hurt me, Nina! I guess you know."

"I guess I do," she tenderly agreed.

"So he must have—something," he hazarded, groping. "What is it, Nina?" And he went on swiftly: "You know—I want people to—like me. I get fat on it. I always got a great kick out of being —popular. I try to figure out how to act so I will be. And Sandy never seems to try. He's not thoughtful of others, or clever, or funny, or—anything, as far as I can see. He just goes plugging along. What has he got, Nina?" He grinned in an apologetic way. "I'd like to know. Maybe I could imitate him." There was a grimace of pain in his smile.

She hesitated, and her eyes filled, and she shook her head. "I don't know, Tony. I just love him."

"You never did love me," he remarked, not accusingly, but as though recognizing a fact.

"I've always been so fond of you," she told him; and she added suddenly: "Never more so than right now, Tony. You're—being fine! You will be fine, won't you?"

"I wish I knew the answer," he persisted, not so much to her as to himself. There was a sudden passion, like fear, in his tones. "I certainly wish I knew. . . ."

She tried to put her feeling into words. "I think I—love the outside of you, Tony. The way you act, and talk, and treat people. The outside of you. But I love the—the insides of him."

And then as she saw the swift comprehension in his eyes, she became rigid with sorrow; she reached quickly to touch his hand.

"Dear, I didn't mean it so," she stammered. "I was just trying to put in words a—thing that can't be put in words."

He shook his head, and he smiled at her reassuringly. "That's all right, Nina," he told her. "Don't take it back. Don't be—sorry! A man can see a lot by the light of a stroke of lightning, sometimes. If he's quick. Can't he? And I'm—quick enough, Nina. Eh?" He was laughing appealingly. "But that makes it harder, doesn't it? I thought a good facial massage would fix me up; but I guess what I need's a major operation. To take something out, or put something in!"

"Tony dear!" she protested.

He came to her side, his arm encircled her. "So we're all straightened out," he insisted whimsically. "Diagnosis complete at one sitting. Smile, Honey!" Then, laughing at her: "Ain't you ashamed, admiring Sandy's insides! I should think a nice girl would have more modesty!" And as her lips did curve in an answering smile: "That's the girl! Now come on. Let's go back in there. I want to give you both my blessing. But—drat his ornery old insides!"

"You're making fun of me," she protested indignantly, yet laughing too.

"Sure I am," he agreed. "I'm amused at myself, too." He opened the door and they emerged into the hall. "Can't you see the laughter bubbling in my eyes?" he challenged grimly.

So they came back into the other room; and Mrs. Caterson's quick, searching scrutiny found in Tony's countenance some comfort. Sandy swung to face them; and Tony crossed directly to his brother, gripped the other's hand. He hesitated, said then straightforwardly:

"Sandy, forget the way I acted, will you. I was sore! Nina's fine, and you deserve her. I acted like a kid, and I'm sorry. I want you to be happy."

Sandy colored with pleasure; he answered warmly:
"That's great, Tony!"

And Mrs. Caterson relaxed, with a slow, deep
inhalation; her eyes closed in a sudden relief too
deep for words.

XXVII

SANDY took Nina home. That is to say, he went away with her in her car; but they did not go home at once. This was a night in May, and warm and still; a starlit night, with a late moon that would not rise till eleven or thereafter. The roadster's top was down, and the air was heavy with the fragrance of flowers along the way, or with the scent of new green leaves. Nina at first drove, and they went silently; they were curiously shy and ill at ease, their tongues restrained.

But when they came near the Buckel home, Sandy said suddenly: "I say, let's not go in yet."

Nina smiled at him. "Why not?"

"Well," he argued. "We've got a lot of things to talk about. This whole thing is a—a sort of a new idea to me." He chuckled provokingly.

"Is that so!" she retorted. "Well, you'll have to get used to it, my dear!" Her head was high, her eyes shining with laughter.

"Then hadn't I just as well begin now?" he insisted. "It's a good night for it. Stars, and a moon by and by, and everything."

She smiled at him with a flashing sidewise glance. "A moon? Sandy, you don't mean to say you notice

such things as the moon? There aren't any carburetors in the moon, my dear."

"Let's drive out into the country somewhere," he
proposed.

"You'll have to do the driving, then," she retorted.
"I'm not going to play chauffeur."

"It's your car," he pointed out. "I'd as soon drive,
if the car can stand it."

She chuckled. "Oh, it's insured!" she declared,
and she pulled in to the curb while he changed seats
with her. They went on more slowly, and for a while
she was quiet by his side; and she was full of a fond
mirth at her own thoughts. It was like Sandy, she
reflected, to confess so frankly that this was a new
idea to him; it was almost a new idea to her. There
had developed between them during these last
months an increasing sympathy; but this feeling had
grown so gradually that Nina herself had scarce
been conscious of its maturity. Looking backward,
it seemed to her now that Sandy, since his election
to the captaincy of the football team, had been slowly
blossoming; like an unfolding flower he revealed at
each new encounter some unsuspected charm. She
was amused at the absurdity of comparing Sandy
to a flower; and she looked up at his rugged features,
dimly illumined by the dash light, searching them
one by one with warm and smiling eyes. Till he
became conscious of this scrutiny, and said without
turning his head:

"Better quit that! You'll take my attention off the

road. What's the matter? Is there still a smudge on my nose?"

"M-hm," she assented happily. "The same one! You didn't wipe it off!"

"I'm going to keep it to remember you by," he assured her; and she laughed, and then she was silent again. Even this was a new aspect of Sandy's character; this aptitude for light, tender jesting. She had long ago come to think of him as sober, almost sombre; it astonished her to perceive that he was not so heavy-witted as she had supposed.

He was not so much like a flower, she reflected; he was more like a lumbering tortoise, a dusty looking creature whose true beauty you do not perceive without a close inspection. And her thoughts flashed back again to that moment an hour or so ago, in Sandy's work room in the basement. He had been explaining something to her, something about carburetors; and in doing so, he had put on a bright garment of eloquence. His words came swiftly, and his eyes were shining with his own enthusiasm, so that while she listened, she forgot his words and remembered only his eyes. She watched the play of his lips as he spoke, and she watched his eyes, and she watched his quick, eager movements, till her long scrutiny began vaguely to embarrass him. He had stopped in mid-sentence at last to cry:

"Say, what's the matter with me? What makes you look at me that way?"

And a moment later—her eyes had for some

ridiculous reason filled with tears at his question—
he was stammering: "Why Nina! Nina!"

Her eyes had cleared long enough for her to see
the smut on his nose and try to dodge it; but then
the grease spot became unimportant, and she forgot
it. It would always be hard for her to discover any
blemishes on Sandy, she decided now; even so conspicuous a blemish as a smudge upon his nose. And
she laughed softly to herself at this thought, so that
he asked a question, and she countered with another.

"What made you do it, Sandy?"

"Do what?"

"Kiss me, tonight," she explained.

He chuckled. "You looked so darned funny, crying," he assured her. "I guess I was sorry for you.
And then you tried to dodge, and that finished me."

"I was trying to dodge that grease spot," she told
him.

Sandy grinned. "Honey, you'll get used to grease
and oil on me, I guess."

"I hope it's going to be good for my complexion,"
she laughingly declared.

"Well, I'll try different brands," Sandy promised.
"There are all sorts of oils on the market. Every
engine has to have the right oil; maybe every cheek
is that way too."

"And noses?"

He chuckled. This nonsense for the time contented
them well enough. He was driving more slowly now,

following a road that was strange to her; and she asked where they were going.

"Down to the river," he explained. "There's a side road, runs along a big marsh. We'll stop and wait for the moon to rise across the water."

"I declare," she exclaimed, "The man's a continual surprise to me! A sense of humor, and a sense of beauty, and everything. . . ."

"It took you to find them, Honey," he told her gently; and her arm slipped through his.

"How long have you known?" she asked presently.

"Known what?" he parried, and turned into the side road.

"Known about you and me," she told him indignantly. "What do you suppose I mean?"

"Why, not till you told me!" he assured her; and she laughed happily there beside him.

"Well somebody had to tell you," she retorted. "And it might as well be me!"

"Better!" he amended gravely. There was that, sometimes, in his slow tones which made her senses swim.

She did not speak for another space, while he threaded his way down the winding road, dirt and sand grinding under their tires. Then abruptly they emerged upon the margin of a starlit opening, with the dim glint of stars reflected on the water beyond the carpet of the swamp grasses. He stopped the car beside the road there, and when the engine was stilled they could hear the shrill, creaking pipe of the frogs. He switched off the headlights, left the dashlight on. "I want to see you," he explained.

She smiled, and let him look at her; and he said at last, in that sober fashion which was his usual habit:

"I've always known, Nina. About myself, I mean. But I thought, till lately, it would be you and Tony." And he added honestly: "He's the one most people like."

"They like him quickly, but they like you long," she amended.

"It was tough on him tonight," he reflected. "I never thought of that, when I brought you upstairs. I didn't even know he was at home. I just wanted —mother and father to know, as soon as we knew. I'm kind of sorry it broke that way." And he added, with relief: "But he came around, didn't he?"

He did not ask what had passed between her and Tony, and she thought this reticence was like him; it was so easy to discover virtues in Sandy now.

"He was sweet," she agreed.

"He's so darned fine," Sandy ungrudgingly exclaimed; and he shook his head. "Gosh!" he protested. "It's funny it should be you and me."

"You want it so, don't you?" she challenged; and he answered gravely:

"Yes. I want it so."

This was not eloquent, but Nina was curiously content with it, content to sit there silently beside him. He was leaning his elbows on the wheel, staring straight ahead of him; and she watched him covertly. Now and then when he looked toward her, she smiled, and he smiled faintly in return; but she saw that his thoughts engaged him. She might have asked to share these thoughts of his, but she did not. Nina had her own reserves, and she could respect reserve in others; so she waited till he should be ready to turn to her.

He began after a while to talk, but not of her; rather of himself, and of what he hoped to do. His tones were low and even and unhurried; there was something in them ponderous and sure, as he himself was. He had dreams, and he shared them now with the girl beside him; and after a while she began to understand that it was his life, the sum of all those things most dear to him, which in this hour he was putting into her hands. All that he had, he gave her, and all that he was, he told her, in words eloquent for their very simplicity. She came to listen with a reverent attention, perceiving in this bestowal of himself a sort of spiritual espousal; a welding of his heart to hers. These were his secret places, and she was bidden in.

He was still talking when by and by she marked the increasing silver light above the trees across the river; but Sandy was not conscious of that which was about to occur until the imperfect circle of the moon, somewhat past the full, did at last lift lazily into view. He checked, roused himself like a man who has been asleep, exclaimed:

"Hullo! There's the moon. Say, it must be late."

She smiled beside him. "The moon?" she repeated in tender irony. "Why so it is!"

"I'll have to get you home," he decided.

"Well, it was worth coming for," she told him softly.

"It is pretty here, isn't it," he agreed. "I used to come out here to try to get a duck, sometimes." He snapped on the ignition and his foot fumbled for the starter button, but she said quickly:

"I mean, hearing you talk so was worth it, Sandy."

He hesitated, grinned awkwardly. "I did get going, didn't I?" he assented, and again he was about to press the starter when she said:

"Sandy!"

He looked down at her. "What, Honey?"

Her color rose. "Sandy, there's a convention about —engaged people, and moonlit nights. You ought to think of such things without my reminding you!"

He laughed in an embarrassed way. "That's right," he agreed. "I forgot!"

"You forgot!" she echoed, in amused indignation. "You've only kissed me that once, you know! Didn't you like it, Sandy? You seemed to, at the time!"

"I've been kind of—paralyzed ever since," he chuckled. "If that proves anything!" He groped for some word. "This whole thing is so—tremendous. And I've had to try to comprehend it all at once, Nina. It—burst on me. It will take me a little while to get it straight in my mind."

"Well, we've all our lives," she reminded him happily.

"That's great, isn't it," he nodded, staring off across the water. "You know, Nina. . . . Of course, I've known you all my life; but I've always thought of you as just a good sport, and a good fellow, and fine, and all that. You're different, now; like a temple, or something. It makes me feel sort of—reverent."

She hesitated, and suddenly she laughed. "I see, Sandy," she remarked, in teasing amusement. "Men always reverence women, they say; and that's very nice, I'm sure. But—an idol must get bored sometimes." Her eyes met his, and she cried in a swift laughing confusion: "Darn it, I want you to kiss me, Sandy!"

He chuckled. "Well, I've been planning to," he assured her deliberately. "When I got you home, came to say good night. I've been figuring out how I'd lead up to it. I'm not a practised hand, you know. Honestly, I'm scared to death of you."

"You're the dumbest thing, when you want to be," she exclaimed appealingly; till he stilled her word.

When a little later they approached her home, she asked with a smile: "Are you always going to act the way you did tonight, Sandy?" And she added: "Because if you do, I'm going to be furious with you, and desperately in love with you, as long as ever I live, my dear."

And he answered, no jest now in his tones: "Honey, I'm going to be that way about you—whatever way you act. As long as ever I live, too."

She nodded; but later, when he had bidden her good night, she whispered reassuringly:

"I wasn't really furious, Sandy."

"But the other?" he challenged.

"The other, always," she promised him.

And he strode away through the silent streets, his heels ringing on the stones.

XXVIII

WHEN Mr. and Mrs. Caterson went up to bed that night, they were unusually silent. Caterson perceived her distress, and in the moment after they had closed the door of their suite, he took her in his arms and kissed her. For an instant then she was limp in his embrace; but after that moment, he went to his dressing room and she to hers, and he was abed before her, a book open on his knees.

"Going to read a while?" he asked, when she came to her bed beside his own.

"I don't believe so," she confessed. "But I don't mind your reading, Joe."

"The light bother you?"

"Not at all."

He knew that she was distracted and unhappy, yet her eyes were calm and her tone serene: so he was willing to affect that all was well with her, and he fastened his attention on the page in front of him.

But after a while she murmured: "Tony—took it finely, in the end, didn't he, Joe?"

Caterson abstractedly assented. "Sure," he agreed. "Tony's all right." And he turned another page.

By and by she said again: "But it did hurt him?"

He read a paragraph before replying. "Oh, I

guess not," he objected. "He's outgrown his feeling for Nina, I think."

And minutes later, she spoke once more. "At least," she amended, "he pretended to take it gracefully, after she had talked to him."

Caterson turned to look at her; he grinned, and closed his book and tossed it on the table beside his bed. "Want to talk about it, don't you, Lady?" he surrendered.

"Don't put your book down, Joe. I didn't mean to disturb you."

He leaned across to kiss her, smiling down at her. "All right, let's talk," he agreed; and he summoned the memory of that moment when Sandy and Nina, their noses mutually smudged with grease, appeared in the doorway from the hall. "Tony certainly was surprised," he remarked. "It knocked him endwise."

She said slowly: "It's the sort of thing that—isn't good for Tony, Joe. To see someone preferred to himself. Of course, I'm glad for Sandy, just as I was when he was elected captain. But Sandy can stand disappointment. Tony needs to succeed, for his own soul's good."

"Why, Lady," he urged. "You don't need to worry about those boys. Tony, in a week, will be wrapped up in this new job of his; have so many new interests. That's what he needs, a new interest to stimulate him."

"Perhaps," she murmured. "And he may learn to—stand failures, if he has enough of them. . . ." There was a whimsical sorrow in her tone.

"Tony'll do well, selling securities," Caterson predicted. "He's naturally loveable; and his enthusiasms always make him even more charming. He'll be a mighty persuasive salesman, I predict."

Mrs. Caterson smiled. "We don't worry about Sandy any more, do we, Lad," she remarked. "Remember how distressed we used to be about him?"

"Sandy's slow but sure," Caterson assented. "The Ganymede people wouldn't have encouraged him in this patent business if it weren't a good thing. If Tony scales the heights, it will be by leaping from one pinnacle to another; but Sandy will trudge patiently up the valleys, till by and by he suddenly emerges upon some fine eminence!"

"I don't think Tony has really wanted Nina, for months past," she hazarded. "But—to know he can't have her will hurt him, just the same." Her voice suddenly broke hoarsely. "I don't want my Tony ever to be disappointed," she whispered passionately. "He's such a sweet boy, when he's happy, and confident, and sure. . . ."

He was silent for a little. "Tony may have to learn," he suggested at last, "that the surest way to—win others is to command yourself. The way to please the world is to please yourself; hew to your own line; choose your own star. The rest comes after that." And he added, more cheerfully: "He'll come to it. There's a head on the top of that young man's neck, after all, Lady."

"Oh, of course," she murmured sleepily. "I know he'll come to the end of the road triumphantly. But

I don't want him to stub his toe too often along the way. . . ."

And presently: "Shall we turn out the light, Joe?"

So they lay in darkness for a while, till Caterson fell asleep. She could hear his slow inhalations, but she did not sleep for a long time. Her thoughts kept her company; thoughts she had not even confessed to Caterson. She was in these days seeing Tony more and more clearly, for her eyes no longer were so completely blinded by the glamor which he wore. The structure and the texture of the boy became as time passed pitilessly clear to her.

And for a while tonight, as she lay there while Caterson slept within arm's reach at her side, tears streamed down her cheeks unregarded, and her heart was aching sore.

Long after Caterson fell asleep, she heard Sandy coming home; heard his swift strong steps draw near, heard the stamp of his feet along the drive. There was something reassuring in the confident vigor of these footsteps; when he came into the house, a certain peace and security came with him. She felt this; fell a little after into a sleep that was restful and serene.

XXIX

THESE things happened on an evening in the latter part of May; and at breakfast next morning Mrs. Caterson smilingly suggested that the date should be printed on the family calendar in red. Tony, a flower in his buttonhole, departed to town with his father; Sandy plunged into the stern business of preparing for his June examinations; and Mrs. Caterson began to consider a fit date for removing to the shore. They would wait, she decided, till Sandy's examinations were ended; thus the routine of his life at home need not for the present be disturbed.

Sandy had already distractions enough. For one thing, whenever he was at home, Nina was apt to appear. Her love for him, as a woman's will, grew by what it fed on; and there was no coquetry in her. She wished to be with him; and she said so frankly, laughing at her own devotion.

"And if I want to see anything of him," she pointed out to Mrs. Caterson, "I have to be the one to do it. If he isn't buried in a book, he's down cellar puttering. He'd never come over to see me."

Nina wore in these days a dizzying sweetness; her affection for Sandy, confessed, somehow transfigured her, so that her face shone with a lovely radiance. But Sandy managed somehow to support his happiness and at the same time keep his head clear; he could have a bright moment with Nina, yet remember that he had work to do. He was as apt as not to leave her with his mother while he departed upon his own concerns. Mrs. Caterson said to the girl one evening, apologetically:

"You mustn't mind him, Nina. Sandy's a young man of one idea."

But Nina cried happily: "Mind? I'm so proud of him I can hardly see! I adore the way he just pushes me into the background when there's something else he has to do."

If Nina alone was not enough to take Sandy's thoughts away from his work, there was the matter of his invention. He had almost daily consultations with the Ganymede engineers, till toward the end of the first week in June he came home one night to report that for the time being the matter was off his hands. There would be road tests at the company's proving grounds during the summer, and if all went well, production would begin in the fall. He had received a thousand dollar advance against prospective royalties, and he spoke of the future with a calm certainty.

Mrs. Caterson was happy in his satisfaction; yet she was practical, too. She asked her husband what this would mean to Sandy in dollars and cents; and he laughed at her cupidity.

"It will be a good thing, undoubtedly," he assured

her. "Some thousands a year, say. How many? Well, Lady, it's early to guess at that, I'm afraid."

Sandy himself professed ignorance on this point. "I'm more interested in seeing how it works," he declared. "I guess I'll get more satisfaction out of that than out of the money, in a way."

And Mrs. Caterson commented, when she and Mr. Caterson were alone a little afterward: "He's like you in that, Joe. If you didn't have Mr. Tedlock to put a price on what you do, you'd be a pauper, my dear."

He nodded cheerfully; but he was thinking not so much of what she said as of the way in which she said it. She was, he decided, happier nowadays than she had been for months past. The old tender gaiety was gone, might never reappear; but there dwelt in her eyes and in her smile a steadier light, as though her heart now were serene. Serene—yet wistful too. Sadness, he thought, must always abide with her hereafter; and this was a sadness not to be relieved.

But he was glad that she had come to accept the situation with philosophy; to take the fruits life offered without repining for those that were denied.

Caterson himself had long since forgotten his own first sense of guilt for this grief that had come to dwell with them. Confession and absolution had brought him peace. So long as Mrs. Caterson wore the garb of happiness, he would be contented too. Yet he was, once or twice, concerned on Tony's account. The boy, he guessed, was drinking more than he should, and sometimes Caterson considered offering a warning word. But in the end, he held his tongue, trusting that time would instruct and discipline the younger man. He was pleased with Tony's enthusiasm for his work; and Champernoon told him one day that Tony showed promise which already began to be fulfilled. Caterson carried the phrase happily home to Mrs. Caterson.

Sandy's last examination fell on the eighteenth; and the next day they removed to the shore. Mrs. Caterson and Sandy went down together in the limousine, and Sandy, exhilarated by the release from the long months of study, had a swift, bubbling humor in him which Mrs. Caterson had never remarked before. She was content to sit silently beside him, happy in his company.

They came by and by to that sharp curve around the high, rocky point of land where long ago Tony and Mrs. Caterson had stopped together. Mrs. Caterson had forgotten the spot till the limousine, lumbering up the grade, suddenly topped the climb; and she saw the steep, broken granite pitching downward to the boiling surges of the sea. An old man —the same old man—in a limp Panama hat, was sitting in the summer house looking out across the water. Mrs. Caterson's color drained away; but Sandy, watching a schooner yacht half a mile off shore, did not see her distress, and a moment later they were past the spot, descending the steep road beyond.

Tony was to drive down later in the afternoon.

Mrs. Caterson found her throat dry with fear till he at last appeared, to sweep her into his arms in the old, familiar way.

After the brief confusion of removal from one home to the other, they settled easily enough into the summer routine. The Buckels had moved down a week before, and other folk were here. Sandy assumed the task of putting the tennis court in order, and Nina came day by day to toil there with him happily, till the task was done. Mrs. Caterson had more and more often to serve tea to clouds of young people. There were familiar faces and new ones too. Audrey Deal was spending a fortnight here before going on to the Lake, and Tony found her suddenly attractive, and was with her constantly. Mrs. Caterson began to like Audrey more and more; certainly she liked Audrey better than Linda Crater, whom Tony had preferred the summer before. She watched them sometimes, smiling hopefully.

Audrey and Nina and Mrs. Caterson had a moment together one afternoon while Tony and Sandy went to change after tennis; and Audrey remarked:

"Oh, Mrs. Caterson, I'd almost forgotten. I saw Barbs Delevan in New York when I came through, and she wanted to be remembered to you."

"I remember her," Mrs. Caterson agreed. She hesitated, and she got up to move a little potted plant from the stand beside her chair to a table near the window, so that her back was toward them. "She adopted a baby, didn't she?"

"He's the sweetest thing!" Audrey assented. "I

played with him for an hour. He's just perfectly adorable." And she added: "Barbs said her show is coming on here early in September. You must see it. She's as funny as she can be, in it; been an awful hit, you know."

"Of course," Mrs. Caterson assented. She remarked Nina's silence, and she looked toward the girl inquiringly; but as she did so, Sandy came through the hall to join them, and Nina's face lighted at his coming, and a moment later Tony appeared, and they were all away on some gay adventure and Mrs. Caterson was left behind.

She watched them go, and her eyes were shadowed; but she shook her head at last to drive the thought away.

Yet it was to return thereafter; for there was a change in Tony that could not be ignored. She tried once or twice to approach him, win his confidence; she asked about his work, but he told her in a jubilant tone that it went handsomely.

"I've earned over a thousand dollars in commissions in six weeks," he assured her. "That's a mark to shoot at, Child! I tell you, you've mothered a promising young man."

"Promise and performance, Tony," she reminded him. "They must go together, dear."

He bent to kiss her, clipped her close. "Leave that to me, young woman," he laughed. "Just leave the details to your charming son. They are his concern!"

She felt faintly baffled and put by. She had come

more and more to discover in Tony's smiling tenderness a sort of barrier between them. But—she could not break this barrier down; could only watch him with an increasing yearning day by day. She was quick to see, in moments when his face was in repose, lines of worry and of weariness; haggard, ugly lines.

And she saw too, with an absurd misgiving at which she laughed without being able to fight it down, the fact that he had suddenly begun to cultivate his father in a fashion new to him. Caterson had always been fond of golf; Tony had played only casually. Now he began to labor at the game, and sought opportunities to play with Caterson; and Mrs. Caterson, watching them go off together to the club, sometimes smiled. But sometimes, too, she frowned in a still concern.

Yet if she intuitively suspected that behind Tony's new attitude toward his father there might lie some sinister explanation, Caterson found the boy's attentions wholly flattering. At the same time, he took advantage of the opportunity to watch Tony, to seek a better acquaintance with this youngster; and so doing, he began to observe circumstances which disturbed him. Little things. An explosion of childish anger at a poor drive; a protracted sullenness after the ball had taken an unlucky bound; a putt missed because someone on the nearest fairway shouted "Fore." Symptoms, Caterson thought, of jangling nerves; nerves over-tired, or over-strained.

He said once, jestingly, after such an incident:
"Late hours, Tony? They'll always spoil your
putting."

And Tony, quick to sense even a hint of disapproval directed toward himself, said in quick
apology:

"Sorry, father! Didn't sleep so well last night, at
that. But I ought not to get sore."

And a little later, when they were following their
drives down the fairway, he added: "It's a relief to
blow off steam, though. In this selling game, you have
to salve your customers; play nice baby all the time.
I get sick of it, by the end of the day." He grinned
endearingly at the older man. "Mind if I take it out
on you, sir?"

Caterson shook his head, chuckling. "Go ahead,
cuss and swear and carry on all you like. You can't
disturb me, son. I've been cursed by experts, in the
old days."

Tony asked curiously: "That so? Can't imagine
anybody cussing you out and staying perpendicular."

"On construction jobs," Caterson explained. "A
young cub always has to take a licking there."

They came to Tony's ball, and he played his
second shot; and thereafter their ways for a while
diverged. But the interchange stayed in Caterson's
thoughts; and when an hour later they were in the
locker room, sprawling at ease, Tony with a highball
near his hand, Caterson reverted to it again.

"That's what licks a man into shape, I sometimes

think," he remarked; and at Tony's quick, curious glance, he continued casually:

"I'm thinking of our talk a while ago. The cussing a youngster has to take. I've seen it work out, more than once. Too much approval isn't good for a man, and especially a young man. I remember one boy . . ."

Tony sipped his drink; he lighted a cigarette, elaborately careless.

"Chap named Pickard," Caterson continued. "He came to us fresh from technical school. He was an honor man there, ranked second in the class, I think; and he took hold so well that we pushed him along. Been better for him, perhaps, if we'd ridden him hard; but I believed more in praise than in blame, in those days.

"Within three years, he was in charge of operations on a power house construction contract down in New Jersey. We thought he was a find, and told him so. But on that job, he failed.

"It wasn't any fault of his own, either. There wasn't a flaw in him, except that he hated to do anything that would make people dislike him. A man turned up down there, a labor organizer, and instead of kicking him off the job, Pickard treated him like a long-lost friend; flattered him, and catered to him, and cajoled him in every conceivable way. The first thing we knew, he had a strike on his hands, and an ugly one. One night a charge of dynamite went off at the wrong time, in the wrong place, and after that it was a matter of militia, and we lost a good many thousand dollars on the job.

"We could stand that, but it ruined Pickard. He'd never had a reverse. He throve on success, but he couldn't stand failure. If he'd put in a year or two under a rough-tongued Irish foreman, and learned to fall down and bust his nose and get up smiling, he'd have come through fine."

He hesitated, watching Tony with a sudden keen solicitude like a prayer. There is a long reticence between father and son, not easily broken down. There were so many things he might tell this boy— if the boy would listen to them. He wished now, with a sudden, poignant longing, that Tony might understand.

But Tony only said drily: "Yeah?" And he drained his glass.

"Pickard came in to see us, last week," Caterson concluded. "That's why I happened to think of him. Tedlock and I laughed at his stories for an hour." He added, his tone sombre: "But he's had nine jobs in the last twelve years. He's never been fired. He always quit because he was afraid he wasn't making good, couldn't bear to face failure. We liked him, but we hadn't any place for that young man."

Tony rose, stretching himself lazily. "I've got to run," he announced. "Drop you at home, shall I?"

And: "If you will, yes," Caterson ruefully agreed. He had hoped for more.

It was three or four days later that his misgivings were at once justified and intensified; for Tony came to ask his father for a loan. They had breakfasted together, and they took the same train to town. It was Caterson's habit to walk from the station to his office; and Tony swung along with him, shortening his strides to match those of the older man. Their talk was inconsequent, yet there was something in Tony's eyes which Caterson remarked there, and he was not surprised when at the entrance to the building where Caterson and Tedlock had their offices Tony asked:

"Mind if I come up a minute, father?"

"Come along," Caterson cordially agreed. "Don't see you here as often as we'd like, Tony."

Tony nodded, and he licked his lips. While the elevator bore them upward he was silent; and when they got off at the proper floor, he followed his father in this silence still. Caterson said good morning to the girl at the switchboard; he spoke to his stenographer; he sat down at his desk to confront the pile of mail waiting his attention.

Tony had crossed to one of the windows that looked down into the street; he stood there now, and Caterson watched him for a moment. Then he asked casually, his hands and his eyes busy with the letters before him:

"Sit down, Tony? Was there something special?"

Tony swung slowly around, stiffened himself by an effort almost visible.

"Why, yes sir," he confessed. "There was."

Caterson nodded to the waiting girl. "I'll ring for you, Miss Swain," he remarked, and she took her notebook and her pencils and departed. Then Caterson revolved his chair till he faced his son.

"All right, Tony," he suggested, with a reassuring smile.

Tony hesitated, and suddenly he grinned. "There's no use beating around the bush, father," he said appealingly. "Can you let me have five thousand dollars? Take it out of my income from the trust fund, perhaps. Five thousand, if you can?"

The instant seemed to Caterson interminable. It was one of those moments when time stands still, while the world revolves. His thoughts raced like a tempestuous wind; yet it was, as a matter of fact, only a second before he smiled and spoke.

"Of course, Tony," he replied. His check book was in the upper drawer; he wrote rapidly, tore out the slip of paper, held it extended. "Here you are!"

Tony, he saw, was pale. The young man took a step forward to receive the check; and he looked at it in a puzzled fashion, half incredulous, before he folded it away.

"Thanks," he muttered then.

"You're welcome," Caterson assured him.

Tony still hesitated; and suddenly he smiled, his eyes shining. "You're a good egg, father," he said swiftly. "Just like that, and no questions asked."

Caterson nodded gravely. "You can always have anything I can give you, Tony," he reminded the boy. "And—no questions asked, son."

Tony tugged his hat tight on his head. He stood a moment longer, and Caterson thought he would have spoken, and hoped he would. But in the end he departed with a movement like flight. The door swung on his heels; his footsteps receded along the outer hall.

Caterson sat very quietly for a while before at last he rang to recall Miss Swain.

XXX

NINA and Sandy suddenly decided to be married in September, before he should resume his work at the Institute. They were themselves almost as surprised as were the older folk, by their decision. The thought had never occurred to them until one Sunday afternoon when it happened that they drove together in Nina's car, turning aside from the thronged roads, seeking byways and unfrequented thoroughfares. It amused them to take the most unlikely turns; they played a sort of game together, driving by rule, the first road to the right and the next to the left; and they made wagers as to where they would be at four o'clock, and at five. But neither could decide these wagers, because by five o'clock they were completely lost; and a little after five, after a long climb in second gear up what began as a country road and ended in a cart track, they came to a set of bars which forbade their passage.

"There, now we've done it!" Nina exclaimed, and looked at the fences to right and left. "We'll not even be able to turn 'round."

"We can take down the bars and drive into the field and turn," Sandy suggested.

They were on a lofty, bare hill top. To the east

lay the lower, wooded lands extending to the distant shore; and the blue of the sea was like a ribbon along the horizon beyond. The smoke of the city made a gloomy blur to the southeast; and in the other direction the sky along the horizon was notched with blue where distant mountains lifted their lofty heads.

"Let's sit here a while first," Nina countered. "We've come so far! There must have been some reason why we came here!" And she turned to smile at him, said laughingly: "Think, if the bars weren't there to let us through, and we couldn't turn around, we might have to stay here all night."

"Or forever!" Sandy cheerfully amended.

"Oh, that wouldn't do at all," Nina protested.

"Why not?" he asked comfortably; and she retorted:

"Without benefit of clergy?"

Sandy nodded, chuckling; and then with a sudden quickening attention he sat more alertly in his seat; and abruptly he caught her hand.

"Say, Nina," he exclaimed. "I've just thought of something." Her eyes questioned him, and he laughed aloud in a rising tide of excitement.

"You know, it's funny, but I never thought of it before. This has been so—satisfactory! But you know, you and I ought to be thinking about getting married. After all, that's where we're headed, isn't it?"

She laughed aloud, her head thrown back, her throat throbbing with mirth. "Sandy, Sandy, you'll be the death of me," she protested.

"But isn't it?" he insisted.

"Why of course it is," she told him; and her mirth passed, gave way to a gentler emotion. "Yes, Sandy, it is."

Sandy was fundamentally practical. He spoke at once of details, urgently. At first she made objections, but in the end, his eagerness infected her; and when they came home they were intoxicated with their plans. They stopped first at the Caterson cottage—since Nina meant to drop Sandy there on her way home—and burst in on Mr. and Mrs. Caterson to tell what they meant to do.

Caterson thought gratefully that this was good; and he particularly approved when he saw that the matter came as a new interest for Mrs. Caterson. During the days ensuing, she and Nina and Mrs. Buckel were more and more occupied with arrangements for the event which already seemed so imminent. Nina and Sandy would be married quietly, at Nina's home; they must find in the meantime some small apartment near the Institute. So the three women searched together till they discovered a place where Sandy could have a work room in the basement, in which he could be as oily as he chose. This much settled, they began to shop for the furniture and furnishings required.

Mrs. Caterson was so absorbed in these activities that she apparently did not remark the accelerating change in Tony which was so obvious to Caterson's troubled eyes. He had not spoken to her of the boy's appeal for money. For a few days after that incident he expected Tony to reconsider his silence, and offer some explanation; but Tony failed to do so, and Caterson once or twice thought that the boy sought in small ways to avoid him, so that the older man began to doubt the wisdom of his own generosity. He had hoped by it to win the boy's confidence; it seemed more likely he had lost it now.

Tony appeared to take no interest in the plans for Sandy's wedding. If the fact that Nina had preferred his brother still hurt him, he concealed the wound. He met her with a surface friendliness that seemed genuine enough; but the boy was in these days less and less often at home, and his contacts with Nina were infrequent.

He did not always come home even for the night. There were sometimes two or three days on end when they did not see him. Caterson heard from Champernoon that the young man was working with a diligent and productive energy; and he remarked in a tone faintly regretful:

"I know we don't see so much of him as we'd like, at home."

"Don't see how you can," Champernoon cheerfully assured him. "By the results he gets, he must be working twenty-four hours a day."

Superficially, all was well with them; and Caterson had the usual masculine readiness to accept the appearance for the fact. Yet though he tried to assure himself that life would mould Tony in a proper fashion, his misgivings always did return.

Late in August Tony went to New York for a

few days. Matters of business, he explained; there were men there, classmates and the like, to whom he expected to sell this or that security. Mrs. Caterson was so much engaged with Nina's plans that she made no protest at his going; she kissed him goodby, and bade him be careful, and come safely home. Caterson added one other word, in a fumbling effort to penetrate the boy's reserve.

"You know you're your mother's life, Tony," he remarked.

But Tony only nodded cheerfully. "She and I've always been sweethearts," he agreed.

So he departed. He drove over, leaving the cottage on the shore at mid-forenoon, offering Sandy a wager that he would be in New York in time for dinner. But Sandy declined the bet.

"If you lost, I'd have to collect from your estate," he pointed out. "The only thing that will stop you is a telephone pole."

"Ten years in the saddle and never pulled leather yet," Tony laughed; and a moment later he whirled away down the drive, his exhaust a muffled roar that diminished and was gone.

Sandy was the first to know of Tony's return. Everyone in the house was long since abed and asleep when a little past midnight, three or four days later, his car slid quietly into the drive. He put it up, and came into the house, and he went at first to his own room. But about half an hour afterward he emerged again, in pyjamas now, and tip-toed along the upper hall to Sandy's room, clear across the house from that in which Mr. and Mrs. Caterson slept. Tony found Sandy's door open. He stepped inside and quietly closed the door, and switched on the light; and Sandy, roused by the glare, turned drowsily and opened his eyes and discovered Tony there.

"Hullo!" he said sleepily. "Back, are you? What time is it?"

"One o'clock or so," Tony told him; and he sat down on the foot of Sandy's bed. "Everyone all right?"

"Yeah," Sandy assured him. "We didn't expect you tonight."

"I didn't leave New York till after four," Tony confessed. "Found at the last minute that I could get away."

"That's moving some!" Sandy commented; and he added, after a moment: "You look it, too! You're pretty well dragged."

"Pretty busy over there," Tony said evasively.

Sandy nodded. "Go grab yourself some sleep," he advised. "Sleep late, in the morning. I'll tell them not to wake you."

Tony shook his head. "I'm not sleepy," he protested. "I feel like talking."

Sandy studied him; and after a moment he pulled himself into a more erect position, nodding good humoredly. "All right, go ahead," he agreed. "I'm wide awake now, anyway."

"Everything all right, is it?" Tony asked again.

"Why, yes," Sandy told him carefully. "Mother's well. She's having a good time buying furniture and things. Father's as usual. Had a forty-one on the first nine, this afternoon, and that tickled him. Nina's fine. Linda Crater's here for the week-end, but she's got a man in tow. Barbs Delevan's show comes to town next Monday. Outside of that, I don't think of a thing."

"How's your patent dingus going?"

Sandy examined his finger nails. "It looks all right," he replied.

"Make your fortune, will it?" Tony's tone was jocular.

"Why, it ought to bring me a few thousands a year," Sandy agreed.

Tony lighted a cigarette with the utmost care; he flipped the match toward the open window beside the bed, and it struck the screen, dropped upon the sill. "If you're feeling prosperous, I'd like to float a loan," he suggested, and the slow color flooded up his throat and cheeks.

Sandy hesitated for a long moment. "How come, Tony?" he asked at last, in the friendliest tone. "Not still short, are you? Market's been going up steadily. If you're short, you must be badly hooked!"

Tony's eyes were sullen. "Have to show you my balance sheet, do I?" he challenged angrily.

"Of course not," Sandy assured him. "Only—it strikes me you've run through quite a little money. Maybe you need advice, as well as money, Tony. I could give you that, anyway; or at least, I could send you to someone who could tell you a few things."

"Anyway?" Tony echoed grimly. "Does that mean you won't lend me anything?"

"I lent you twenty thousand," Sandy reminded him apologetically. "That sort of put me back on a cash basis, Tony. And—I'm getting married in two or three weeks, you know."

"You must have five or six thousand on hand," Tony urged shrewdly. "And you get four hundred more, the first of the month."

"So do you," Sandy pointed out. "I haven't that much, though, Tony. Mother's buying our stuff, but I pay the bills. She's used to father's income, and buys accordingly; and she enjoys it, so I've let her go along. But if we put off getting married till October, she'll have me in the poor debtor court."

"I could use four thousand," Tony persisted.

Sandy watched him evenly. "How bad is it, Tony?" he asked; but when the other made an angry movement, he said reluctantly: "I can let you have three thousand. That will leave me about six hundred. That's the best I can do."

Tony smiled with a quick gratitude. "You've got your points, Sandy," he declared, something almost affectionate in his tones. "I—can't tell you about this. But you're giving me a lift when I need it."

"I'll have to arrange to get the cash," Sandy explained. "But Tony, why don't you go to father? He's an able citizen, you know. He knows his way around. And—he'd do anything for you."

"I can manage this alone," Tony insisted, but his

lips were white, and Sandy thought they were quivering. He was young enough to be terrified into silence by this sign of weakness; and he said quickly:

"All right! I'll fix it in the morning." He yawned elaborately, added in a tone cheerfully abusive: "Now go to bed, you darned owl! I want some sleep. My office hours are in the daytime."

Tony stood up. "Where'll you be?" he asked. "When can you let me have it?"

When they had arranged a rendezvous, Tony did at last depart to his own room again. As he went, Sandy called to him to turn out the light, leave the door open. Then he settled himself in bed with a great creaking of springs; and lying utterly still, he listened to Tony's soft footsteps as the other departed along the hall. Sandy was full of concern. Without putting the thought into words, even in his own mind, he perceived something akin to tragedy in Tony's haggard eyes. He lay for a while, puzzled and anxious, but in the end sleep overbore him, and he forgot Tony in his dreams.

Yet on waking the thought returned to him, nor could he shake it off. When he met Tony in town, to deliver the promised check, he tried to find some way to win his brother's confidence; but Tony laughingly put him aside. Last night he had been weary and haggard, something hopeless and sullen in his eyes; but today Tony was as confidently masterful as he was used to be, and Sandy could make no impression on the other's grateful good humor.

But when Sandy got his teeth into a problem, he

was not likely to abandon it until the enigma was solved. During the next day or two, he watched his brother with a strict attention, weighing the other's every word; and the more he saw, the livelier became his certainty that Tony was fighting to avert some hideous and imminent disaster. Sandy seemed to discover in the other a restlessness not unlike the twisting, frantic straining of a trapped animal; and as the first suspicion became certainty, he considered what to do.

The obvious thing, he decided, and the wise thing was to go to his father. He had a profound respect for Mr. Caterson, a deep appreciation of the other's sound sense. For him to take this matter to their father would be in Tony's eyes a shameful betrayal, and Sandy knew this. But he had never any lack of moral courage, and this consideration would not deter him. Yet there was enough of youth in Sandy still, so that when he did on Sunday seek a word with Mr. Caterson, he moved circumspectly.

He had led his father down to his work shop in the garage, and when they were alone there, he said slowly:

"I wanted to suggest something, father. I didn't want mother to know, and worry."

Caterson knew by Sandy's tone that this was serious; and he thought wearily that he was in these years becoming used to the shock of abrupt disclosures.

"Tony needs you," Sandy continued, without waiting for the other's question.

Caterson met his son's eyes. "He does?" he echoed.

"I've been watching him," Sandy explained. "I'm sure he's in some difficulty. I suppose he dreads coming to you."

Caterson nodded. "Tony dislikes all unpleasant-nesses," he agreed. "But—they must be faced, sometimes."

"I thought if you gave him a chance to talk to you."

"Have you anything definite, Sandy?" the older man inquired.

"You'll have to get it from Tony, sir," Sandy steadily replied.

"I dislike to seem to—force his confidence," Cat-erson explained, something like an appeal in his tones, as though he found a sudden strength in Sandy upon which he would have liked to lean.

"Well, I think it's time you did," Sandy insisted.

Caterson stood a moment silent; and then abruptly he recognized this reluctance which he felt for the business of cross-examining his son. This was that ancient vice of his, that desire to avoid any unwel-come responsibility. And with the recognition, as in these years he had learned to do, he stiffened himself to meet the task demanded, to fight his weakness down.

So he nodded reassuringly to Sandy. "I will, then," he promised. "Thank you for the suggestion, son."

Sandy seemed about to speak; but in the end he turned back toward the work bench, and began to arrange the tools scattered loosely there; and Caterson knew himself dismissed. He smiled faintly at Sandy's youthful dignity, and he departed toward the house again.

He asked, directly, whether Tony had come home. If this must be done, it had best be done quickly. But even though the day was Sunday, Tony was not about. He had driven to town immediately after dinner, Mrs. Caterson explained, on some matter of business; and he expected to be back by supper time. When Tony did not come for supper, Caterson felt like a man reprieved; yet this respite did not shake his resolution. Tony might come late, as he often did; and Caterson sat up long after Mrs. Caterson was abed, waiting for the boy.

But his vigil was vain, for Tony did not appear.

At breakfast time, he learned that Tony had not come home at all. This was not unusual, yet it did excite a wistful word from Mrs. Caterson.

"We see less and less of him," she remarked regretfully. "Are you sure he's not working too hard, Joe?"

Caterson shook his head. "Hard work won't hurt Tony," he assured her stoutly. "It might Sandy, but you don't have to worry about Tony, I'm quite sure."

There was something in his tone which vaguely affrighted her; she asked a quick question. But Caterson mustered his resources to comfort and deceive her, and Sandy abetted him in this hypocrisy. She was—or she seemed to be—at ease again before her husband departed presently for town.

He thought, when he reached the office, that he

might seek to locate Tony through Mr. Champernoon; but he delayed doing this till he should have
attended to his morning's mail; and when the letters
were done he decided to wait and try to catch Tony
at lunch time; and at lunch he reminded himself that
Tony would certainly be at home tonight.

But he was to have word of Tony before then.
About half past two, Champernoon telephoned to
ask:

"Will you be there for the next half hour, Mr.
Caterson?"

"Yes, certainly," Caterson agreed. His lips were
dry.

"I'll drop in on you, if I may."

"By all means." Tony's father hesitated, but an
irresistible impulse forced the question from him.
"Anything in particular?"

"I'll explain when I see you," Champernoon
evaded.

So Caterson was left to wait the other's coming.
There was work on his desk, but he could not fix
his mind upon it. Miss Swain came in to announce a
caller, but Caterson almost petulantly bade her send
the man away. He told her he was expecting Mr.
Champernoon, and she nodded and withdrew. Caterson crossed to one of the windows above the street;
he stood there looking fixedly down into the deep
gorge between the buildings, staring at the small
human figures interweaving so intricate a pattern as
they hurried to and fro. Thus, he thought, all lives
interwove.

When Champernoon arrived, Caterson turned to meet the other man, and he saw instantly the grim distress in the broker's countenance. For a moment the two confronted one another, the length of the office between them. Then Caterson nodded, as though in understanding, and he crossed to his desk and sat down there; he bade Champernoon take the chair at the end of the desk. He spoke with a grave courtesy, the sort of courtesy a duellist uses to the man with whose sword his own is about to cross; and Champernoon sat down.

Caterson, after a moment, was the first to speak. "I see this is serious," he remarked with a steady dignity. "We need use no indirections. I foresee you have some complaint to make of Tony. Let me have it please."

Champernoon hesitated, nodded. "I'm sorry, my old friend," he said gently. "Yes. Tony has converted to his own use a bond that belonged to one of his clients."

Caterson shivered faintly under the shock. He felt as though every nerve in his body were laid bare, quivering to the faintest touch, contracting in spasms of pain utterly unendurable. Life had gone out of him, as water goes out of a bucket when it topples on its side; he had to wait for it to seep slowly back into his veins, for the tide to rise again.

He felt his lips twist in a grimace like a smile; and he thought Champernoon must be astonished to see him smile at such a moment; and he caught this astonishment in the broker's eyes. So, with a meticulous courtesy, he spoke; and he was smiling still.

"I perceive your astonishment," he remarked, "at what seems to you mirth on my part. But if I smile, it is at one of those thoughts, utterly incongruous, which nevertheless arise at moments of great stress."

"I know what a shock this is," Champernoon ruefully agreed. "But—to come to you seemed the friendliest thing to do."

"I was smiling at myself," Caterson repeated, with that calm precision which had in it a frightful agony. "I was smiling at myself, because my first thought, after your remark, was that there had never been a thief in my family, nor in Mrs. Caterson's."

"Not theft exactly!" Champernoon evaded, in a keen sympathy with this stricken man.

"One unconsciously seeks," Caterson persisted, "to discover certain family resemblances, in one's own son."

XXXI

THIS disclosure of Tony's dishonor had upon Caterson an effect like that of a stunning physical blow, which while it does not render the victim actually helpless, does produce a sort of babbling garrulity. He was ordinarily silent, almost taciturn, slow to form opinions or to express them; but now in the first moments after the impact of Champernoon's revelation, an irresistible impulse drove him to find easement for his pain in many words.

There was an old friendship between him and Champernoon. Champernoon was the younger man, and Caterson's first association had been with his father; but the elder Champernoon had been dead ten or fifteen years; and the younger had since his father's death been Caterson's adviser in matters of investment, and his friend besides. So now Caterson was able to speak to him without reticence, exposing to the other all those flickering impressions which raced through his benumbed mind. He was like a man alone who talks aloud with only himself to hear.

"Tony's charm is his greatest handicap," he remarked. "He has been liked so much that he has become an addict to affection and friendship. The thought of provoking dislike or criticism terrifies him. I think he might go to any length to avoid it."

Champernoon shifted uncomfortably in his chair. "He's a lovable youngster," he confessed. "Yes. This thing . . ."

But Caterson paid him no heed; he went on, in a lowered tone, almost dreamily; and his cheek was white with pain.

"I remember an episode in one of his football games," he murmured. "He had been the hero of the game; but in its closing moments, through an accident, he became responsible for a reverse. A bounding punt struck him on the leg and rolled across the goal line, and an opposing end fell on the ball for a touchdown.

"Tony felt the ball touch him; he whirled around, but too late to recover it. He had to make, in that moment, under fifty thousand pairs of eyes, some decision. To accept the blame for this mischance would be to tarnish the glory he had won that day; and he—lacked the courage. Instead, he denied that the ball touched him, protested to the referee."

Champernoon urged reassuringly: "He was excited! Maybe he didn't feel the ball. I've come out of a game with a lump on my jaw as big as an egg, and no memory of the blow that caused it."

Caterson ignored this kindly suggestion. "That incident lost him the captaincy," he persisted. "And that loss demoralized Tony for a while." There was an impersonal detachment in his tones. "Later, there was a girl who preferred—another man. I don't be-

lieve Tony loved her; but he had asked her to marry
him. The reverse jarred and loosened his moral
fibre; it was like a slap in the face which cannot be
avenged, and it left a scar."

Champernoon could find no word, and after a
long moment, Caterson murmured: "And so many
little incidents besides." His eyes grew blank as he
withdrew among his own memories.

It seemed to the broker that Tony's father remained as motionless as stone for minutes that
dragged interminably, before he roused himself at
last and shifted in his chair and turned again toward
the other man.

"I'm sorry," he apologized. "This is all beside the
point. What has happened? What is there to do?"

Champernoon said earnestly:

"You know I'm ready to do anything. Damn it,
Caterson, I love the boy."

Caterson nodded. "Yes," he agreed. "Many
people love him."

"You know I've no intention of—taking any
action. But—I had to tell you. He can't very well
stay with us, after this."

"How much has he stolen?" Caterson asked
calmly.

Champernoon made a swift gesture. "Not out-
right theft," he objected. "But—an indirection!" He
hesitated. "Tony's done well for us," he explained
then. "He's built up a good line of customers, increasing all the time. One of them is Dan Rimmon,
the contractor. You know him?"

"A good man," Caterson assented. "He does honest work, and pays his bills. He built the tennis courts and the club house at our country club, down at the shore."

"I suppose Tony met him down there," Champernoon suggested. "At any rate, he persuaded Rimmon that we could make money for him if he'd put his surplus capital to work, whenever he wasn't using it to finance his jobs. Rimmon had never tried the investment market at all, and he knew nothing about us, but he trusted Tony. Tony brought in the account, and handled it; and Rimmon always insisted on dealing only with him."

"I understand," Caterson nodded.

Champernoon continued. "Well," he said, "Rimmon telephoned the office this morning, two or three times, asking for Tony. Tony wasn't there and we couldn't locate him. I offered to take the call, but he insisted on speaking to Tony. But at last, since Tony did not come in, he reluctantly talked to me. He said he had spoken to Tony last Friday, asking him for forty-eight hundred dollars to meet a bill for material. He directed Tony to bring him the check to-morrow at noon. But today he found it necessary to leave town for a few days, so he wanted to get the money before he left. I promised to send it to his office at once."

Caterson sat in silent attention.

"Rimmon's securities were in our office," Champernoon explained. "Tony—since he handled the account, and the circumstances were somewhat unusual —had access to them. I went to the box, and I found that a five thousand dollar bond—Preston Electric Convertible four and a half, 1942—was gone. It was not checked off on Rimmon's card, but it was gone.

"And I find that Tony borrowed thirty-six hundred on this particular bond at the Prince Street Trust. Jim Dane is their credit man. You know Jim."

"Certainly!"

"I got the information without—arousing any questions," Champernoon explained. "But the facts are sure."

Caterson seized on a straw of hope. "Perhaps Tony got the money to take to Rimmon."

Champernoon shook his head. "Rimmon didn't speak to Tony till Friday, but Tony had already pledged the bond on Wednesday. Also, Rimmon wanted forty-eight hundred, and Tony only borrowed thirty-six hundred. And—Tony made no report of the transaction at our office."

The other man considered, and the lines in his face seemed to deepen. "Of course, you sent Rimmon the money?" he suggested.

"Of course."

A heavy silence fell, and it persisted for minutes on end, till Caterson asked at last quietly: "Have you any information as to why Tony might need money?"

"None at all," Champernoon confessed.

"He has no margin account with you?"

"No. We don't encourage our men in that sort of thing."

"He came to me, some time since," Caterson remarked, "to borrow five thousand dollars. I was— surprised, because he has a liberal income from a trust fund, and he had ten thousand in cash on his graduation. It worried me, but I gave him the money, without asking any questions." He hesitated. "Tony thanked me for not questioning him," he remembered wistfully. "But—perhaps I was wrong."

"He made no explanation?"

"I hoped he would," Caterson admitted. "But he did not do so."

Champernoon could find nothing to say to this. Caterson sat thoughtful for a while, and at last he drew his check book from the drawer and wrote a check and handed it to Champernoon. Champernoon made some protest, but Caterson only smiled.

"That of course comes first of all," he insisted mildly. "As for the rest—— Champernoon, do you mind if I wait to see what Tony will do? It may be that he had a sudden need for money, and was reluctant to borrow again from me, and took this means, intending to correct the situation in a day or two. He must be planning to get the money for Rimmon somehow, and he may come to me, if other means fail. I'd like to have the first move come from him."

Champernoon said steadily: "You know I'll do whatever you want."

"We will wait, then," Caterson repeated. "See what Tony decides to do." And he added slowly: "I—can't help thinking he'll choose the straightforward way, in the end."

The other man rose, nodding, relieved that this interview was done. "I don't know where he is," he remarked. "He hasn't been in the office today."

Caterson smiled in a weary fashion. "I suspect he is trying to borrow from his friends," he suggested. "I—believe I know Tony. He will exhaust every means before he comes again to me." And he added: "You might let me know if he corrects the situation, in the office."

"Of course," Champernoon assented. "I'll keep you informed."

When he was gone, Caterson did not move. He sat quietly at his desk, in a sort of smiling stupor; and he waited all that afternoon, vainly hoping that Tony would come to him, or telephone. But Tony did not come, and when it was time for Caterson to start for the station, his anxiety drove him to phone Mrs. Caterson.

"Anything I can bring home?" he asked, too casually. "Anything you need from town? Will Richards meet me? Or Sandy, or Tony?"

Tony, she replied, planned to spend the night in town. He had telephoned earlier in the afternoon.

"I wasn't here," she explained, and she added laughingly: "He left word that it was business, but Miss Delevan's show opens tonight! I expect he'll be there!"

She was, Caterson thought, not so much amused as she pretended; and it occurred to him that perhaps she felt a mother's quick jealousy of her son's attention to any other woman. He smiled at this reflection.

But later, on the train, he found his thoughts returning to Miss Delevan.

XXXII

HE and Mrs. Caterson were alone that evening in the cottage at the shore. Caterson had hoped that Sandy might be there; he was more and more apt to discover in Sandy a comforting strength and solidity, and it seemed to him that to discuss this matter with the young man would in some degree relieve the burden which he himself was called upon to bear. But when he reached the house, Mrs. Caterson told him that Sandy and Nina had driven to town, to dine there and see Barbs Delevan's show.

"I think her friends are planning to give her a riotous reception," she explained.

Caterson stifled his regret at Sandy's absence. "I expect so," he agreed; and he added in a tone he tried to make jovial: "We might go in ourselves, Edith! Lend our voices to the huzzas!"

She smiled, shook her head. "I'd rather be here with you," she assured him. "I always like being just with you; and somehow, I never cared so very much for Miss Delevan." And a little later, she linked her arm through his and they moved toward the dining room. "We get along pretty well together, don't we Joe," she remarked. "After all these years."

"Well," he said judicially, his eyes laughing down at her. "I have a feeling sometimes that we're too

serene. Need a little fireworks, now and then. I sometimes try to start a row, a good old hair-pulling;
but you're a hard person with whom to quarrel, my
dear."

"That's not very complimentary," she protested,
while he seated her. "You mean I haven't any
character!"

"There's something lacking in you," he assented
with a sober mirth. "Perhaps that is it. I've often
wondered."

She made a wry face at him across the table.
"Beast!" she exclaimed. "I've as much character as
you, only it isn't all one kind."

And Caterson chuckled, and made some teasing
retort. It was a relief to him to find her tonight thus
ready for empty talk; for the interchange of foolish, tender pleasantries that rippled the surface of
their lives as warm summer breezes ripple the surface of a still pool, without disturbing the depths. He
was able almost to forget that hideous thing which
did in fact possess his mind. He saw her happy, and
this did always tend to his own happiness; it was
only when now and then he thought how agonized
she must be if she knew that a shadow swept across
the mirror of his eyes.

Yet he played his part so well that she, who knew
his inmost heart, did not suspect him. After dinner
they read aloud together for a while, as they liked
to do; and later, just before going to bed, they
walked arm in arm down across the lawns to the
rocky shore. Although this was September, the night

was warm and the stars were clear and the surges broke lazily on the shingle beach below the boulder strewn point on which the cottage stood. The salt air filled their nostrils searchingly, and made them drowsy, and they came contentedly back to the house by and by, and so to bed.

When they were almost asleep, Mrs. Caterson, in that semi-conscious state which precedes actual slumber, sensed the fact that Caterson was lying unnaturally still, and she murmured affectionately:

"Everything all right, Joe?"

"Eh?" he exclaimed. "Guess I was asleep."

His pretense half-deceived her. "I'm sorry! Did I wake you?"

"What did you say?"

"I just asked—is everything all right?" Her tone was dreamy; and he reassured her, and she whispered something, and so spoke no more.

Caterson, though not so readily as she, did eventually fall asleep. He woke to bright sunshine, a cloudless sky, a warm and radiant morning. Mrs. Caterson was still asleep beside him, and he rose and departed to the shower. He heard her stirring presently, and they went down to breakfast together. Sandy, she suggested on the stairs, would have been late in coming home the night before, would doubtless sleep till noon; but he was as a matter of fact only a moment behind them at the breakfast table. At the boy's appearance, Caterson felt a quick lift of relief, as though in Sandy he would find a strong and sure ally.

Sandy kissed his mother cheerfully, and he dropped his hand upon Caterson's shoulder as he went around to his own chair. "What a day!" he cried. "September's the best month of all, for me!"

Mrs. Caterson smiled in affectionate derision. "You're so good humored lately, Sandy! I wonder if the fact that you're going to be married so soon has anything to do with it. Do you suppose it has, Joe? He's a regular Sunny Jim, isn't he? If it rains, he loves the rain; and if it shines he loves the sun. You're so cheerful that you're tiresome, Sandy!"

Sandy grinned. "All right," he agreed, and he managed a frown. "I'll grouch a bit, then! What's the matter with this grapefruit? Tastes like straw! Gosh, this coffee's rank! Where the whoop-de-do is my eggs, woman, anyhow?"

Mrs. Caterson threw up her hand in laughing surrender. "Mercy! I like the other better," she protested. "Go ahead and be happy, then, if you must, Sandy. I'll try to bear the strain."

Sandy chuckled. "Well, it won't be long now," he reminded her. "Nina'll soon take me off your hands!"

Caterson saw his wife's hand stray to her throat in that gesture which always suggested a sudden, wistful pain. He thought they would miss Sandy; and he asked:

"How was the show, Sandy? Good party last night?"

"Yes," the boy agreed, though with no particular enthusiasm in his tone. "The house wasn't big, but we made enough noise to make up, I guess."

"Did you like the play?" his mother prompted.

"Pretty good," he assented. "It's not just the sort of thing that hits me. The girl in it's not so hot; sort of a vampire, or gold digger, or whatever. I'd have wrung her neck, if it was me."

"That was Miss Delevan?" Caterson suggested; and Sandy nodded.

"She was good in the part, too," he admitted. "Of course, she's just the same on the stage as off, just her natural self. It must come easy to her."

Caterson, after a moment, inquired in a carefully casual tone: "You mean she's a—gold digger—off the stage as well as on?"

Sandy hesitated. "Well," he confessed at last. "She's loaded down with stuff, rings, and bracelets and things. She must be getting a whopping big salary or—something."

Caterson lighted a cigarette, and his eyes were bleak; and Mrs. Caterson poured Sandy a fresh cup of coffee.

"I suppose you all went back to see her," she remarked.

"Oh, sure," he nodded. "Regular party on the stage after the curtain. Lob Dudley had ordered a big supper sent in, and we managed some music and so on." He chuckled. "Dudley's crazy about her, they say. He gave her quite a rush in London, a year ago last summer, till they had some sort of row; but I guess they've made it up now. They act so, anyway."

"Tony was there, of course?" Mrs. Caterson suggested; but Sandy shook his head.

"He was around after the first act," he explained. "He had to beat it before the party, though. Business, I guess. He's certainly a busy man." He lifted his coffee cup. "I thought he might come back later, but he didn't show."

Caterson asked slowly: "How did you like Miss Delevan? As well as ever?" It occurred to him, as he put the question, that Sandy's judgment in this matter would be worth having; that Sandy's appraisal of the girl would be sound.

Sandy answered, a little awkwardly: "Why—she's changed, seemed to me." And he added, after a moment: "Of course, Barbs was always as hard as nails, or pretended to be. That was her line. But I think it's more than a line now; more like the real thing. Maybe she's worn it so long it's come to fit her."

"How do you mean, Sandy?" Mrs. Caterson inquired. "How has she changed?"

"Well, I had a feeling that she's just as hard as she pretends to be," he admitted. "And—there's something defiant in the way she talks. As though she thinks people are criticizing her in their minds, and wants to show them she doesn't give a hoot. And she's so darned patronizing; treated the rest of the girls like so many country cousins."

"Conceited? Inflated by her success?"

Sandy hesitated, and he chuckled doubtfully. "Why—no," he replied. "It didn't seem to me so.

It rather struck me that she was—that her attitude was defensive. You know how a little man will sometimes sort of strut, to make himself seem bigger. That sort of thing."

Their breakfast was done, and Caterson pushed back his chair. Mrs. Caterson asked: "Did Nina think as you do?"

"Nina—thought she was hateful," Sandy confessed, with a sudden grin. "She was furious at her, all the way home. I never saw Nina so worked up about anything. Honestly, she was funny."

Mrs. Caterson nodded contentedly. "Then I'm glad Tony didn't go back for the party," she remarked. "He probably felt as you do about her. I expect that's why he stayed away." She rose, spoke to her husband. "Richards will be up in a few minutes, Joe, to take you to the train."

Caterson nodded, and as Mrs. Caterson departed on some business connected with the administration of her household, he asked his son hopefully:

"Going up to town today, Sandy? Go along with me?"

Sandy hesitated. "I'm planning to see Nina this morning," he confessed. "But I expect to go up this afternoon."

"Then perhaps we can come home together, Caterson proposed. He was increasingly hungry for the companionship of this boy he was so soon to lose.

"Right," Sandy assented readily. "I'll drop in at the office, in time for the train." He filled his pipe, and looked toward the door through which his mother had departed. "See Tony yesterday, did you, father?" he asked, in a lower tone.

"No, he was busy all day," Caterson explained.

"I didn't tell mother," Sandy confessed. "But—I had a word with him last night." He hesitated, then went plunging on. "That's why I'm going up today. To try and get hold of him." And he added: "He was—ugly drunk, last night; and, father, he looked terribly. Sick, and—frightened—and tortured, and wild!"

Caterson asked quietly: "What was he doing? Making himself conspicuous, Sandy?"

"He tried to borrow money from Lob Dudley," Sandy explained, and there was a half-terrified bewilderment in his tones. "And—he hates the sight of Lob! I don't understand his doing that. Lob laughed at him, and they came near a fight in the smoking room. I got Tony out into the air, thought I'd bring him home; but I had to go in to explain to Nina, and Tony got away before I could get outside again."

There was in him now none of that loyal reticence which is the habit of youth; this was an emergency, demanding the truth. He went on steadily: "If he'd try to borrow from Lob—feeling about him the way he does—he needs it mighty bad, father. That's why I'm worried." He hesitated. "And I—thought I'd see Barbs, too."

"You think there is some—relation between

them?" Caterson asked, his tone steady, but his lips as white as marble.

Sandy met his father's eyes reluctantly; but before he could reply, Mrs. Caterson came in to say that Richards was at the door, and Caterson had to depart to catch his train, his question still unanswered.

He rode alone to the station. The newsboy there gave him his usual morning paper; and once on the train he opened it, and his heedless eyes scanned the columns. Then Mr. Buckel got on at the next station, and sat down beside him, and they talked together all the way to town of many things. They spoke only casually of Nina and Sandy, avoiding that topic with a masculine reticence; their talk was rather of politics, of the market, of business conditions. In such impersonal concerns Caterson found for his pain an anodyne.

In the city, they walked together from the station toward their offices, till at a certain corner their ways separated and Caterson went on alone. He moved slowly, heavily. His problem now was pitilessly definite. He must somehow this day get in touch with Tony. He had asked Champernoon for delay, but—he could delay no longer. Tony needed him, and this need was desperate; it was his task to find and to defend the boy, against himself or any enemy.

Yet it was hard to know how he should begin. He half expected to receive word from Champernoon that Tony had returned; but no such word came, and when Caterson asked Miss Swain whether Champernoon had phoned, she shook her head. So he attacked his mail, trying to focus his thoughts on the problems it presented. Tedlock came in on some matter of the firm's business, and they were together for a while; and Tedlock, departing, saw the sudden sagging of Caterson's cheeks as the man's thoughts returned to this grief that gnawed at him, and he asked a question.

"Feeling all right, are you? Look a little tired."

"Quite all right," Caterson assured him rigidly. He might later call on Tedlock for help or sympathy; but this was not the time.

So the other man went away, and Caterson continued to plod through his mail, dictating the necessary replies. But his attention wandered; he broke off sometimes in the middle of a letter, to sit in staring silence, and he had to ask Miss Swain to read what she had recorded before he could go on.

She perceived his distraction, and watched him with a sympathetic scrutiny, for she had served him long and loyally. His concern now was plain for her to see, and it puzzled her.

She had by and by some answer to the question in her thoughts; for Caterson's desk phone rang, and since it was near her chair, she answered it.

"It's your son," she reported. "He's outside, wants to see you!"

Caterson came convulsively to his feet. "Tony?" he whispered, through dry lips; and at her assent, "Send him in," he said huskily.

She conveyed these directions to the operator, and when she had returned the receiver to its hook, Caterson nodded her dismissal.

"I'll ring for you," he told her.

Miss Swain, departing, met Tony face to face on the threshold. The boy's countenance was a mask of agony. As she closed the door, she looked back and saw Caterson, at his son's entrance, drop limply in his chair.

XXXIII

THIS boy who had been his son these twenty years was become a stranger! Thus ran Caterson's first thought. Tony came in, and closed the door behind him, and leaned against it, his shoulders pressing the panels as though he might collapse there. And Caterson looked at him as upon a stranger!

Yet he must not let Tony see. This was like one of those encounters in a crowd when someone whose countenance is vaguely familiar hails you by name; when you have to pretend a recognition that is pretense and nothing more; when you must carry on an extended conversation without revealing your own bewilderment. This young man who had been for twenty years his son was a stranger now.

Caterson had time to muster resolution; for Tony stayed a moment leaning against the door, as though to wait while strength flowed into his limbs. His eyes were angry with congested blood; his cheeks sagged and there were deep lines in them; his shoulders drooped. He wore in only the shabbiest fashion any resemblance to the Tony whom Caterson had known and loved; to that fine youngster of whom he had always been so proud. This could not be that young man; this haggard boy was a stranger!

The word rang persistently in Caterson's ears;

yet as Tony moved, and came slowly toward the desk, the other man found his strength again. He even smiled; and he said mildly:

"Good morning, Tony."

Tony nodded. "Morning, father," he returned, and he sat down in the chair at the end of the desk. There, Caterson remembered, Champernoon had sat the afternoon before. Caterson tipped back in his chair, pressed his finger tips together, nodded amiably.

"Missed you at home, Tony," he remarked. "You ought to try to be there more. Your mother can't do long without you, you know."

Tony grimaced. "I've been—tied up," he explained. "Couldn't get away."

"You might telephone," Caterson urged cordially. "She likes to talk to you, even over the wire."

"Yes, I ought to do that," Tony agreed. He took out his cigarette case. His hand was shaking, and his lips were pale, and he broke one match before his cigarette was lighted. Caterson lighted one of his own.

"Busy?" Tony asked, with a glance at the desk where unanswered letters still waited in a little pile.

"Not particularly," Caterson assured him. "And —I'd always put off business for a visit from you, you know." He wondered if his tone was natural. It seemed to him that even Tony—who was sometimes apt to be blind to the distress of others—must remark his perturbation.

But if Tony did see his father's distress, it was

without comment. He stubbed out the freshly lighted cigarette in the tray at the end of the desk; and abruptly, with that old gallant lift of his head, something defiant in the gesture now, he said:

"You told me one day that if I needed anything from you, I could have it, father."

"Of course," Caterson assured him. "You must have known that without the telling."

"I need some money," Tony blurted.

Caterson nodded cheerfully. "Yes?" He reached for his check book, and without looking at the boy, he nevertheless saw Tony's quick movement, at once of relief and of despair. Caterson opened the book; he dated a check, and wrote Tony's name on the proper line, and without filling in any amount, he set his own signature below. He tore the slip out and passed it across the desk top.

Tony stared at it, and he swallowed hard. "I need four thousand," he confessed uncertainly.

"You can fill it in," Caterson suggested. "Take more, if you require it."

The young man slowly folded the slip of paper between his shaking fingers. He tucked it into the pocket of his vest, and for a moment he did not move. Caterson, watching him, hoped so desperately that Tony would speak; would tell him even a part of the truth, so that he might find some opening to offer the boy a help more tangible. He said no word, waiting upon Tony; but after an interminable time, Tony only mumbled:

"Much obliged."

And he got to his feet, turned slowly toward the door.

He was half way across the office before Caterson spoke. The older man said then: "Tony, wait a minute. If you've time?"

Tony checked, stood with his back to his father. When he did turn at last, there was something like a sneer on his lips, as though this recall were expected, as though he had known from the first that the older man's generosity was too good to be true. He came back with dragging feet, sat down once more in the chair.

"All right, fire away," he said sullenly. "What do you want to know?"

Caterson shook his head, and he smiled reassuringly. "Nothing, son," he insisted gently. "I don't propose to question you, Tony."

Tony slumped in the chair, motionless, his head hanging.

"But—I am glad to listen, any time you want to talk to me," Caterson reminded him.

"I—haven't wanted to distress you and mother," Tony explained miserably.

Caterson, after a moment, replied: "I've not spoken to your mother. There is no need of that. As for distressing me . . ." He hesitated, shook his head. "Never mind me," he said. "But Tony, even though I don't interrogate you, I must ask myself questions."

And after a moment he continued:

"That's a part of my obligation as your father,

son; to try to keep an eye on you, and if I see you are on the wrong road, to try and set you right."

Once he had begun, he spoke more readily.

"You know, I'm not likely to reproach you for anything. I only want to help you, if I can. Obviously, you are under some heavy financial drain. It may be through speculation. I'm not an expert in such matters; but Mr. Tedlock is, and Mr. Champernoon is, and either one of them would be glad to advise you, if you require advice. I need not even know about it, if you prefer I should not know.

"And I can see that your health is suffering, Tony. That must be clear to you, as it is to me. Good health is an important asset. You know that."

Tony said rebelliously: "I'm all right. Short of sleep, that's all."

"It occurs to me as possible that you are drinking too much," Caterson suggested.

Tony looked at the older man with a quick glance in which there was a faint alarm. "Who said so?" he challenged.

"Your appearance," Caterson replied. "Your hand shakes, and there is a stale odor about you, son."

Tony laughed bitterly. "Sandy tell you he saw me last night?" he asked suddenly.

Caterson met his eyes. "You mean by that that you were drinking, and that Sandy saw you? It was a mistake, Tony, whether anyone saw you or no."

And he added, preventing the other's word.

"That need not be argued, I suppose. But—

another thing has seemed to me possible; there may be some entanglement of a more personal nature."

His eyes suddenly clouded with old memories. "Tony," he said frankly, "I've lived through a good many chapters of life, myself. If you ever come to me for advice, you may find me ready with first hand experiences upon which to draw for counsel." He relaxed in his chair, spoke very casually. "I've been drunk in my time, and I've—made other mistakes that young men are apt to make. I know something about such matters."

Tony grinned in a sudden affectionate respect. "Oh, I guess you were a devil in your day," he said, in cheerful raillery. "Yes sir, I expect you were a gay young dog!"

Caterson smiled in acknowledgment of the other's jesting tone, yet he insisted:

"No one ever came to be fifty years old without having first been twenty-three or four, you know."

Tony's eyes became sombre, and there was something hopeless in them. "You think I'm—mixed up with a girl?" he asked, his tone sullen.

"I think only what you tell me," Caterson assured him. "But whatever you may tell me, Tony, you'll find me—capable of understanding." And he added in a wistful appeal: "I don't think you've ever found me the sort of father who flies into a rage, storms and scolds and threatens. I don't think I've ever sought to terrify you, have I, son?"

Tony shook his head, grinned faintly. "I've never been scared of you, no sir."

Caterson made a gesture with one hand. "I'm—groping, Tony. But I'd like to make some contact with you, son. Give me a hand, if you can."

Tony sat silent for a while, his brow twisted in thought. He said at last, almost explosively:

"There's nothing wrong, father! I need some money on a matter of business, that's all! Maybe I'm tired, working pretty steady, out late and so on. A fellow just starting in has to dig like a woodchuck to get a foothold, and I'm digging. And—I'm swinging a deal, just now; but I'll come out of it all right."

His eyes for a moment wavered with mounting terror.

"I'll come out of it!" he persisted. "It may all straighten out today, sir. Really. But give me credit, whether it does or not. I'm working like a terrier, father."

Caterson nodded. "Mr. Champernoon told me so, yesterday," he assented.

"Champernoon?" There was a gasp of dismay in Tony's word. "Where'd you see him?"

"He dropped in here," Caterson casually explained; and he added: "They've handled my account for twenty years, you know."

He saw reassurance fight with fear in the boy's countenance; but in the end Tony seized on reassurance hungrily. "Well, that ought to satisfy you," he insisted, and he got to his feet. "Thanks again for the lift," he repeated, fumbling in his pocket where the check lay as he turned toward the door

"All right," Caterson desperately agreed. "But that's enough of business. Stop a while, Tony. I enjoy visits from you. Tell me about yourself."

"Nothing much to tell," Tony protested.

"I suppose you'll see a lot of Miss Delevan while she's in town," the older man remarked; and Tony's head jerked around, and Tony's eyes bored into those of his father, and Caterson saw a fear like panic in the boy's glance. For a long moment they were rigid thus; then Caterson added calmly:

"You've known her so long!"

"Oh, I probably won't see much of her," Tony replied at last, huskily, and he turned once more toward the door.

Caterson said no more; there was no more he could say. But when Tony was half way across the office, the boy stopped and stood for a moment as though in thought; and then he swung around to face his father again.

"You know, you're mighty decent to me, sir," he said uncertainly. His cheek was crimson now. "I do appreciate it."

"I want to go along with you, shoulder to shoulder," Caterson reminded him, almost pleadingly.

Tony nodded. "I guess I do need you," he confessed, sullenly, yet yielding too. "I'll see you tonight," he promised.

"You'll be home?"

"Yes. Maybe I'll get straightened out today." He hesitated, and his eyes were shadowed by a dreadful fear. "I think so! But if I don't—or anyway, sir, I'd like to talk it over with you."

"Tonight?"

"Yes. If mother needn't know."

Caterson smiled in a rush of gratitude and thankfulness. "Tony," he promised. "Whatever this is, it's between you and me. You can make any conditions you want. I'm ready to go to any lengths to have your confidence, son."

Tony stood a moment longer, as though he might speak even now; but in the end he cried, with a curt nod: "Tonight, then!"

And he bolted through the door, something like flight in this departure.

A moment after he had gone, Caterson started from his chair. The rigid self control which during this interview he had exercised gave way; he was lashed by a sudden hideous terror. That door which had closed between him and Tony was so firm, so fatally decisive. There was to his tormented imagination a finality about it; it was as though that closed door was never to reopen.

He lunged across the office and wrenched the door wide, and he stared along the corridor toward the elevators.

But Tony was not in sight. The boy was gone.

XXXIV

TONY left his father's office in a state of mind that was strange to the young man, a sort of wistful humility. Caterson's attitude had almost melted him, had almost brought him to the point of crying, "Mea culpa!" and throwing himself at his father's knees. But with the stubbornness of youth he deferred that surrender; he broke away, yielding only the promise that tonight, at home in the cottage at the shore, he would make some explanation.

If he had stayed a moment longer, his composure must have broken in a flood of forthright tears. Like an erring small boy, he had thought it would be incredibly sweet to tell the whole ugly truth, and be forgiven. But once away from the office, he knew he could never do that. To do so would be to bring upon his father and his mother a sorrow and a grief which he could never deliberately inflict on them; it was unbearable to him to see, even in anticipation, the tender reprobation in their eyes. He had scarce reached the street before he began to seek to devise some tale to tell his father, in order to evade that promise he had made.

He had no scruple in planning this deception. It was for their happiness.

Yet after a moment, matters more pressing drove

that problem from his mind. Dan Rimmon wanted forty-eight hundred dollars at noon, and it was already past eleven. It would be necessary first to repay his own loan and redeem the Preston Electric bond which he had pledged; then to arrange the sale of that bond; and after that to get a check from Champernoon for Rimmon. The time was desperately short; and he hurried his steps, dodging through the crowds, nodding inattentively to the occasional familiar countenance.

He had almost reached the Prince Street Trust before he perceived a way to save time. The thought came to him like a reprieve, so that he slowed his pace, and smiled, and his breathing slackened. He even stopped for a moment outside the bank to exchange a word with a casual acquaintance; and once inside, he crossed at a leisurely pace to the writing counter and drew out the blank check his father had given him and filled in the amount. But he made it for forty-eight hundred dollars, instead of the four thousand he had asked. Caterson's account would stand it, he knew; and Tony could thus avoid the necessity of any immediate redemption and resale of the pledged bond. At the teller's wicket he drew the cash, in denominations up to twenty dollars. Rimmon had asked for a check, but he could assert that he had misunderstood, could say he thought the contractor wanted payroll money. There was no time to get a check from Champernoon; and a cashier's check might seem to Rimmon strange.

So Tony took the cash; but before he left the bank

he stopped to instruct Dane, the credit man, to sell the pledged bond and repay the loan, and credit the difference to Tony's personal account. There would be time enough later to arrange the matter on the books at Champernoon's.

Thus Tony, with the quick resilience of youth, was by the time he left the bank completely at his ease again. All his present difficulties were solved, and the terrific burden which for three or four days past had threatened to crush him was lifted from his shoulders. He felt a tremendous gratitude to his father; and so greatly was he moved by this emotion that his eyes filled with sentimental tears. He must, he vowed, always strive to avoid distressing the older man, and his mother, too; they had been so finely generous to him.

He went smilingly toward Rimmon's office, as jubilant as a small boy who has evaded the punishment that seemed inescapable; he had a ridiculous impulse to run, and he called a cheerful word to every passing face that was in the least degree familiar.

He felt like bursting into song.

He reached Dan Rimmon's office at five minutes before noon, and he remarked the fact with a jubilant satisfaction. This was good business, this prompt exactitude. Forty-eight hundred at noon on Tuesday; those were Rimmon's orders. Well, this was noon, and the money was here on the dot. The girl at the switchboard was pretty. He smiled at her and asked for Mr. Rimmon.

And she replied:

"Mr. Rimmon is out of town!"

Tony's smile faded. "Out of town?" he echoed, in a dawning dismay. He had been, a moment before, a conqueror, astride the world; her simple phrase made him totter like a colossus about to tumble to destruction. "Out of town?"

"I'll let you speak to Miss Judson," the girl suggested; and Tony nodded eagerly. Miss Judson was Rimmon's secretary, a middle-aged woman of a proved efficiency and wisdom. Tony had sometimes been faintly afraid of her, but he was hungry now for any reassurance; and when a moment later she appeared, he strode swiftly toward her, and he produced the roll of bills.

"Here's the money Mr. Rimmon wanted," he explained. "I suppose he left word with you. And when she stared at the fat bundle of currency in a quick astonishment, he added hurriedly: "He wanted it for a payroll, he said, so I brought the cash."

She shook her head. "But Mr. Rimmon attended to that yesterday, before he left," she said severely. "He had to meet a bill for material. It wasn't due till today, but he wanted to pay it before he left, so he got a check from Mr. Champernoon."

Tony was back on his heels; he had to fight for balance, as though he had received an actual physical blow.

"A check?" he repeated. "Mr. Champernoon?"

"Mr. Rimmon telephoned the office, tried to get

you," she assured him. "But he couldn't catch you in, and so finally he talked to Mr. Champernoon."

Tony's dry lips scraped one against the other as he tried to speak. His thoughts were racing, in a swift comprehension of what must have happened. Champernoon, having talked with Rimmon, would have gone to the contractor's box to select a security to be sold. So—Champernoon knew! And—Champernoon had seen his father yesterday!

The revelation blinded and confused Tony; he could not wholly grasp, in this first moment, all the implications of the situation. He heard himself babbling:

"I see! I've been out of town, hurried back to attend to this, didn't happen to see Mr. Champernoon. Sorry. I'll straighten it out at the office."

Miss Judson, he perceived, was watching him with a disapproving intensity, and he backed away from her, stuffing the money loosely into his pocket, tremulously anxious to get it out of sight. . . . A little later, he found himself on the street, wandering at hazard. Champernoon knew, and Champernoon had seen his father yesterday.

So—his father knew!

Tony might, if he had remembered his father's forbearance an hour before, have found some comfort in this memory; but in this moment, characteristically, his thoughts centered wholly on himself, and on his own dark guilt, thus by mischance exposed. Champernoon knew, and Champernoon would discharge him. His father knew, and tonight he must face his father! The very flesh on Tony's bones crawled with dread of that encounter. The boy, who had learned to love success and approval and praise, cringed and shuddered at the thought of facing blame; his thoughts twisted in a pitiable despair, seeking some evasion. There must be a way to becloud the issue, to gloss the truth; there must be some garment in which he might dress the black facts more becomingly.

A street clock by and by told him it was past one; he had promised to be home in time for dinner. Five hours remained at his command; five hours in which to find some protective subterfuge.

Tony was not used to feeling hatred; he had a natural affection for the world and all its works, but now his soul twisted in a sudden fury. He hated Sandy, who might have averted all this ugly business by a larger loan a week ago; and he hated Lob Dudley, and he thought of Barbs Delevan, and his muscles constricted murderously. Fear had long since taught him hate for her; he had learned under the lash. When he turned now toward where she dwelt, he was half mad with rage.

Then a quick panic flicked him on the raw. His father had spoken of Barbs. This, too, perhaps, his father knew! True, Caterson had not revealed that knowledge; but neither had he given any sign that he knew what Champernoon must the day before have told him. Yet desperately Tony seized on hope; this much at least from the wreck could yet be saved.

And he hurried toward the hotel where Barbs had her suite, moving more and more swiftly, racing to stop her mouth, to silence her by some persuasion. His fingers curled around the roll of bills in his pocket. Here was a weapon successful heretofore, now ready to his hand.

He saw her hotel a block ahead; then half a block. He was within twenty paces of its portals when a familiar figure emerged, and without having seen Tony, turned in the opposite direction. Tony rubbed his eyes and stared again to be sure; but there could be no mistaking. That was Sandy, coming out of Barbs' hotel!

The implication, that Sandy had seen Barbs, shattered for a moment the last structure of strength in Tony: yet instantly, like a drowning man, he seized on one straw of hope. It might be merely coincidence that brought Sandy here; and Tony, hurrying lest his brother turn and discover him, dodged into the revolving doors. He did not wait to telephone up and announce his coming. In an instant he was in the corridor outside Barbs' suite; in a moment more her maid had admitted him.

He saw Barbs across the room at her desk. She rose to receive him, and Tony stumbled toward her. Then he remembered the maid, and stopped to give the girl his hat, and to wait till she was out of the way.

When he swung back to Barbs, she was smiling in a dry amusement at his haste; and he asked her sharply:

"Was Sandy up here?"

She nodded tauntingly. "Yes. We had such a pleasant call!"

"Did you tell him?" he demanded.

She chose a cigarette from a little silver box on the desk and lighted it; she crossed the room with that swaggering walk which had proved so amusing on the stage. "I? Tell him?" she echoed; and she chuckled. "There's not much your brother needs to be told."

"Did you tell him?" he insisted.

"I didn't have to," she assured him, and she smiled again, maddeningly; for her word had worked a physical change in the boy. He seemed to shrink before her eyes; and he looked to right and left, despairingly. So, Sandy knew! But if Sandy knew, then his father and mother too would know. Sandy would feel bound to tell them. They would know! Not only the other, but this blacker business, too!

The world collapsed about him, and he began to laugh. This laughter of his was a shudder of sound; the hideous mirth of one in a delirium of pain. But there was in it something which loosed in the woman who faced him the springs of an ancient hatred, long by cupidity restrained.

"Laugh, you idiot!" she cried. "Laugh, you poor fool!"

He said apologetically: "I'm sorry, Barbs. I wasn't really laughing. Shock to me, that's all. You see, Sandy'll tell the folks! He'll think it's his duty to."

She was staring at him with lowered, furious head. "You want to laugh? I'll give you something to laugh at!"

"I wasn't laughing," he protested defensively. "But Golly, Barbs, if they know, there's nothing left! What do you want of me?"

"I don't want anything of you!" she told him stridently.

"You've had—quite a lot," he reminded her.

She threw back her head again, and her harsh mirth lashed him like a whip. "I don't want anything from you!" she repeated. "Except to see the look on your face when I tell you—this!"

She strode suddenly to the desk, took from a drawer there a sheaf of papers, swung back to him.

"Listen, idiot!" she cried. "You may not laugh at this, but others will, when they hear! You see, my asinine child, the joke is on you. Listen to me! I adopted a baby in Switzerland. Adopted, do you understand? His father's name was Johann Lutz, an Alpine guide. The mother was dead, and Johann Lutz was killed in a fall while I was there. I adopted the brat! Do you understand?"

"Adopted?" he echoed, in a dull bewilderment. He dropped blindly in a chair that chanced to be beside him. He tried to understand. "Adopted?" And he urged soothingly, as though to humor her: "Why, sure you did, Barbs. . . ."

She was convulsed with a hideous mirth. "Adopted, yes!" she repeated. "You don't believe me! You conceited idiot!" He felt the torrent of her scorn and hatred pour over him; he heard now and then a word, a phrase, the name of a town, of a Swiss canton. She rattled a paper before his eyes; he saw that it was some legal form, in a foreign tongue. And the world about him, like a house of blocks, went tumbling in confused destruction. . . .

Later, as this chaos passed and some order did emerge, one solid, hopeless fact remained. His father had heard truth from Champernoon; Sandy had heard another truth from Barbs. So they knew! This he must face; this hopeless grief in the eyes of those most dear to him; this shame for him where had dwelt only pride. The pride he had loved to see. . . .

He found himself by and by outside the hotel. He did not know how he came there, nor greatly care. The sun shone calmly, and the faces of the folk who passed him by were all serene. These people were happy and content and absorbed in their own concerns. They did not notice him, and Tony thought this strange; for it seemed to him there must be marks upon him, plain for all to see.

The fact that he was free of Barbs for good and all scarce occurred to him. He thought vaguely that with Lob Dudley at her beck she had no need of him; but she was no longer significant or important. The only certainty remaining was—that his father and his mother knew the worst of him, and he must face them presently.

His car was housed in a garage down town; he found himself entering the building, without knowing

how he had come so far. It was, he discovered, a
little past four; and he need not start home for
another hour. But the garage attendant had recognized him and wheeled his roadster out into the
floor; and Tony automatically got into place under
the wheel. He nodded to the man and meshed his
gears and turned into the street outside.

Traffic held him for a while in sluggish bonds, and
he fretted at this restraint; but by and by the road
began to open, and he pressed the throttle down.
There was relief in the routine of driving; there was
peace in this wedding of himself to a machine that
became a part of himself, responsive to his least
touch, the creature of his will. Just as a pianist plays
upon his instrument, so Tony manipulated the roadster now; he achieved a rhythm, the rhythm of the
road; the engine purred a pleasant song; he impro-
vised amusing cadenzas. Once when he dropped to
second gear at a traffic light, he found the louder
song of the motor, fierce and turbulent, sweet to his
ears; and he pressed the throttle hard, and at the
swelling, metallic roar of the gears, like the roar of
a great beast, he wished to shout in triumphant
response as to a challenge.

But presently he remembered that this abuse was
not for the engine's good; and he dropped into high
and went more easily. He began to relax at the
wheel. His emotions were in abeyance now. That
which awaited him, the hour in which he must confront his father and mother, had filled him with such
an agony of dread that his suffering brought its own

easement. They knew; there was no saving that; the case was a hopeless one.

There is peace in despair.

The road became at once easier and more difficult. There was less traffic, but the curves were sharper, and they were often blind. Once or twice he was near collision; and each escape acted on Tony like an intoxicant. And once, as he whirled past a roadside garage, he saw a motorcycle leaning against the gasoline pump. The roadster leaped under his thrust at the throttle; and he saw, in his mirror, a man in uniform run out and wheel the motorcycle into the road. Tony laughed delightedly; he trod the throttle and breathed deep, like a war horse which scents the battle afar.

He was almost disappointed when beyond the next town he came to a mile-long straightaway which revealed the fact that he had left his pursuer hopelessly behind.

A little later, the road approached the sea; it began to wind along the shore.

Tony's senses were in this hour keenly attuned, alive to every least impression. There was in him an alertness almost superhuman; he had in the smooth manipulation of the machine under his hand a sense of power and strength unbounded. It was as though destiny lay in the grip of his two hands. Nothing, in this moment, seemed beyond his reach and grasp; and his thoughts were as swift as his muscles were sure in their control of the throttle and the wheel.

He scarce saw the cars he passed, the pedestrians

along the road; but sometimes he caught the whisk of a white face turned to watch his roaring progress, and he laughed aloud at the dismay his speed evoked. The road ran uphill and down, but the power under his toe levelled these inequalities. His speed slackened only when on the narrowest curves his wheels threatened actually to leave the ground. For the rest, it amused him to keep the throttle pressed down to the floor.

He began to climb a steeper ascent; and since he had driven this way so many times, the spot was instantly familiar. Two or three hundred yards ahead, at the top of the grade, the road rounded a rocky shoulder, high above the sea. There was a cottage above the road, and a summer house below, and the turn was not an easy one. He grinned as at a challenge, and held the throttle down; in the briefest seconds, he came to the top of the ascent, could see what lay before him here.

There was an old man in a limp Panama hat, directly in his way. The old man must have come up from the summer house below the road; he was crossing to climb to his cottage above, where dinner would presently be ready for him. He had been down, no doubt, to watch the ever-changing sea; to watch the slow rollers break in a boiling confusion on the shards and boulders a hundred feet below.

Tony swerved toward the left side of the road in order to pass in front of this old man; but as he did so, a car appeared around the curve, coming up the grade beyond, not twenty yards away.

This was one of those moments when time stands still; it seemed to Tony that he had leisure for a long consideration of the situation, for a deliberate determination of what it was best to do. The approaching car blocked half the road; the old man in the Panama blocked the other half. On the left, solid ledges rose; on the right, beyond a low, flimsy wall of loose stones, there was a hundred foot plunge to sure destruction.

Tony nodded in a calm decision. The old man had lived long, and no doubt happily. He was about to die.

This much he thought while he swerved back to his proper side of the road. The old man was scarce ten yards ahead of his fenders; and not even a young man could have leaped to safety now.

But there was still time for Tony to think; for a sudden and a jubilant comprehension. Here was offered him, in the last moment before he faced the bitter fruits of shame, triumph and fine victory. If he went on, he must endure long years of slow striving to retrieve the errors that were entered on his score; he must stand for an interminable time on trial, must labor to redeem himself by the slow drudgery he hated. And at best there could be only a partial redemption at the end. There would always be these red ink entries in the ledger of his life.

But—here was glory! Instead of grief and shame, he might bestow upon his father and mother at last a legacy of pride. He imagined headlines. "Sacrifices Life for Old Man. Former Football Star Drives Car

Over Cliff to Avoid Hitting Pedestrian." They
would grieve, yes; but with a tender sorrow that was
almost happiness, and with a fine and lofty pride.

Tony had always loved applause. Here was glory
now!

He had long since tried his brakes, but his speed
was too great; the car lurched, threatened to over-
turn. There was no time for brakes, nothing left for
him but this decision.

He embraced death like a lover. His wheels
plowed through the low wall. The car lurched and
toppled forward. Behind him he heard from the
other car a woman's shrill, terror-stricken scream.

His was a cry of triumph! Long after the sodden
crash far below the road, that cry, like the shout of
a victor in battle, seemed to hang ringing in the air,
before it receded and was lost in the serene blue
deeps of the cloudless sky.

XXXV

A DAY or two before Christmas, Mr. and Mrs. Caterson dined with Sandy and Nina in their apartment; and these four were happy there together. Time is a physician worth respecting; he can heal a grievous wound.

Caterson, watching his wife as he was apt to do, saw that she was happy. She grew older, but this became her. She was a little more quiet; but her happiness had deeper roots than in the old, laughing days. She had, he thought, met life, and comprehended it, and wedded with it willingly; she went forward now at peace and all serene.

He was learning serenity from her. There were in her depths of understanding which he glimpsed now and then, and in these glimpses seemed to perceive eternity. Tangible things of every day lost their dark reality seen through her eyes, which saw the deeper verities.

He wondered, sometimes, how much she did know and comprehend. He had never told her the truth about Tony; yet he sometimes suspected her of knowing without words. If she knew, she yet found happiness in the rightful pride which by his end Tony had bequeathed them. Even while the hurt was still an aching wound, she had said, almost contentedly:

"If Tony had time to know, he was glad, Joe. He'd love to end with so fine a gesture!"

Caterson did not speculate too deeply on how much she did understand. Her content was manifest; and in her peace, he found contentment too. So long as she was happy, he could not dwell in any final sorrow. . . .

Tonight Caterson watched Nina, too; and his eye on Sandy was full of pride. Life lay plain before Sandy, inviting him not to easy successes, but to battles in which by strength he might be always victor. And Sandy, growing stronger through each victory, went forward from one trial to the next with a steady eye.

By and by Richards rang to announce the car. "Ten o'clock already," Mrs. Caterson protested smilingly. "It doesn't seem possible!"

"Stay a little longer," Nina urged; but Mrs. Caterson shook her head.

"No, dear. I saw Sandy yawn an hour ago."

Caterson brought her coat, her overshoes. "Still snowing, Richards says," he reported. "We'll have a white Christmas, this year."

"Dinner will be at seven, Christmas Eve," Mrs. Caterson reminded Nina. "Then we'll drive in afterward to hear the carols, perhaps, if you'd like that. Suppose I send Richards to fetch you. Sandy's is an open car, and you mustn't risk a cold, now."

Sandy nodded his thanks, and they moved toward the door.

"And next Christmas Eve," Nina pointed out,

"you must be with us, to help us hang up his little stocking where Santa will be sure to see."

Mrs. Caterson smiled, her eyes full of happy tears. She kissed Nina; and Sandy slipped his arm through hers and went down the stairs with them to the door, Nina calling goodnight from above. Outside, they looked up and saw her at the window, watching; and she lifted her hand in a gay farewell.

Sandy kissed his mother, tucked her in; he helped his father into the car beside her. "Good night, folks," he called; and he added whimsically: "You know, you're awful nice, and we like you very much."

A moment later he had shut the door, stood back to watch them go. Mrs. Caterson twisted around to wave to him through the rear window of the absurd old limousine; and when he was out of sight, she settled herself again by her husband's side.

"Nina's made him so much sweeter," she said happily. "I love having him so demonstrative, and affectionate. Just as Tony used to be."

His quick glance caught no grief in her eyes. "He's come along in so many ways," he assented; and he added, a moment later: "You can count on him! You can almost predict just where Sandy will be ten years from now, or twenty-five."

And after another calm interval of silence, he confessed:

"I find myself—leaning on him. There's a lot of strength in the boy, Edith."

"And sweetness, too," she insisted contentedly. "He's so dear to me, to us both, now."

The snow was deep; the car lurched and lumbered through the uncertain footing. They turned aside to pass a plow already at work to keep the streets open through the storm.

"Things do work out, don't they," she said at last, half under her breath. "For so many griefs there are—compensations long before prepared."

Caterson looked at her with a quick attention. She had never said as much as this before; never come so near confessing her complete comprehension. He was startled and dismayed; and she caught his glance, saw his swift concern, and touched his hand reassuringly.

"It's all right, Lad," she told him. "Don't be distressed for me!"

She knew, then! His cheek stiffened, and at his stricken countenance, she urged warmly: "And—never blame yourself, Joe! You—recognized your enemy, and beat him down. Taught your heart courage. There was no more you could do than that, dear man."

He muttered an incredulous question. "You know?" And he saw her smile.

"Know?" she echoed. "Yes, Lad, I know! Oh yes, I've known, in my heart for ever so long, my dear."

They sat thereafter in a silent communion, till the big car stopped before their own door. When arm in arm they entered the great hall, warm memories, in which no ugly sadness lay, were there to welcome them.